Only for the Holidays

ABIOLA BELLO

SIMON & SCHUSTER

First published in Great Britain in 2023 by Simon & Schuster UK Ltd

1 3 5 7 9 10 8 6 4 2

Simon & Schuster UK Ltd
1st Floor, 222 Gray's Inn Road
London
WC1X 8HB

www.simonandschuster.co.uk
www.simonandschuster.com.au
www.simonandschuster.co.in

Simon & Schuster Australia, Sydney
Simon & Schuster India, New Delhi

A CIP catalogue record for this book
is available from the British Library.

PB ISBN 978-1-3985-1690-8
eBook ISBN 978-1-3985-1691-5
eAudio ISBN 978-1-3985-1692-2

This book is a work of fiction. Names, characters, places and incidents are either
the product of the author's imagination or are used fictitiously. Any resemblance
to actual people living or dead, events or locales is entirely coincidental.

Typeset in Times by M Rules
Printed and Bound in the UK using 100% Renewable Electricity
at CPI Group (UK) Ltd

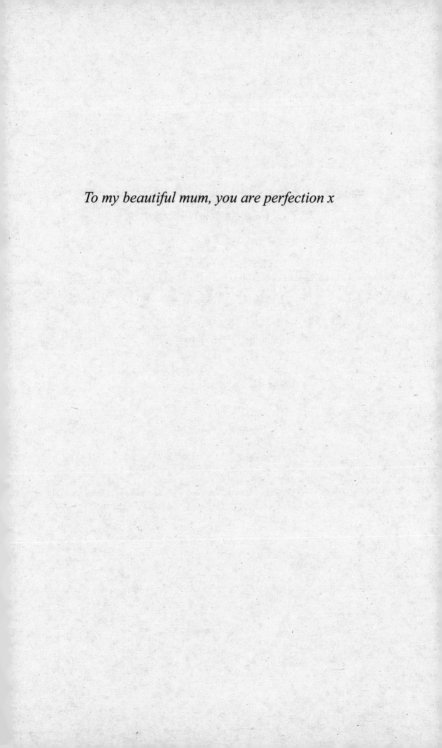

To my beautiful mum, you are perfection x

ONE

Quincy

8th December

I've been in the supermarket for no more than five minutes when I hear, 'Oh, Quincy.'

I turn to see Mrs Huntington, a sixty-something white woman in a fur jacket who is decked out in pearls. Under the jacket she has a powder-blue shirt and matching skirt. She owns the Huntington's, a range of luxury cabins that she lets out here in the little market town of White Oak.

'Hello, Mrs Huntington. How are you?' I ask.

I'm surprised when she rests a gloved hand on my arm. Her face falls, and for a second I think she's going to tell me Mr Huntington has died – he's been ill for years. 'I heard about you and Kali, dear.'

And there it is. It's been a couple of months since we broke up, but word spreads fast, especially in somewhere as small as White Oak.

'What happened?' she presses, taking a step closer and wafting her floral perfume in my face. 'You were together for years, weren't you? I always thought you were such a gorgeous couple.'

I shrug like it's no big deal, but I can feel that familiar lump forming in my throat whenever I think of Kali. Despite everything, I miss her. How am I meant to move on when people keep bringing her up? Everyone wants to know why we broke up, but if I told them what went down, her reputation as a sweet and innocent girl would be ruined. God knows I've thought about spilling the truth, though. I bet if I told Mrs Huntington what happened, she'd die from shock right here in the supermarket.

'It just wasn't meant to be,' I reply then gesture at the full shopping basket in my hand. 'Cameron's in the car, so I better go and pay for this.'

'Oh, of course, dear. Don't keep your brother waiting. I'm sure you'll find another lovely lady to take to the Winter Ball,' Then her voice goes up an octave: 'I'm so pleased your family are hosting it this year.'

I force a smile, because even though I like Mrs Huntington, I know from her voice that she's lying.

The Winter Ball is a massive deal. It's held annually on December 23rd in the Renaissance Ballroom of the Tudor manor house that I used to think was a castle. Centuries ago, it was owned by a super-wealthy family who left it to the town back in the 1800s. The Winter Ball has been a tradition ever since.

My family are one of the few Black families here, and no Black family has *ever* hosted the Winter Ball before, despite my parents bidding every year to do it. This year the committee agreed.

'Yeah, we're very excited,' I say cheerfully. I start to walk away and her gloved hand falls from my puffer jacket. 'Say hi to Mr Huntington for me.' As soon as my back is turned, I roll my eyes.

Once I've paid, I carry the bags to the black 4×4 parked on the side of the road. The windows are down even though it's freezing, and Kendrick Lamar is blaring out of them. I'm convinced it's going to snow, but Mum says I shouldn't put that out in the world, because when it snows here, it *snows* – the roads close and everyone is housebound. All that time and money spent on the Winter Ball for nothing.

My older brother Cameron, or Cam as we call him, is bopping his head to the music. His long locs are swinging back and forth. Inside the boot are his DJ decks and business cards printed with the words KING CAM under a logo of a crown with headphones over it.

I go to his window and yell over the music, 'Cam, your decks are in the boot. Should I put the shopping in the back seat?'

'Nah, me and Stacey had sex on that blanket, and I still need to wash it.'

What the hell? I glance into the back of the car, and there's a grey fleece blanket bunched up on the seats. Stacey and Cam went to school together. I had no idea they were hooking up.

'I'll wash it when we get back,' he adds.

'That's nasty, man,' I say, and Cam laughs in response. I head back to the boot, rearranging it so I can fit the shopping in.

'Got everything?' he shouts when I get in the car.

The bass feels like it's in my bones. I lower the volume. 'The whole street can hear you,' I snap, and Cam grins.

Cam's twenty-one, three years older than me, and we couldn't be more different if we tried. He's loud; I'm more reserved. He has girls blowing up his phone all day and night; I've always been in a committed relationship. He has light brown locs down to his waist; mine are darker and only reach my shoulders. But we do resemble each other physically, both being over six foot with a slender build, rich brown skin and dark eyes. He's the local DJ and, when he pulls up anywhere, everyone knows it's him. Mum and Dad used to get constant complaints, but now that he's the go-to person for parties the whole town seems to put up with it.

Cam presses the gas, and the car pulls off fast. I put my hands out in front of me, catching the dashboard before I smack into it. He couldn't even wait for me to put on my seat belt. That's another thing: my brother drives like a maniac.

'Dickhead,' I say, pulling the belt over me.

'My bad,' he replies, not looking the least bit sorry. I cross my arms and sigh. 'What's up with you?' he asks.

'Nothing,' I mumble.

'Q, what's up?' he presses.

'Just drive, man,' I say.

Cam looks at me before reaching over to change the playlist. Wizkid sounds out of the speakers – my favourite. One good thing about Cam is he knows when to drop something and let music do the talking instead.

The roads are long and bendy in White Oak, making it impossible to see what's approaching round corners. We've driven up and down these lanes our whole lives, but I still drive with caution. Cam, on the other hand, drives like he's in *Grand Theft Auto*. He's no better at night when there aren't any streetlights. To this day I catch my breath every time we meet another car on the road, but so far he's never crashed. Not yet anyway . . .

We turn left at the sign that says SAIYAN HEDGE FARM and drive up to the main house, a three-storey Georgian building with cream pillars along the front. On one side fairy lights twinkle in the ivy that covers the brickwork. Our gardener, Harry, puts them up every December to make the house look Christmassy.

Our parents bought Saiyan Hedge Farm from the Saiyan family just before our older sister Drew was born. They'd met when Mum visited White Oak on holiday with her girlfriends. Dad's lived here his whole life, but Mum was a city girl. She's a great cook, adores animals and loves the countryside, so it made sense for her to move here to be with him.

The farmhouse sits within sixty acres of greenery. As well as the main house, there are three holiday cottages that we let out. We employ a small group of staff but we all chip in to help. We've got horses, cows, sheep, chickens and rabbits. I mainly run the horse-riding sessions for the guests. I've been riding since I was a kid and I love it. There's something so free and calming about galloping through the open fields on the back of a horse.

Cam's usually on reception in the main house, which gives him an excuse to flirt with any hot girls staying at the farm, but lately he's been so busy DJing due to the festive period that we've had to cover for him, which is annoying. I don't like being on reception, but I haven't really got a choice. Maybe when Drew comes back for Christmas she can help out.

It feels like forever since I've seen Drew. She lives in London with her fashion photographer boyfriend Daniel in this amazing modern apartment that has skyline views. She's just celebrated her twenty-fifth birthday. Drew's an actress and was in a soap opera, but she left a few years ago to focus on films. Recently she starred in a thriller on Netflix that got strong reviews and now she's being invited to all the award ceremonies and after-parties. Last week she was on the cover of *Rebel Pop* magazine. There's nothing weirder than seeing your sister's face smiling out from a newsstand.

Cam's phone beeps as he's parking the car. 'It's Drew,' he says. 'She said it'll just be her and Regal coming down next week. Daniel's going to join later for the ball.'

'Regal's coming?' I ask, and Cam bursts out laughing.

'You gotta let it go, man,' he says, still chuckling to himself as he types back.

Everyone, including Regal, knows that I used to have a major crush on her back in the day. I even wrote poems and made love-song playlists for her. I was just a kid ... but no one lets me forget it.

I've known Regal Majekodunmi since I was a baby. Her mum, who we call Aunty Shola, used to be housekeeper here when she first came over from Nigeria, so Regal practically grew up with us. She's the same age as Drew and they've been inseparable ever since they met. She's always looked on Cam and me as her little brothers, which used to annoy the shit out of me. And did I mention she's a famous model? It's wild that I ever thought I stood a chance.

Cam chuckles again, and only then do I realize he's been texting back and forth with Drew.

'Let me see,' I say, reaching for the phone. He leans back, dangling it out of the window. 'The fuck, Cam?'

He's too busy laughing to answer me back. I know he and Drew are taking the piss out of me. I jump out of the car, purposely slamming the door hard so he has to pay attention.

'Watch the paint!' he shouts.

Technically, we share the car, so I can slam it if I want to. I don't bother grabbing the shopping from the boot. He can sort it out himself.

I head into the house. Mum, dressed smartly in a black pencil skirt and cream shirt, is behind the reception desk, checking out three women who have been staying for the past week. Oreo, our black, brown and white Border Collie runs up and licks my hand. Mum mouths, 'Wait,' so I lean against the wall and Oreo lies down by my feet. Drew named him. She thought we were getting a Dalmatian, but Oreo does love to eat Oreos, so I guess it makes sense.

Our house and the holiday cottages have been decorated identically for Christmas. There are fairy lights and large white candles everywhere, Christmas trees decorated with gold, bronze and white baubles, boxes wrapped in cream paper stacked underneath, and three stockings hanging at the fireplace with large, white appliqué letters spelling out JOY but with the 'O' replaced by a wreath that has red ribbon tied around it. The communal areas look impeccable, but behind closed doors it's a different scene entirely. Stock for the Winter Ball clutters up every available space – chairs, tables, candles, cloths ... and we don't get access to the ballroom for another week.

'Thank you for staying at Saiyan Hedge Farm,' Mum says to the women. 'I hope you have a great Christmas.'

'You too, Mrs Parker,' they chorus. As they walk by, they smile at me, and I wave back.

Mum sighs. Cam and I both resemble her, whereas Drew looks more like Dad. Mum's skin tone is darker than ours, but she's just as tall, with large brown eyes and curly black hair.

'Gia's sick,' she says.

'Again?' I groan. 'What's wrong this time?'

'Tummy bug.'

Gia's been the head cook here for four years and knows how to execute all of Mum's dishes to perfection, but this is the second time this week she's been off. When we first opened to guests, Mum used to cook everything and we soon developed a reputation for the best food in White Oak. People began coming from all over and, as we got busier, Mum had to hire and train cooks to implement the dishes. I've picked up some of her recipes just by watching her over the years.

There's not just a problem with Gia, either. We've had staffing issues for a while now. As more holiday homes open up in the town, it's got harder to recruit people. Mum's never liked anyone's housekeeping as much as Aunty Shola's and she thinks our current cleaners aren't as good. Maybe we'll attract better staff after the ball.

Mum clasps her hands together in prayer. 'Can you make dinner for the remaining guests, Quincy? Pretty please?' she adds before I can object. 'Dad's picking up more chairs, I've got admin to sort out, and Cam has a gig tonight.'

'Why is it always left to me?' I complain, for the millionth time.

'Because you're the best.' Mum gently nudges me, and I can't help but smile. 'Plus, your carbonara is delicious. Hey, why don't you invite Simon over for dinner? I haven't seen him in ages.'

It takes all my strength not to react when I hear Simon's name. He was my best friend for years. Scratch that – he was more like a brother. That's why it's still a mind fuck, knowing he slept with my girlfriend.

I told Drew and Cam about it because they'd clocked that I'd stopped mentioning Kali and Simon. Drew was livid, Cam was even worse. He immediately jumped in the car and drove off. It only took me and Drew a minute to realize where he was headed, so we got in her car and chased after him. We managed to stop him banging down Simon's house, but he carried on screaming and cussing. I could see how frightened Simon was from his face at his bedroom window. Sometimes I wish I'd just let Cam punch him up, to really make Simon understand how I felt. But I didn't tell Mum any of this. She and Sophie, Simon's mum, have been close friends for years and I don't want my issue with Simon to ruin that.

'No, it's fine,' I say. 'Are there any more guests coming tomorrow?'

'Yes, the Adelaides and Johnsons, but I'll double check with Cam as he sorted the booking. Where is your brother, anyway?'

'I left him in the car, texting Drew. I can sort out dinner tonight, but we have to find someone who can step in for Gia if she keeps getting sick, or we're gonna really struggle with the food for the ball.'

Mum sighs. 'I know. I'll sort it. That reminds me – we need to buy you a new suit.' I groan in response, making Mum frown. 'Look, I know you're worried about the ball now that you and Kali aren't together and you don't have a date—'

'This has nothing to do with Kali,' I argue, even though it does.

I've gone to the Winter Ball with Kali for the past three years, so of course the one year my family host it I'm single. There's an old-fashioned rule that you need a date to attend, but there's no girl I'm remotely interested in taking.

'You've still got time to find someone,' Mum says gently. 'I can ask around?'

Ask around? How sad would I look if my mum had to find me a date!

'It's fine, Mum. I'll sort it. Maybe someone from college is still available.'

As Mum smiles and walks off, I know I need to find a date, and fast.

TWO

Tia

8th December

'Shit.' My white press-on nail falls to the floor, and I quickly pick it up and pocket it, keeping my hand in my coat out of sight. Great. I don't have any money to buy a new pack.

'All I'm saying is, she should have told me how she felt,' my best friend Remi says, mouth half full of Bounty chocolate.

We're walking out of media class together, ready for the weekend. Remi uses her hands to talk, showing off her fresh new set of acrylics, and I watch her enviously. I haven't been able to get my nails done professionally for over a year now. Remi's offered to treat me, but I always decline because it makes me feel weird, even though we've been best friends since secondary school. Remi is tiny, at only five foot, so whenever we're standing next to each other I always feel like I'm towering over her.

'Definitely,' I say for what feels like the hundredth time. I love Remi, but she knows how to exhaust a dilemma. 'Just talk to Ashleigh. I'm sure she'll understand. You shouldn't fall out over some guy.' *Especially one as clueless as Aaron.* But I don't say that part out loud.

'Yeah, maybe,' Remi responds, also for the hundredth time. 'Anyway, what are you wearing to Mike's birthday? You better come with all the sauce.'

I laugh. 'Oh, trust me, I will.'

My boyfriend Mike's eighteenth birthday party is *the* party that everyone at college is talking about, and I'm organizing it. First is bowling with close friends, followed by the party in Rye Levels, this really cool creative space that looks like a warehouse. Mike wanted an exclusive guest list, but the space is pretty big and I was worried we wouldn't fill it, so I invited most people from college. He was pissed when he found out, but I know he'll be happy when it's packed. Mike's obsessed with Diddy's white parties, so the theme has been influenced by that. I'm making an all-white birthday cake, but when he cuts into it, there will be three layers of chocolate – white, milk and dark.

'Tia!' I turn to see Mike jogging down the hallway towards me in baggy jeans and a hoodie despite it being freezing outside. I catch my breath when I see him. Mike's half Black, half Indian, with the most amazing hair. It's long and wavy, and he usually wears it in a top bun. A few weeks ago he shaved off the sides, and I thought I'd hate it, but it somehow made him look even more hot.

We've been with each other for almost a year, and sometimes I can't believe he's mine. We'd always hung out in the same friendship circle so would often find ourselves at social events together. He also dances, so we go to his shows and competitions to support him. I'd always thought he was fine, even though I don't normally go for short guys and Mike, at five foot six, isn't much taller than me. I never thought he was into me, but then something changed one night at our friend Winn's birthday.

It was around the time Mum had broken up with Paul. She lost her job as a chef when the restaurant she worked at closed down and couldn't keep up with the rent, so we had to leave our home in Peckham and move into a small, cramped flat ten minutes away where my big sister Willow and I have to share a room, while Mum shares a bed with my three-year-old sister Banks. I try not to complain, but I hate it. There's zero privacy, and Banks' toys are always everywhere. I take every chance I get to escape from it all.

The night of Winn's party, everyone was drunk. I'd gone outside to get away from the loud music and sloppy college kids, and was thinking about all the massive changes that had happened to my family recently. I started to cry and had no idea Mike had been watching me from inside. He followed me into the garden and asked what was wrong. I told him everything, and he was so sweet, not caring that my foundation rubbed off onto his shirt while he was comforting me. We started to talk more after that and began to get closer, then he asked me out on an official date. We went to a virtual reality arcade, and as soon as the game was over and we took off our headsets, he leaned in and kissed me. It was perfect. A few months of dating later and he asked me to be his girlfriend. He's been my rock ever since.

'What's good, Remi?' Mike asks.

'You want a Bounty? I've got a pack.' Remi reaches into her bag.

Mike shakes his head. 'Nah, I'm good, thanks. I don't like coconut.'

'Oh, fair enough. Right, I need to go find Ashleigh.' Remi pronounces it 'Ash-a-leee', dragging it out, and Mike laughs.

I frown at her. 'Be nice, okay?'

'Yeah, yeah.' She waves as she walks off.

'So ... erm ...' Mike seems nervous in a way I've never seen him be before. He runs a hand over his hair and my heart starts to race. *Is he going to say it? Here in the hallway?* I look around at the students walking up and down. It's not the most romantic setting, but I'll take it. Despite how long we've been together, Mike's never said *I love you*. Whenever I say it, he only smiles in response, which I've always thought is a bit weird, but I know deep down he feels the same way about me. Why else would we be in a long-term relationship?

'Yes ... ?' I ask expectantly.

He glances at my bag. 'You're buzzing.'

What? I put my hand inside and sure enough my phone screen reads WILLOW.

'Sorry, it's my sister,' I say before I answer it. 'Hello?'

'Balloons,' Willow says, sounding breathless. 'We need more balloons.'

'Okay, cool. I'm on my way.' I hang up then turn back to Mike. 'Mum got a new job so me and Willow are going to decorate the house to say congratulations. I need to pick up more balloons, apparently.'

Mike's face softens. 'That's great. I'm really happy to hear that.'

'Thank you.' I smile. 'Now hopefully this shitty year is on the up. At least I've had you by my side. You've been the best thing to happen to me this year.' I take his hand in mine and squeeze.

Mike smiles, but I notice it doesn't reach his eyes. My stomach suddenly flips. What if he wasn't going to say *I love you* and it's actually bad news instead?

'I better go,' I say quickly, dropping his hand. I don't want to stick around to find out. I button up my coat that I bought last week from a secondhand shop. It's a vintage faux fur forest green number with a leather collar, not made for the rain, but very cool.

Mike frowns. 'Can you sneak out later?'

'I don't know. I might be able to,' I say as I start to walk off, trying to ignore the way my heart's racing and my stomach is in knots.

'I'll text you,' he calls after me, and I give him a thumbs up.

I can feel him watching me, but I don't look back. As soon as I'm outside, I take a deep breath and my heart calms down.

We've been so good recently, so why do I feel like I just dodged a bullet?

Willow is balancing on the sofa arm trying to straighten out the massive CONGRATULATIONS, MUM! banner. She glances at me when I close the door.

'Got them?' she asks, and I wave the packet of pink balloons. She notices my missing nail and arches an eyebrow.

'I know! Now I've got to take them all off.' I slip off my coat before starting to blow up the balloons.

Willow leans back and looks at the banner from left to right, narrowing her eyes. 'Is it straight?' she asks. It's not, but Willow is a perfectionist and if I tell her she'll be fussing with it all night.

'Yeah,' I say as I tie the neck of a full balloon into a knot.

Willow jumps down from the sofa and brushes imaginary dust off her shorts, showing off her long, slender legs. Her gold hoop nose ring shines as it catches the light. We got them done together last year for my birthday.

'How was college?' she asks grabbing some balloons. She holds one up next to her pink hair. 'Love the colour match.'

Willow makes wigs as a side hustle. She only used to do it for herself and a few friends, but she's got a loyal customer base now and charges upwards of £200. With Mum out of work, Willow has been helping to pay the bills from what she earns from her wig business and her job at Nando's. She's always experimenting with colour and is eager to get her hands on my long, black bob, but it's a firm no from me. The only experimenting I like to do is with baked goods. Baking is a hobby at the moment, but one day I hope to do it professionally. I've seen bakers on Instagram that charge hundreds of pounds for one cake.

'It was all right, but something was up with Mike,' I confess, and Willow perches on the sofa arm.

'In what way?' she quizzes.

I shrug. 'He just seemed off, like he was nervous or something, and then I got this weird feeling that he was about to tell me something bad.' I shake my head. 'I'm probably being silly. What could he possibly have wanted to say?'

Willow holds the half-blown-up balloon between her fingers. 'Maybe something about the party?'

Of course! Mike pretty much asked me to organize it … there must be something he wants to change.

'You're right, that must be it.'

Willow points at herself. 'I'm so wise.'

I roll my eyes and laugh. I really lucked out with Willow. She's two years older than me and one of my best friends. I lucked out with my mum too. She's first-generation Nigerian-British and a lot more laid back than my grandparents, who are very traditional. She loves quoting Regina George's mum's line in *Mean Girls*: 'I'm not like a regular mom. I'm a cool mom.' She's always encouraged me and Willow to be close because she's close with her sister, so we grew up telling each other everything. I was the first to know when Willow had her first kiss and even when she lost her virginity – nothing is off limits between us. But Willow has never fully warmed to Mike. She thinks I'm too good for him. It baffles me why

18

she doesn't like him, because I think he's perfect, but I guess she's just being protective.

We blow up the rest of the balloons and place them around the living room. Willow's brought food back from her shift at Nando's, so that's dinner sorted. I could eat the same thing from Nando's every day and still love it – extra-hot quarter chicken, spicy rice, peas, coleslaw and a side of halloumi. Mum's an amazing cook, especially her Nigerian food – jollof rice, egusi stew and moi moi – but Nando's will always be a firm favourite in this household. I plate up and put everything on the dining table just as the front door opens.

'Congratulations!' we both yell, and Willow pops a party popper that makes Mum jump and Banks clap her hands.

Mum puts a hand to her chest. 'Oh, girls, this is amazing! Look at what your sisters did, Banksy!'

'Come on, queen,' Willow says, helping Mum out of her leather coat.

Banks' eyes light up as she takes in the balloons. The wind has messed up her light brown curly hair, but when I try to smooth it down, she dodges out of my grasp. Unlike Mum, Willow and me, with our dark brown skin, wide-set eyes and pouty lips, Banks is mixed race with light brown skin, blue eyes, small lips and brown hair that goes blonde in the summer. I can't tell you how many times people ask Mum, 'Is she yours?' as if she's kidnapped her.

Mum's ex, Paul, is Banks' dad, and he's the nicest guy ever. I still have no idea why they broke up; all Mum said is that they're better off as friends. Mum's friends with all her exes. Take my dad, for example. They met and fell in love at secondary school, built a life together and had Willow and me. Some years later, when we were still little, he got a promotion that meant we moved to San Diego. Then, while there, Mum and Dad began arguing all the time and Mum eventually decided to move us back to London. Dad has stayed in America. But even though it didn't work out between them, and they live thousands of miles apart, they talk on the phone all the time and still manage to make each other laugh. Willow is the type of girl that would set fire to an ex's house if they broke up with her. Me? I have no idea what I'd do. Mike's my first boyfriend.

'Thank you so much, girls. This is lovely,' Mum says as she eats a chip, closing her eyes as she savours it. 'I haven't eaten much today.' She catches me and Willow sharing a look. Mum used to skip meals to save money. 'Don't worry, it's only because I've been so busy meeting all the new team and learning the ropes. I'm so excited!'

Mum's new job is head chef at Simone's, this really pretty and expensive restaurant in Chelsea. Before she got into cooking, she worked all sorts of odd jobs, but there was no turning back when she realized her passion for food.

'This is a new start for us. I can feel it.' Mum looks at us with a huge grin on her face. 'Come the new year when I start there properly, the extra money is really going to help us. But before that, I have a surprise for you all!'

'For me?' Banks asks, her mouth covered in peri-peri sauce.

'For everyone!' Mum pulls out a brochure from her handbag and places it in the middle of the table.

I turn my head to the side trying to read it. 'Saiyan Hedge Farm?'

'What's that?' Willow asks, glancing up from her food.

'We're going away for Christmas!' Mum claps her hands.

My stomach lurches. *I can't go away for Christmas!* Mike's party is on the twenty-first – I have to be in London for that. Plus, I like our family Christmas dinner. Mum fuses Nigerian and British culture, so we have turkey with stuffing, jollof and plantain, and finish with mince pies and puff puff. I'm just about to tell Mum this isn't going to work when my phone beeps and I see a text that makes my stomach fall completely to the floor:

Tia, I'm sorry, but I need some space.

THREE

Quincy

8th December

Dinner for the guests is usually served between six and eight p.m. in the dining hall, unless they choose to eat out. Once they're done, our family sits down to eat. Guests used to be able to choose from a wide range of dishes, but because of the lack of staff we now offer a set menu with a smaller choice. I'm a pretty good cook, but it's not my job and I don't love doing it.

I put the dirty cooking pots in the dishwasher as the guests finish up. Thankfully, there was only one family eating tonight. The kitchen door swings open and one of the young waiters, Evan, a white man with curly black hair, brings in a tray of used dishes and puts them on the side.

'I'll sort it,' I say, and he gives me a thumbs up before he leaves.

From the dining hall I can hear Mum chatting away to Emma, the restaurant hostess, with Dad occasionally adding his two cents' worth. When I've cleared up, I stay in the kitchen, not wanting to make small talk, and start thinking about the Winter Ball. How am I going to find a date in time? My mate Sean has a hot cousin that I met a few months ago, but he's in Bradford visiting his grandma in hospital, so I don't want to ask. I don't even know if he'll be back in time for the ball. I quickly send a message to my friend Eliza. Her, Simon and I have been a trio since nursery. Then Sean joined our group in secondary school; he's Filipino, so one of the only other ethnic minority people around here. And then Kali tagged along when she and I started dating. Eliza always tries to fly solo to the ball, but somehow every year her mum manages to find a backup guy ready to swoop in at the last moment. But her mum runs the hairdresser's in town, so Eliza always has the gossip on everyone round here.

> I need a date for the ball. You know anyone?

She replies straight away:

> Yeah, but you can't be picky

> What do you mean?!

> What about Amber? She's annoying but pretty

> Spending all night with Amber would drive me crazy!

Eliza's typing so I wait.

Okay, that might solve my problem.

'You all right, love?' Mum asks walking in and surveying the kitchen.

'Yeah, I'm cool. Is it time to eat yet?'

Mum nods. 'I've just told the staff to head home. You sit down and I'll bring the food in. Thanks again for stepping in, Quincy.'

'No problem,' I say pocketing my phone. I go through to the dining room and sit next to Dad and Cam. Oreo's lying by Dad's feet. Dad's his favourite because he's the only one who gets up in the early hours of the morning to let him out. I'd like to think I'm a close second.

'I thought you had a gig tonight,' I say to Cam.

'Later,' he replies, his eyes not leaving his phone.

'So you could have helped me with dinner, then?' I look at Dad for support, but he's leaning back in his chair with his eyes closed, his hands clasped on top of his round belly.

Dad kind of reminds me of a bear – big and tall, with a full beard and a stern face, but he's friendly really. He's up at the crack of dawn, tending to the animals, checking on the fields and the farm in general. Normally, the only times I see him is when I'm in the stables or at dinner. But now that preparation for the Winter Ball is well underway, Mum's got him running round picking up whatever she's convinced we need.

24

'You all right, Dad?' I ask, and he grunts in response, his eyes still closed. A man of few words.

Mum comes in and taps Dad's shoulder. 'Food's here, Will.'

Dad sits up straight and rubs his red eyes as Mum dishes out the garlic bread and carbonara I made earlier. I pour myself a glass of juice and start to down it. Out of the corner of my eye, I can see Cam grinning as he messages some girl. He catches me looking and turns the phone towards me.

'What do you think?'

I splutter and have to hold my hand over my mouth to stop the juice from flying out.

'Quincy!' Mum says disapprovingly, but I can't take my eyes off the picture.

She's fucking hot. Dark brown skin, curves I could drown in and a sexy smile. There's no way she's from around here.

'Who is that?' I ask slowly when our parents start talking, inevitably about the ball.

'This girl Kelly who lives in Manchester. Met her at an event a few months ago,' Cam says smugly.

'Is she your date?' I ask and he shrugs. He's always meeting cool people through his DJing.

'Might ask her,' he says. 'May have a better offer, though.'

'A better offer?' I reply incredulously. How could Cam do better than Kelly? If I showed up at the Winter Ball with *her*, Kali would lose her shit – and that's exactly what I want.

'What happened to Stacey?'

Cam pulls a face. 'What about her?'

'You know . . .' When Cam looks blank, I add, 'The blanket?'

'Oh, that was just a ting. It's nothing mad.'

Typical Cam. I don't know why girls are so drawn to him. He loves the chase, but as soon as he gets the girl, he moves on. Drama always quickly follows. I bet Stacey has brought a dress for the ball just to impress him.

'Have you told Stacey you're not interested?' I ask.

Cam scoffs. 'No! Why you in my business like that?'

'Erm, you made it my business when you told me about the—'

'Boys!' Dad says at the same time Mum asks, 'What are you two looking at?'

Cam locks his phone and puts it on the table. 'Nothing. I was just asking Quincy who he was taking to the ball.' Cam grins evilly at me. I elbow him in the side, and he winces.

'Aren't you going with Kali?' Dad asks before he slurps up a mouthful of spaghetti.

Mum tuts. 'Will! I *told* you about her and Quincy . . .'

Dad looks at her blankly and then at me. Can I not even get through dinner without hearing my ex's name?

'They broke up, and now Quincy hasn't got a date for the Winter Ball.' Cam jumps up before I can punch him and runs to sit opposite me, beside Mum. Pussy.

'Cam, you should be helping your brother, not teasing him,' Mum scolds. 'There must be someone available.'

'Everyone's taken,' Cam insists.

My heart drops. He must be joking.

'All the hot girls have a date,' he continues, and then starts counting on his fingers. 'Maria Hunter, Sarah Gibson, Harley

Sutherland, Lisa Shah … even Eliza is taken, and she always says how pointless the balls are.'

Eliza has a date?! I wonder who she's going with.

Mum and Dad share a look, and I know they're silently stressing. The Winter Ball is a massive deal. What's more, Drew and Regal are coming to this one, which means more local press will turn up. Some high-end fashion magazine will probably do a feature on Regal's dress. The point is, having no date isn't an option. *Wait* … Cam just said everyone's taken, but who's Kali going with … ?

I clear my throat. I really don't want to ask this question, but I need to know.

'What about Kali?' Dad asks and I could kiss him.

Cam glances at me. 'I don't know.'

And Simon? Does he have a date? Are they thinking of going together? My heart starts to race and it suddenly feels really hot in the dining room. I roll up the sleeves of my jumper to try to cool myself down. Mum and Cam are talking, but all I can hear is a buzzing in my ears. What would I do if Kali and Simon walked into the ball hand in hand, with everyone watching? My mouth can't catch up with my brain and before I know it I've blurted out five little words:

'I actually have a date.'

I focus really hard on my bowl of pasta and instantly the chatter stops. No one says anything, so I look up and catch Dad's eyes widening, Mum looking confused and Cam frowning.

'You what?' Cam eventually asks.

I take a deep breath. 'I have a date, so it's all good.' I stand up quickly, grabbing the empty water jug. 'I'm just gonna fill this up.'

No one says anything as I walk to the kitchen and shut the door behind me. I turn on the tap so the water gushes loudly and lean against the counter, my head in my hands.

Fuck.

FOUR

Tia

8th December

Mike needs space. From me*?* Mum is still talking about the Christmas getaway, but my ears are ringing and my breaths are coming quickly. Why did Mike send me that text? *What did I do?* Questions are running at lightning speed through my head.

'What the hell!' I shout, and everyone falls quiet.

'Tia!' Mum snaps, and she glances at Banks, who's staring at me with her mouth open.

'I'm sorry ... Banks don't repeat that ... Two secs, I – I'll be back.'

I hurry out of the living room, holding my phone so tightly that I'm sure it's going to leave an imprint in my hand. I shut my bedroom door and rest my back against it, breathing heavily. *Space?* I call Mike's number and it rings through. I call again and again, until I remember his dance rehearsal has just started and he won't be done until eight.

'Tia?' Willow opens the door. 'Are you okay?'

Her face is filled with so much concern that my eyes start to well up. I pass her the phone and her eyebrows shoot up when she reads the message. 'Why does he want space?'

'I don't know!' I cry. 'Everything's been fine. More than fine . . .'

Hasn't it? I'm racking my brain, trying to work out if I missed any signs, but nothing's coming to mind. But I *knew* he was going to say something in the hallway earlier, didn't I? *I've been with him for almost a year, and he sends me this shit by text?*

'What a dick,' Willow says.

'Maybe I'm reading it wrong,' I suggest, holding onto hope.

Willow scoffs. 'You're not. If he doesn't respect you enough to tell you face to face, good riddance.'

Good riddance? I don't want Mike to go anywhere. I just need to talk to him. As soon as we talk, things will be fine, I'm sure of it. The last thing I want is to give him space. What if he likes the space and then we break up? Oh, shit! Are we going to break up?

'Willow, I can't go on this family trip! And what about your clients? Christmas is a busy time. Why don't we both stay here in London and Mum and Banks can go?' I beg.

Willow sighs. 'It's not ideal, and I'd love the extra money, but a break away from the city will be nice. Besides, we can't *not* be with our family for Christmas.'

'We could join them after Mike's party,' I reply.

'Mike? Tia, he just asked you for space!' She narrows her eyes at me. 'You're not still helping this boy with his party, are you? And you're definitely not going!'

'I have to! I'm not losing my boyfriend.'

Willow looks at me like I'm crazy, and, okay, I know I sound a bit hysterical, but she doesn't get it. I *love* Mike. We've never had any problems before, so I'm certain we can work this out and get things back on track.

'Girls?' Mum comes in and looks from me to Willow. 'What's going on?'

Willow hands Mum my phone and she reacts the same way my sister did, her eyebrows rising. But Mum is more comforting than Willow and immediately pulls me into a hug.

'I'm sorry, baby.' She rubs my back and I sink into her, tears now falling down my face. 'He doesn't deserve you. Maybe you're better off as friends.'

'Friends?' I pull away from her, wiping my wet cheeks with the back of my hand. What is wrong with these two? They're acting like Mike just dumped me, but asking for space isn't the same as breaking up ... is it?

'Mum, I can't go away to that farm for Christmas.'

She smiles sadly. 'It's already arranged.'

I stamp my foot like Banks does when she doesn't get her way. Am I talking a different language? No one is listening to me!

'It's not cool that you booked a holiday without even asking us. You know I've been planning Mike's party for months.'

31

Mum crosses her arms and glares at me. *'Ask* you? The last time I checked, I'm the parent and you're the child. You need to watch your tone, Tia.' I fall silent, because when Mum gets really mad she has no problem cussing me all the way out. 'This holiday is a lovely and thoughtful gift from Aunt Bimpé, a "well done to me" for getting my new job. I've been so excited to tell my girls that they're going to spend Christmas in a luxury house in the country. You both spent Thanksgiving with your dad and had such a brilliant time. I can't match that. But now this trip has been organized for us – and you're being a brat about it.'

I glance at Willow, who avoids my eyes. Great, so she's pissed at me too.

'Now I know you're upset about Mike, and you definitely need to talk to him, because that little boy should not be asking for space via text,' Mum continues, and I stay quiet. She's right. 'But after that message, I'd have thought his party would be the last thing on your mind.'

'You would think so,' Willow mutters, and I glare at her.

'Can both of you come back into the living room? Let's finish our food and I'll carry on explaining about the trip.'

Mum walks out with my phone in her hand, so I have no choice but to follow her. I sit down next to Banks, who frowns at me.

'It's okay,' I say, kissing her cheek, and she smiles. Then a lightbulb thought hits me. 'Mum, when's the holiday booked for?'

'We go Monday and stay until the twenty-seventh,' she says.

I try to stop myself from cheering. 'But I've got college until next Friday,' I say. 'I can't miss the last week.' The last week before Christmas is always more relaxed and I'm up to date with my work, but surely Mum wouldn't want me to miss college?

Instead, she waves her hand. 'You can copy Remi's notes. She's in all the same classes as you. Right, where was I?' Mum puts my phone on the table, which I reach over to grab, and proceeds to open the brochure.

Damn it! I thought college would change her mind. Clearly not. I can't help checking my screen to see if Mike's messaged me, but there's nothing there. I cross my arms over my chest and slump in my seat.

Mum grins as she points at the pictures. 'Look how gorgeous it is! Bimpé and your cousins went a few years ago, and they said it was one of the best holidays they've had. There's a farm with horses and other animals for Banksy, lots of cute shops and cafes in the little town, and residents put on a travelling Nativity every Christmas.'

'Horsey!' Banks says loudly.

I *hate* horses! They freak me out. Did you know Superman was paralyzed from falling off a horse? Ever since I found that out, I can't look at their hooves without shuddering.

'And there's an annual Winter Ball.' Mum points at a picture of a very pretty hall filled with people dressed in ballgowns and suits. 'It's like that show we watched the other day, Willow. Bridgey something.'

'*Bridgerton*,' Willow says. 'Yeah, it's giving those vibes.

33

Who knows, we may meet our own Duke of Hastings.' Willow smiles at me, and I can't help but laugh a little. I'm obsessed with Regé-Jean Page.

'It's going to be so fun dressing up. There's even a separate party for the kids, so Danks can make some new friends. And the best part of all is that the farm is owned by a Black family!' Mum looks at us, excitement shining in her eyes. 'Bimpé said the family have sons that are around the same age as you both.' She nods at me and Willow.

Great, now Mum's trying to play matchmaker. It's like she's already forgotten that I'm in a committed relationship.

'And guess who their daughter is?' Mum asks. Willow and I look at her blankly. Mum huffs when we don't respond. 'Drew Parker!'

'No way!' Willow says. 'We just watched her in that Netflix film.'

Okay, this is kind of cool, but I'm not going to let Mum know that. She's looking at me expectantly, but I deliberately don't react. She taps her long nails on the table.

'So Drew Parker will probably be there. I read in a magazine that she goes home to Saiyan Hedge Farm every Christmas with her best friend, Regal Majekodunmi.'

Willow gasps and, I can't lie, I almost fall out of my chair. Mum smirks knowing she's just thrown down her trump card. Regal is one of the highest paid supermodels in the world, on every magazine cover that's currently stacked up on my desk. She's perfection.

I turn to Willow and see her quickly scrolling through

her phone before she gasps. 'Look!' She passes it to me, open on Instagram, and there's a stunning picture of Regal and Drew in a car, blowing kisses and holding up the peace sign. The caption reads *Just a couple of farm girls*, followed by Christmas tree and house emojis. 'They must already be heading home!'

'This is the part where you say *Thank you, Mum*,' she says, looking pleased with herself.

Willow gives her a one-armed hug. 'Thanks, Mum! This is *very* cool.'

Mum looks at me. 'Tia?'

It's true, I want to meet Regal Majekodunmi and Drew Parker. When else will I get the chance to meet actual celebrities? And it might be fun to do something different for Christmas ... But the middle of nowhere is so not my vibe. And why does it have to be *this* Christmas? Not only have I worked hard on Mike's party, I've been looking forward to it massively. Now I'll have to let him and all my friends party together while I'm on a farm in the country. And if I'm away for the holidays, am I not technically agreeing to the space Mike is requesting? It's the one thing I really don't want to do.

Willow flicks her eyes towards Mum and her look says it all. *Don't ruin this for her, Tia.*

So I swallow the urge to argue and force myself to smile. 'Thank you, Mum.'

FIVE

Quincy

9th December

The sound of glass shattering echoes around the house. My eyes fly open and I jump out of bed looking from left to right. My windows are intact, and nothing seems to be broken on the floor. *What was that?* Break-ins are unheard of in White Oak – some people even leave their doors unlocked – but there's a first time for everything. Without thinking, I hurry downstairs, not even bothering to put a T-shirt on over my shorts. The dining room is empty, and for second I think it might have been a bad dream, but then I hear the word 'Fuck' from the kitchen.

I pick up a vase from the side table and walk slowly towards the kitchen. Why am I down here by myself? Oreo's useless. I bet he's still asleep with Mum and Dad … I probably should have woken them up, now I think about it. I wish Cam wasn't working late. Taking a deep breath, I push open the door and see two figures in black.

'Who's there?' I yell as I turn on the light. Two girls quickly put their hands over their faces, squinting at the bright light.

'Quincy, what the hell?'

'Drew!' I lower the vase.

My sister glares at me like I'm the idiot creeping around at one in the morning smashing glass. She swipes her long, straight, black hair over her shoulder, frowning at the mess on the floor. Regal stands next to her, tall and willowy, with dark brown skin, thick black hair, sharp cheekbones and flirty eyes, which are currently fixed on me.

'What are you doing?' I ask, until I realize that the mess on the floor is a couple of smashed beer bottles. Why are they even here? Drew told Cam they wouldn't be down until next week.

Drew groans. She's just as tall as me, but she has Dad's heart-shaped face. All my friends fancy her. It doesn't help that she's recently been photographed wearing a load of skimpy outfits on various shoots and red carpets. No one wants to see their sister half-naked on Instagram. My friends used to tag me in the posts just to mess with me. You'd be amazed at the number of followers I've got. They just want to interact with me to get to Drew and Regal. I've had to make my account private.

'I'll sweep up,' I say, fetching a brush. Drew, too lazy to get the mop, uses a few sheets of kitchen roll to soak up the alcohol.

As I start working, Regal takes the brush off me. She looks me up and down slowly, and I remember I'm topless. Thankfully I've been working out. My schoolboy crush on Regal may be a thing of the past, but she's still the most beautiful girl I've ever seen.

'You haven't got any shoes on,' she says eventually. As Drew picks up the larger pieces of glass, Regal bends down in her stilettos to sweep up the remaining pieces. Her short skirt barely covers her arse. I turn away quickly so she won't see me checking her out.

'Hey, Q, have you seen her around?' Drew asks, dumping the glass in the bin. She pulls out the bin bag in one swoop and places it in front of Regal to empty the dustpan. 'Kali, I mean.'

I swallow that familiar lump in my throat and shake my head.

Drew looks at me sadly. 'You okay?'

'Yeah, I'm cool,' I say, but it must come out weird because Drew and Regal give each other a look. I clear my throat. 'I am ... Look, if you're fine down here, I'm gonna go back to bed.'

'No, stay!' Drew says, walking slowly towards me. 'I haven't seen you since your birthday. We need to catch up. Is Cam asleep?'

'He's at a gig. He'll be back soon.'

Regal puts the brush to the side, the floor now clean. 'I'm starving. Anyone want French toast?'

'Yes!' Drew says. 'Q?'

Drew and Regal look at me eagerly. Eating this late always makes me feel a bit sick, but, now they're back, I realize how much I've missed them. Anyway, it will be impossible to sleep if they're down here gossiping and laughing loudly.

'Sure. Thanks, Regal,' I say before Drew grabs my hand and leads me into the dining room.

I'm barely sat down before Drew asks, 'Are you really okay? I swear, if Kali's done anything else . . .'

'She hasn't. I haven't seen her around. I don't really go into town any more.' I look down at the table, but Drew puts her hand under my chin and forces me to look at her.

'You shouldn't be hiding away. You did nothing wrong!'

'I know,' I mumble. 'I just don't know how I'm going to act when I do see her, you know?'

Drew nods. 'And what about Simon? Have you seen him?' I shake my head, and Drew sighs. 'His part in this hurts me the most. He was practically family, and on your birthday too . . .'

'Drew, please, I don't want to talk about it,' I say, desperate for this conversation to be over.

'Sorry.' She waits a beat. 'Have you spoken to any of your other friends about it? Don't keep your feelings bottled up.'

I shrug. 'Eliza knows a bit, but she's friends with all of us, so I guess she's heard various versions of the truth.'

'Eliza still speaks to them?' Drew asks outraged.

I felt the same way until Eliza pointed out that she's known Simon for as long as I have and that she and Kali are the only girls in our friendship group so of course they're close. She swears she backs me, but the selfish part of me wants Eliza to cut them both off for good.

Drew kisses her teeth. 'When I next see Kali …'

The door swings open and Regal walks in carrying three plates of French toast covered in maple syrup. She places them in front of us, making the whole dining room smell like vanilla and cinnamon.

'What are we talking about?' Regal asks, sitting opposite me.

'Kali,' Drew says.

'Bitch.' Regal waves her fork at me. 'I will destroy her.'

I sigh. 'Please, can we talk about something else?' These two could easily carry on all night talking about my ex. 'How about the Winter Ball? Are you guys excited?'

'It's going to be epic,' Drew says. 'All those haters that acted like we weren't good enough to host the ball are going to have to eat their words. Look at us now, bitch!'

'Shh!' I hiss as Drew and Regal cackle. 'You're gonna wake up the whole house.'

Drew takes a bite of her toast. 'Mmm, this is so good!'

'I added a bit of salt this time. It really helps to bring the flavours out,' Regal says. 'We should have pancakes tomorrow. Remember that place in Paris – Holybelly?'

Drew groans. 'That food! Maybe we should go to Paris for a few days?'

'You just got here!' I say. 'And may I remind you, you're meant to be helping with the ball.'

Regal cleans her plate and leans back in her chair. 'Speaking of which, who's your date, Quincy?'

I glance at Drew, who's looking at me expectantly. 'Oh … erm … well …' I stammer.

At that moment, the front door swings open and we all hear Cam's music playing loudly through his headphones.

'Cam?' Drew calls, getting up from her seat to meet him in the hallway.

I sigh with relief, but Regal's still watching me. I should just tell her the truth. She knows everyone, so if I admitted I needed a date, she'd call in a favour and I'd be walking into the ball with a serious ten on my arm. But I can't now admit that I've lied. Every time the Winter Ball rolls around they'll bring it up, laughing their heads off.

'You don't know her, but she's really cool. You'll meet her at the ball,' I eventually say.

Regal frowns. 'How do I not know her? I know everyone. Is she new around here?'

I take a bite of my French toast to stall. If I say yes, then Cam will know I lied, and I'll never live it down. 'No ... she's from London?' I clear my throat, because why is it coming out as a question? 'She's from London,' I repeat with more conviction.

Regal's expression is hard to read and I'm not sure she's bought my lie. My hands start to feel clammy, and I discreetly wipe them on my shorts. I keep my eyes on her, because, if I look away, she'll know I'm lying. She leans forward, her face shining with excitement. 'Where did you meet?'

'Regal!' Cam walks into the dining room with his arms outstretched. Regal breaks into a grin and jumps up to hug him.

Thank you, God, for the perfect timing.

'I've missed you,' Regal says, pulling away from Cam to stare at him. 'How was the gig?'

41

'Ah, it was sick.' Cam sits down and nods at me in greeting. 'It was at the Vauxs' – an early Christmas party because they're travelling for the holidays. Bunny Vaux said they're gonna host the Seven Days party at theirs this year.'

In White Oak, the Seven Days party is almost as notorious as the Winter Ball. It happens seven days before Christmas Eve. I don't know when the first one was held. Mr Huntington once told me he'd attended one at least forty years ago. Unlike the ball, which has old-fashioned rules about dress code and dates, Seven Days is a party where all the adults turn a blind eye and there's dancing, drinking and hooking up until sunrise. It's way more fun than the Winter Ball.

'How did Bunny get her dad to agree to that?' Regal asks just before Drew says, 'What's wrong with the barn where it's normally held?'

'I'm not sure how Bunny pulled it off,' Cam replies, 'but there was a fire at the barn a few weeks back. No one was hurt, but the barn's still being fixed up, so we can't use it for Seven Days. Anyway, Mr Vaux's party tonight felt like a rave . . .'

I tune out as Cam talks. Drew and Regal are lapping up every word and seem to have forgotten about my date. I sigh with relief, but I still need to find someone to take. If they catch me out, I'll never hear the end of it.

SIX

Tia

9th December

I groan in my sleep and turn onto my side, clutching my bloated belly. After dinner yesterday, I brought out the cake I'd baked especially for Mum – red velvet with vanilla buttercream. Mum took a bite and sighed with pleasure like she always does when she tastes my baked goods.

'You, my girl, are an exceptional baker,' she said.

I don't even know how I learned to bake. Maybe I picked it up by watching Mum in the kitchen, but I've really stepped it up this last year. We've all needed cheering up, and nothing has made us happier than eating cake. Lately, I've been thinking how cool it would be to own a bakery someday.

We all had a slice of the red velvet before collapsing on the sofa to watch a re-run of *Ramsey's Kitchen Nightmares*. I hadn't been able to relax because Mike still hadn't contacted me. It wasn't until one a.m. that he texted to ask if we could meet up the next day. I couldn't get back to sleep after that, so I headed to the kitchen, cut myself a huge slice of cake and ate it in one go. I'm suffering the consequences of overeating this morning.

'You on your period?' Willow asks, sitting up in her bed and looking at me.

'No, I had too much cake,' I mumble. My stomach's so full it hurts. 'Mike wants to talk today.'

'What do you think he's going to say?'

'I don't know,' I reply, feeling nervous already.

All night I tried to figure out what had gone wrong between us. I'm not trying to big myself up, but I'm a fantastic girlfriend. I'm supportive, I go out of my way for him, I love the guy! It's like he doesn't even realize any of that.

My phone buzzes and a message from Mike pops up, almost like he knew I was thinking about him.

I'll be outside yours in 30

'I'm going to shower,' I say before Willow can ask me any more questions and drag my bloated body to the bathroom.

It's Saturday so I try to dress quickly and quietly not to disturb anyone and then wander over to Willow's desk, where her make-up bag is lying open. Thankfully there's a set of eyelashes inside because I've run out. I grab them, glancing at Willow, but she's fallen back asleep. Luckily, I've perfected my make-up routine so it can be done in under ten minutes. I sigh at my missing press-on nail and remove the rest of them. I'm about to head out when I hear Banks talking behind her and Mum's closed door. I open it, and my little sister is in bed in her teddy-bear pyjamas, playing with my old Barbies. Mum's lying next to her, looking at her phone.

Mum glances at me. 'Morning, darling.'

'Morning, Mum. Morning, Banksy. I'm just heading out to meet Mike. Won't be long.'

'Good luck,' Mum says, smiling sadly at me.

I hurry out of the door and down the stairs of our council estate tower block which smell of bleach, my footsteps echoing in the stairwell. I still find it weird living in a flat and not a house. When I reach the bottom my heart is racing and outside the main door I see Mike in a black coat, beanie hat and Timberlands. Thank God it's winter, because my layers are conveniently hiding my full belly, but my jeans are pressing uncomfortably on my abdomen.

'Hey,' he says, and he makes no gesture to greet me with a kiss or a hug. My heart sinks.

'Hi,' I say. 'Let's go sit in the park.'

We walk in silence up the road. I glance at him out of the corner of my eye, and he's looking straight ahead, hands in pockets, a determined look on his face. Before yesterday, I used to be able to read him so well, but right now I don't know what to think. He said he wanted space, but the vibe I'm getting right now is that our relationship is over.

Because it's early, there are only a few kids with their

parents in the children's playground. We head away from them towards a bench near the fountain. Just this summer, during the heatwave, we sat on this very bench, laughing as we tried to catch the ice cream that was melting onto our hands. I sit down first and Mike joins me, close enough that his leg presses against mine. A familiar shiver races through my body. Can he feel it too?

'How was your party yesterday?' he asks awkwardly.

'It was a celebratory dinner, but Mum appreciated it. How were rehearsals?' I say, wishing it wasn't so tense between us.

'Good. Just getting ready for our last show of the year.' Mike sighs. 'I'm sorry I didn't call you back. I was . . . I didn't know what to say.'

I glare at him. 'You sent me a text asking for "space". A text, Mike!'

He looks at me guiltily. 'I'm sorry.' He rubs his face. 'I wanted to talk to you about it at college yesterday, but you ran off. I should have waited to have the conversation in person instead of texting, though.' He falls silent but remains looking at me. I don't know what he expects me to say, so I don't respond. Instead, I look at the fountain and the litter round the bottom of it.

'I've been feeling kind of lost for a while now,' he continues, and I can't hide my surprise. Mike is the most put-together, sure-of-himself person I know.

'What do you mean?' I ask, my words tinged with concern.

'I'm trying to figure out what I want to do with my life. If I want to dance or go down a different route. But it's been difficult to think when I've been so focused on you . . .'

46

Me?

'Wait, let me finish,' he says as I go to object. 'I'm not saying I haven't wanted to be there for you. You and your family've been going through a lot, and I get it, but I realized recently that it's been draining all my energy and I need to think about myself too. You know?'

Hearing those words come out of Mike's mouth is like a punch to the gut. He's never, ever acted like my problems were an issue, but now he's telling me I've taken up so much of his time that it's started to impact him.

'I'm sorry I'm such a burden,' I spit back. 'I didn't choose for my family to go through everything we've been through!'

Mike jumps up, throwing his hands in the air. 'This is exactly what I wanted to avoid!' he says loudly. 'I don't want to be dick, but I need to tell you how I feel, Tia. It's been one thing after another, and I've been there for you whenever you've needed me. All I'm saying is I want some space to figure out what *I* need now.'

'Space from me!' I yell back, standing up so we're face to face. 'The whole point of being in a relationship is to be there for the other person.'

'Tia, I am here for you,' he says softly before gripping my hands. They're warm against my freezing ones. 'Is it so wrong to want to figure out what I need from life?'

'No, I'm not saying that,' I reply, feeling myself wavering. Sometimes I really annoy myself. I want to tell Mike that throwing my family's situation back in my face is hurtful and he's never mentioned it until now, but I can't get the words out.

47

'I think space would be good for both of us, to decide if this relationship is what we both want,' Mike continues.

I want you! I feel like screaming in his face.

'So this isn't a break-up?' I ask, desperate for clarity.

'No ... I mean ...' He sighs. 'I don't know.'

I glance around the park. This must be a joke, right? Mum told me about this prank show she used to watch called *Punk'd*, and I must be the star of an episode, because this isn't making sense.

'But I love you,' I say, and Mike responds by rubbing his thumb across the top of my hand.

'I really care about you, Tia,' he says softly.

Realization hits me. *He didn't say it back. He's never said it back.*

I desperately want to ask *why* he doesn't love me, but I can't bear to hear his answer.

'I'm actually going away for Christmas,' I suddenly say, taking my hands out of his grasp.

'Oh, when are you going?' he asks.

'Monday.'

He frowns. 'Why so soon?'

I shrug. 'My aunt booked it and I only found out about it last night. We won't be back until the twenty-seventh, so I guess you'll get the space you want.' I try to make my voice light, but it comes out hard and sharp.

Mike slowly sits back down. I follow suit, waiting for him to say something.

'What about my party?' he eventually says.

48

'I won't able to come now,' I reply.

'But I need you there.' Mike grabs my hands more urgently this time.

'You still want me there?' I ask. Does this mean we're not completely over?

'Well, you've been organizing the whole thing. How am I meant to do it without you? What about my cake—?'

'Wait.' I pull my hands away. 'Is that the only reason you want me there? To make sure everything runs smoothly and you get your stupid cake?'

Mike looks at me blankly. 'I love your cakes.'

I scoff. 'I'm glad you love something!'

He frowns. 'You're upset that I love your cakes?'

'IT'S NOT ABOUT THE CAKE!' I yell.

A couple walking by pause and look at us. Mike smiles back at them reassuringly, but I can see by the way his jaw is tensed that he's pissed. *I'm* pissed! Why is it so easy for him to say he loves my cakes, but he can't say he loves me?

'Tia, what the hell?' Mike hisses once we're alone again. 'Why are you shouting?'

'Do you … ?' I want to ask him how he really feels about me. 'Do *you* … ?' *Please get the hint, Mike!*

His eyebrows crinkle together. 'Do I what?'

Ask him, Tia! But I can't do it, because I know if I do and he says no then we can't stay together, and I'm not ready for us to be over. We're going to get through this. I'm sure of it.

'Do you … really want me there?' I finally ask.

Mike smiles. 'Of course I do. I'm sorry. I wasn't saying I

49

only want you at the party because you're making the cake. I want you there because you're important to me, and you should be there at my eighteenth, even if it's just for an hour. Please, Tia.' He kisses my hand. 'Promise you'll come?'

My head is screaming at me that Mike's using me, but my heart doesn't want to listen. All I want is for us to be back in a good place again, and if helping him with his party will do that, then I'll find a way to be there.

SEVEN

Quincy

9th December

We didn't go to bed until past four a.m. but somehow managed not to disturb Mum and Dad. After we'd had our French toast, Drew randomly decided it would be a good idea to play charades, so me and her teamed up against Regal and Cam, but every time someone guessed wrong, they had to take a shot. It didn't take long for all of us to get drunk and start shouting out the stupidest suggestions. Then Cam got his keyboard from upstairs, and we each had to play a tune while the others guessed what it was. The only song I can play is 'Gangsta's Paradise' because Cam taught me it years ago. He was so drunk that even with his musical ear he couldn't work out my obvious song choice. We went to bed when Dad came down to do his morning rounds and cussed us out. He was even angrier when he saw we'd drunk his good rum. I'm going to try to avoid him today.

I sit up in bed, head pounding and throat feeling like sandpaper. I reach for my phone and my stomach sinks when I see a message from Kali on the screen.

Please can we talk?

I leave her on read just like the other forty-odd messages she's sent me. I should block her, but there's something satisfying in knowing that she'll see I've read her messages and ignored her. I keep expecting her to get the hint, but she hasn't yet.

A knock sounds on my door and it's Drew who walks in, wearing a purple dressing gown and black sunglasses, her hair piled on top of her head.

'What's with them?' I ask gesturing at her face.

She touches the glasses. 'Ugh, it's too bright. I feel like shit!'

Drew sits on the edge of my bed and looks around my room with interest. She spots the picture of me, her and Regal taken at Regal's penthouse. I'm halfway through buttoning up a dark blue shirt, and my head's thrown back in laughter; Regal and Drew are laughing too, but they're leaning on each other struggling to stand. I can't remember what was so funny, but Daniel, Drew's boyfriend, captured the moment perfectly.

I love that picture. It was taken on my eighteenth birthday when Drew had organized for me to come to London. We spent the whole day as tourists – visiting the London Eye, Big

Ben and Buckingham Palace, followed by lunch at the Ivy and then drinks at Soho House. After that we met Regal at her penthouse so we could pre-drink before hitting the club. She had a rail full of designer clothes waiting just for me! I'd never tried on Balmain, Tom Ford or Louis Vuitton in my life, let alone worn them out.

Drew stands and smiles as she holds up the picture. 'That was such a good day, wasn't it?'

'Yeah, the best.' Until it wasn't. I'd come home two days later and that's when I found out about Kali and Simon. 'I like London,' I say instead, to focus my attention elsewhere.

'Why don't you come back? It might do you good to be in the city, meeting new people and figuring out what you want to do with your life. You can stay with me and Daniel. I think Cam is thinking of moving up. There are way more music opportunities in the capital.' Her eyes may be hidden behind dark shades, but I know Drew's looking at me eagerly, wanting me to say yes. Unlike her or Cam, I've never known what I want to do. I think I'm good at lots of things, just not great at anything. The creative gene definitely skipped me. For as long as I can remember, Drew was set on moving to London as soon as she could, and Cam has always wanted to be a global DJ. I know he can't wait to leave the countryside, but, me, I like living here. Maybe one day I'll take over Saiyan Hedge Farm. Drew and Cam reckon I need to dream bigger – like if I'm not thinking about world domination, then what's the point of existing? But what's wrong with staying here?

'I don't know,' I say.

Drew sits back on my bed. 'I just want you to have a plan for after college, Q. It's a big world out there, and you need to see it. You don't have to be stuck in White Oak for the rest of your life.'

'I don't feel stuck,' I protest. 'It's hardly like life is hard out here.'

'Isn't it?' Drew challenges. 'We're one of the only Black families. London is so much more diverse. No one there would ask you about your religious beliefs just because you have locs.'

'But we belong here just as much as the next family,' I argue. 'Ignorant people exist everywhere. I don't go telling you about knife crime statistics in London, do I? I support you in whatever you want to do, wherever you want to do it.'

'And I support you, Q! But is it that bad of me to want you to have a plan?'

'A plan that fits you,' I mumble.

Drew opens her mouth to argue back, but my phone rings. I pick it up. 'Hey, Mum.'

'Hi, darling. Is Drew with you?'

Wordlessly I hand the phone to her.

'Morning, Mum ... What? But I feel sick too ... Tell him to get his behind up ... I *am* being nice!' She groans loudly. 'Fine ... No, I'll go with Quincy.' She glances at me, and I raise my eyebrows. 'It might be too heavy for him ... Okay, bye.' She hands me back my phone. 'Mum wants us to go to the vineyard to pick up more wine for the ball.'

Great. The vineyard is the last place I want to go. It's Simon's family who own it. I've only seen him around college, and we haven't spoken since him and Kali. We used to speak every day; we practically lived in each other's houses. To be honest, I miss him more than Kali. His parents probably don't know what happened, so they'll for sure question why I haven't been round recently.

Drew puts her hand on my leg. 'Mum's going to cover on reception because Cam's sick – so useless. Let's get ourselves sorted and then head to the vineyard. I've always got your back, Q.'

'Thanks, Drew.' Even though she's a pain in the arse about my future, my sister is as loyal as they come, and I love her for that.

She smiles. 'Leave in an hour, yeah?'

I shower and dress and then head downstairs. My head's still pounding, but I'm hoping some fresh air will help. Mum and Drew are talking in hushed voices when I reach reception, but they stop when they see me.

'What?' I ask looking at them. Mum looks away, but Drew, now dressed in baggy jeans and a long jacket, hands me a bottle of water.

'Thanks,' I say gratefully, downing it.

'Okay to drive?' Drew asks.

'Yeah, sure.' I look again at Mum, who is now busying herself tidying the already tidy reception desk. I ignore her odd behaviour and head for the car.

'What was that all about with Mum?' I ask Drew.

'Oh, she told me you had a date!' She's looking out of the window so she misses how hard I grip the wheel as I steer through the bendy lanes. 'She wasn't sure if you wanted me to know, but I got it out of her.' At this, Drew turns to me. 'Did you meet her online?'

I nod.

'She must really like you to come all the way down here for the ball.'

'Yeah,' I say weakly. *Eliza, you better come through with a date.*

The vineyard is only a ten-minute drive away, and the closer we get, the more clammy my hands become. I'm not nervous about seeing Simon, I'm more worried about getting angry. My brain still can't comprehend that Simon, of all people, betrayed my trust. I think of Cam shouting outside his house, Simon looking scared from his window, and I wish I'd confronted him then, when my feelings were raw. Now all my emotions are simmering inside me, and I know one day it's going to get too much and I'll explode. I just hope that day isn't today.

I park by the farm shop that's also owned by Simon's family. I get out, shivering from the icy-cold weather, and follow Drew into the shop, passing the bare vines that Simon and I used to spend our summers running through. The door heater blasts in my face, and I take in the familiar sight of the wines, cheeses, chutneys, jams and pâtés lining the shelves, all homemade products.

'Quincy!' A short, round woman with wavy blonde hair

breaks into a smile when she sees me. 'How are you, love? I haven't seen you in ages.' Sophie, Simon's mum, opens her arms and I hug her tightly.

'I'm good, thanks. Just been busy with college. Me and Drew are here to pick up some more wine.'

'Hi, Sophie.' Drew hugs her too.

'Wow, look at you, Drew! Our very own celebrity!' Sophie pulls away, smiling at the both of us. 'You must be so excited about the ball. Oh, I can't wait! I went into town a couple of weeks ago and bought myself a pretty little number. I spent way more than usual – Peter was rather annoyed at me – but like I told him, it's not every day our favourite family get to host the Winter Ball!' She's beaming so lovingly at us that it's obvious she doesn't know what went down.

Drew links arms with me. 'I'm sure you're going to look beautiful,' Drew says. 'Sorry to rush you, Sophie, but Mum's short-staffed.'

'Oh, of course, love. Let me grab the bottles. Simon! Watch the till, will you?'

Simon comes through from the back and Drew grips my arm. He stops mid-step, his green eyes widening as he sees us. He's wearing an oversized hoodie and baggy jeans, and the silver chain he's had for ever dangles round his neck.

'Hey, Q,' he says, putting his hands in his pockets and bouncing on his feet, something he only does when he's nervous. His shoulder-length blond hair falls in front of his face. 'How are you?'

57

It's weird seeing him. For a moment, it feels normal, but then I remind myself of what happened and my emotions start to bubble.

'I'm cool ... You?'

He shrugs. Simon is usually full of energy, but he looks broken, like he can't even muster a smile. He turns to my sister. 'Hi, Drew. I saw your film. You were great.'

Drew glances at me before she says, 'Thanks. You look like shit.'

'Drew!' I mutter at the same time Simon says, 'I feel it.'

That's when I feel the bubbling sensation reaching boiling point, my whole body getting hot.

'As you should,' Drew continues, oblivious of how I'm feeling. 'What the hell were you thinking, Simon?'

'I just ... we ...' He sighs and shrugs.

I clench my fists. Simon notices and takes a step back. 'You feel like shit?' I hiss, looking him square in the eye. He winces like I've hit him.

'Not here,' Drew warns.

'I messed up. Bad. I know that. But, Q, please, can we talk?' Simon pleads. I don't even realize I've lunged for him until Drew pulls me back.

'Car! Right now!' she yells.

I brush her off and march out, breathing hard like I just ran the length of the vineyard. And *he* feels like shit? I'm the one who lost my best friend and girlfriend. And *he* feels like shit?

I lean against the car, my head down on my chest, arms folded in a poor attempt to keep warm. When the shop door opens, Drew uses her body to wedge it and I hurry over, grabbing the boxes of wine from her.

'You okay?' she asks gently, and I nod. 'Put those in the boot. There's a few more.'

From the corner of my eye I see Simon staring at me, and I purposely avoid looking at him. If I never see him again, I'll be more than happy.

EIGHT

Tia

9th December

When I get home, Mum's cooking lunch in the kitchen and singing along to the radio. She looks up. 'Hey, darling. How did it go?' I lean on the counter and sigh in response. 'Oh. That bad?'

'Not bad but not brilliant,' I reply.

I agreed to go to Mike's party, and I'm so annoyed with myself. Why did I say yes when I don't even know my status any more – his girlfriend, his special friend, his soon-to-be-but-she-doesn't-know-it-yet ex-girlfriend? And how will I get there from the countryside? With a cake, no less. When Mum says no, she usually means it, but maybe I could try one more time . . .

'He wants me to be there for his birthday party. Mum, I have to go!'

'Tia, we'll be in the middle of nowhere. There's not even a train station nearby.' Mum takes the chips out of the deep-fat fryer.

I frown. 'So how are we getting there?'

Mum avoids my eye. 'Paul's taking us.'

Paul? Banks' dad, that she broke up with a year ago? *Are they getting back together?*

'Don't read too much into it,' Mum says, as if my thoughts are written all over my face. 'He won't get to see Banks for Christmas this year, and you know how he loves hanging out with us. He's happy to do it.'

I reach for a homemade chip and pop it into my mouth. *Damn, it tastes so good.* 'Why doesn't he just stay with us at the farm?'

Paul is great. Even though he's not mine or Willow's dad, he treats us like we're his own children. He was always really invested in what was going on in our lives, took us out on shopping and cinema trips and never prioritized Banks over us. Even my dad likes him. And when Mum and Paul broke up, it still didn't change our relationship with him. I would love for them to get back together. People that nice don't come around often, and I think Mum made a huge mistake letting him go.

'Stay?' Mum looks at me bewildered. 'Stay where?' She bursts out laughing. 'Tia, you're too funny. Anyway, where do you and Mike stand now?'

'Well, we're still together.' *Kind of.*

What I really want to ask Mum is how long you should wait

for a boy to say he loves you, but she's never had that problem. Her issue is getting guys to *stop* being in love with her. My mum is beautiful, and I don't mean that in a 'she's my mum so she's beautiful to me' way. No, she's completely stunning. Clear skin, high cheekbones, her thick dark hair natural and long; one of those 'I woke up like this' photogenic women I'd give anything to be.

Mum shaves parmesan cheese over the chips and dresses them with truffle oil. The chef in her won't allow her to serve basic chips, but I haven't seen truffle oil in the flat since we moved here. I grab the bottle and raise my eyebrows at her.

'Ezra sent me a hamper to say congratulations about the new job. Isn't that lovely of him?' she says. Mum glances over my shoulder, and I turn my head. I don't know how I missed the wicker basket tied with a red bow by the kitchen door.

'As in Ezra, your ex-boyfriend from years ago?' I walk over to the basket. Inside is a bottle of champagne and a range of foodie items, from caviar to smoked salmon pâté. 'Mum! This must have cost a fortune.'

'I know,' she says, opening the oven to check on the burgers. 'I'll call him later to thank him.'

'How does he know where we live?' I question.

Mum shrugs. 'Maybe Bimpé told him. I think they still work together.'

I spy a white card peeking out from behind the champagne. I pull it out and clear my throat: '"Tope, I always knew you could do it! You're the definition of never giving up on your dreams. Would love to take you out to celebrate properly, but, until then, enjoy the hamper. Miss you. Love Ez. Kiss.'" *So even Ezra, who she dumped years ago, isn't afraid to say the word 'love'.*

Mum laughs, breaking my thoughts. 'Typical Ezra! Always trying to shoot his shot.'

I can't help looking at the hamper with a twinge of jealousy. *More like typical Mum, always having guys after her.* I sigh. Not me being jealous of my mum's love life.

'Where's Willow?' I ask, changing the subject.

'She had to get some bits ahead of the trip. Banks went with her. Are you going to start packing today?'

'I dunno,' I mumble, taking another chip. I swear nothing bangs more than triple-cooked parmesan truffle fries. Mum frowns at me. 'What? I'll do it later, I promise.'

'We're leaving on Monday morning whether you're packed or not,' she says.

I roll my eyes as she hands me a plate of food. The beefburger is filled with cheese, lettuce and a homemade onion relish. Mum's burgers taste better than any fast-food restaurant's. Once I'm done, I head to the fridge, carefully remove a slice of the red velvet cake and wrap it in foil.

'I'm going to see Remi. You know, now that I won't be seeing my *best friend* for weeks.'

Mum waves her spatula at me by way of goodbye, then adds, 'If you think of anything you need for the trip, message Willow.'

'I will. See you later,' I call over my shoulder.

*

Remi and I used to be neighbours, but when we moved to the flat we had to deal with the fact we're now a ten-minute bus ride away from each other. I get off outside a two-storey house with a green door and look wistfully at the house a few doors down. Remi said an Asian couple with two kids moved in, and I can see they've painted over our pink door that I loved. The left window on the top floor was mine. I wonder which family member has my old room, and if they've painted over my lilac walls too.

Remi opens the door as soon as I ring the bell.

'I come bearing gifts,' I say, holding out the cake.

'Stop!' Remi's eyes light up, and she reaches for it greedily.

We head up to her room and I take a seat on her bed. 'How did things go with Ashleigh yesterday?' I ask.

Remi rolls her eyes. 'I managed to catch up with her before she went home, and she tried to act like Aaron had been the one moving to her. But we know how Ashleigh is – she'd flirt with a brick wall if she thought it would respond.'

I chuckle. Remi's not wrong. We met Ashleigh in college, and she's part of our friendship group, but she and Remi always seem to be clashing over something,

Remi unwraps the cake and takes a bite, closing her eyes and groaning. 'Damn, girl, you're too good at this.' She squints at me. 'Are you buttering me up?'

'Maybe ... Mum's taking us away for Christmas.' Remi's eyes widen in surprise. 'Oh, it gets worse. We're going to a farm.'

At this, Remi bursts out laughing. 'You're joking!'

'I wish! It's going to be shit, cold and boring as fuck.'

'I don't think I've ever been to a farm. Where is it?' she asks.

I shrug. 'It's called Saiyan Hedge Farm. My aunt booked it for us to celebrate Mum's new job. And get this: apparently, they don't even have a train station. I know!' I add when Remi gasps.

She licks the buttercream off her fingers before picking up her phone from her desk. 'Let's see what godforsaken place your mum is taking my bestie.' Not long after she smiles. 'Wow! This actually looks nice, Tia.' She sits next to me and shows me the Instagram page. I barely look at it. A brochure and an Instagram page don't show you real life. It's a filtered fantasy. I bet the place smells like horse shit.

Remi squeals and grabs my arm. 'Is that Drew Parker?'

'Yeah, her family own it. And Regal Majekodunmi grew up in the town as well.'

'Erm, why didn't you say that first? This sounds well cool! Imagine spending Christmas with them.'

I roll my eyes. 'If they're even there.'

Remi points at a picture and wolf whistles. 'Who's this hottie?'

I can't help my curiosity, so I look over at the screen. *Wow. Who* is *that?* Remi's finger is pointed at a tall Black guy with shoulder-length locs, a light goatee, a hard body and eyes that look like they're trying to seduce me from the picture. He's standing next to a gigantic black horse in the middle of a field. I try to block out the horse because they freak me out, but, I can't lie, the guy is beautiful. Maybe he's a model.

'"Riding lessons for children and adults led by the horse whisperer, Quincy Parker,"' Remi reads. He's tagged in the photo, but when she clicks onto his page, it's set to private. 'Fuck it,' she says as she requests to follow him. 'I can think of better things to ride than the horse.'

'Remi!' I laugh and shake my head.

'What?' she says, feigning innocence. 'I wouldn't be complaining about spending Christmas with him! Oh, wait . . .' She glances at me. 'You have a boyfriend.'

Do I? But instead, I say, 'Just a small problem.' It takes all my effort to take my eyes off Quincy Parker and focus them on Remi.

'Wait!' Remi says loudly, making me jump. 'If you're away for Christmas, how are you going to Mike's birthday?'

I raise my hands. 'And that's the big problem.' I fill her in on what happened with Mike but don't mention the love issue or the fact he doesn't know if he wants us to be together. To be honest, I'm embarrassed. Mike and I are usually joined at the hip, and everyone thinks we're madly in love, so what would they say if they knew he's never even said he loves me?

'Space from *you*?' Remi asks with her mouth open. 'But it's not a break-up?'

'No, definitely not, but how is space going to help our relationship?'

'I hear that,' Remi says.

'And if I miss his party, I feel like it'll make everything worse. Plus, he asked me to still be there, which is a good sign, right?'

'Don't there have to be clear rules when someone asks for space? Like you know when Ross and Rachel went on a break in *Friends*, but then Ross cheated because he thought they'd broken up,' Remi explains.

I frown. 'But we're not on a break. He just said he wants space.'

'What's the difference?' she asks, and my stomach knots because I honestly don't know.

'Do you think Mike and I should have clear rules, then?'

Remi nods. 'What if he meets someone during this "space"? You need to set boundaries so nothing like the Ross thing can happen.'

My stomach bubbles and I feel like I'm going to be sick. Is that why Mike's not sure about us? Is there someone else?

Remi squeezes my arm. 'I'm not saying it will happen, but it could, right? And what about you?'

I frown. 'What about me?'

'Erm, hello?' Remi taps on her phone and the picture of Quincy Parker lights back up. 'What if he asks you out?'

'Why would he ask me out?' I reply, bewildered. 'I'm sure he has hundreds of tourists falling at his feet. And I have a boyfriend, remember? But you're right. I'll talk to Mike and set some boundaries. It'll be fine. I know it will.'

It has to be, I think to myself.

NINE

Quincy

9th December

Drew drops me home before continuing into town to meet Regal. She asked me if I wanted to come, but I'm still annoyed after seeing Simon and I don't want to risk bumping into Kali too. The one person I do want to see is Eliza, but she's busy helping her mum at the hairdresser's today.

Dad helps me carry the boxes of wine into the cellar.

'Ava Duffy's cancelled her riding lesson today,' Dad says, leaning on the cellar wall. 'She says it's too cold.'

I scoff. 'She didn't know it would be cold in December when she booked the lesson?' Dad raises his eyebrows at me. 'Sorry, Dad – I'm not having the best day.'

'Nor am I. My best rum's been drunk.' I look at the floor guiltily. 'Was it Drew or Cam's idea to drink it?'

I don't even remember, but Drew's a daddy's girl meaning Dad will go easier on her so I say, 'Drew.' All Dad does is tut in response. 'Can I help with anything else?' I ask to soften the blow.

Dad shakes his head. 'Check with your mum, though.'

I head towards reception, where I assume Mum will be. As I walk by the kitchen, I'm relieved to hear Gia's distinctive singing, something she always does when she cooks, which means I won't have to sort dinner tonight. But when I reach the reception, it's empty. I take off my coat and sit behind the desk. I'm just about to text Mum to ask where she is when Cam walks round the corner and I get a waft of something delicious.

'Better, then?' I ask as he stands next to me.

Cam laughs. 'Was Drew pissed?' He offers me his bowl of halloumi chips covered in breadcrumbs – crispy on the outside, gooey on the inside.

'Of course she was.' I take one and bite into it. *So good!*

'Where did you two go? I couldn't find you,' he asks.

'To the vineyard.' Cam's eyes widen. 'And, yes, before you ask, he was there.'

'And?' Cam presses.

'It was awkward, and I got mad all over again.' I take another halloumi chip, and for once Cam looks at me seriously.

'I'm really sorry you're going through this, Q. You're for real the last person that deserves it.'

Hearing Cam say those words, I instantly feel better. I smile. 'Thanks, man.'

A red car pulling up outside catches my eye. A familiar blonde girl steps out of it.

'Hey, isn't that Stacey?' I ask Cam, but he's vanished. 'Cam?'

'Get rid of her!' he hisses from under the desk.

Stacey opens the front door. Her pale cheeks are flushed red from the cold, and she smiles brightly when she sees me.

'Hey, Quincy! How are you?'

'I'm good, thanks. What brings you here?' I respond as normally as possible.

Stacey comes closer and I glance down at Cam, whose eyes are wide with panic. 'I came to speak to Cam about the Winter Ball. I'm hoping he might be my date. He hasn't responded to my messages, but I know you guys are super busy with the prep.'

I feel bad for Stacey. If Cam had just told her he's not looking for anything serious, she wouldn't be putting herself out there, and he wouldn't be hiding under a desk to avoid her. Cam hits my leg and I have to stop myself from jumping. I flick my eyes down towards him and he shakes his head quickly.

'So, is he about?' Stacey asks.

'No, sorry. He's not well.'

Stacey's shoulders sink in disappointment.

'Do you want me to pass him a message?' I offer.

'Yeah, can you tell him I stopped by? Ask him to let me know about the ball ASAP. I have a dress on reserve.'

'No problem. I'll see you soon.' I smile tightly.

She waves as she goes. Cam only stands up once he hears the car driving away.

'Bloody hell,' he says, putting another halloumi chip in his mouth. 'She's intense, isn't she?'

'You shouldn't have slept with her,' I point out. 'It obviously meant a lot more to her than it did to you.'

Cam shrugs. 'What can I say? I'm good at what I do.' I elbow him in the ribs and he groans and holds his side.

'Don't be a dick,' I say. 'Be upfront with these girls so they know where they stand from the start.' It annoys me that Cam treats girls like that. I bet Stacey will continue to text him despite him ghosting her. I've never ghosted a girl in my life, except Kali, but she deserves it.

Cam chews slowly as if he's really contemplating what I've just said, but I know he'll be back to his old ways in no time.

'I'm going to check on Legend,' I say, pulling on my coat and walking towards the door.

The stables are a fifteen-minute walk away from the house. I usually drive down, but I'm not in a rush today. It doesn't matter how many times I've been down here, the stables never lose their ability to cast a spell. The sight of the horses and all their tack, the sound of their hooves rustling the straw, the warm smell of manure – to me, it's a magical place. Ethan gives me a wave as I get closer, and I wave back. He's the stablehand who looks after all the horses.

'Didn't think I'd see you today,' Ethan says, sitting at the small table with a cup of tea. 'Your lesson got cancelled.'

'I know, but I thought I'd take Legend out for a ride.'

Ethan is in his late forties with dark brown hair and blue eyes, and his white skin always seems to be tanned whatever

71

the season. He's worked at Saiyan Hedge Farm for years, and he was the one who taught me how to ride.

'Sure,' he says. 'I'd prepped her for your lesson so she's all ready.'

We have five horses and three ponies at the farm. A few of them are out in the field grazing, including Legend, who trots towards me when she hears me calling her. She's a black Selle Français and we've had her for years.

'Hello, girl,' I say, rubbing her neck.

Legend's tall, and beginners are always scared of riding her, but she's a big softie. I climb onto the saddle, and Ethan walks over with a helmet for me, which I take from him reluctantly. Yes, I know helmets should be worn for safety, but it always feels like a mission with how thick my hair is. Still, I strap it on, grab the reins and tap Legend's side with my foot and she starts to trot. Instantly, I feel calmer.

Ethan starts to take the other animals into the stables as Legend and I trot around the fields. From this height, I can see in the distance the Tudor manor house where the Winter Ball will be held. Once word gets out that Drew and Regal are back and will be attending the ball, I'm sure more people than usual will want to catch a glimpse of them. There'll be even more attention on us as a family. One small problem – I still don't know who's going to be my date. *Maybe I could join a dating app . . . ?* I shake my head. How exactly am I going to convince a stranger to come here from wherever she lives to attend a ball in two weeks' time?

I put my lack of date out of my mind and, after a good hour

of riding, I'm feeling refreshed. Back at the stables, I dismount and press my face close to Legend's.

'Making up a fake girl wasn't smart, was it, Legend?'

Legend whinnies in response. Yep, even she thinks I'm a total idiot.

TEN

Tia

9th December

I spend the rest of the day at Remi's, and when it's time to go I hug her tight, as if it's the last time we'll see each other.

'So you're coming back for Mike's party?' Remi checks, once we let go.

'Hopefully. I definitely won't make it back for bowling, but fingers crossed I'll be at Rye Levels. I'll let you know once I work out the logistics,' I promise.

'Send me pics,' Remi says. 'And say hi to that hottie for me.'

I laugh. 'See you later.'

When I get home, clothes are strewn everywhere, open suitcases line the hallway and Banks is running between rooms with her toy horse in her hand. She's topless and wearing patterned shorts, cowboy boots and sparkly pink fairy wings.

'Tia?' Mum calls, poking her head out of the living room. 'There you are! I didn't realize you were planning to stay at Remi's the whole day.'

'Sorry. I did text you to let you know.' I take off my coat. 'How's the packing going?'

Mum looks at Banks and pulls a face. 'She wants to try on everything. It's taking for ever.' She rubs her face. 'Can you get on with your packing, please? I'll relax once I know everything is sorted.'

'Yeah, sure.'

I head to my room and Willow is folding up jumpers with her air pods in. She looks up when she sees me and removes one. 'Were you at Remi's?'

'Yeah. I wanted to see her before we left,' I reply.

Willow nods. 'I had to tell all my clients and my boss at work that there had been a family emergency and I was going to be away for the next couple of weeks because of it. There's no way I could have had all that time off at such short notice otherwise. I hate lying to people and letting them down.' She shrugs like it doesn't matter, but I can tell she's upset. 'And I met Zarah in town and had to tell her I can't go to her party now.' Willow slumps on her bed. 'Everyone is going.'

'Sorry, Willow. That's shit,' I say sympathetically. Here's me moaning about all the things I'm missing out on when Willow's in exactly the same boat.

Mum's not-too-out-of-tune singing reaches us. Willow jerks her thumb at the door. 'She's been so happy lately, hasn't she?

I know the timing of this trip isn't ideal, but I think we should make the most of it, for Mum's sake.'

I nod. Mum really has been happier, and it's starting to feel like our family is returning to the way we used to be before everything went wrong. I just wish this trip wasn't now.

I pull out a bunch of clothes from my wardrobe and dump them on my bed. What exactly is farm attire? I start to fold up jumpers and jeans, even ones I never wear. It's not like I'm trying to impress anyone.

'How did things go with Mike?' Willow asks.

I pause mid-fold. 'Erm ... yeah, it was okay.' If I tell Willow how our conversation really went down, she'll probably go beat him up before we leave, and I already know there's no way she's going to help me sneak back to London for his party. For some reason, I remember that guy Quincy, and look down at the clothes on my bed. Some of them are ugly as hell. Maybe I should give my outfits a bit more thought ...

'How's it going?' Mum asks, walking in and dragging two suitcases behind her. She lays them in the middle of the room. 'They're empty.'

'What do we wear for this ball?' Willow asks.

I totally forgot about that. I glance at my wardrobe and catch the gleam of the white dress I bought for Mike's party. I need to remember to sneak that into my suitcase without Mum or Willow clocking.

'Bimpé says there's this shop in the town where everyone goes to buy their ballgowns. I thought it would be fun to buy them there,' Mum says.

Willow and I look at each other, both thinking the same thing.

'Sounds expensive,' I say gently, and Mum frowns. 'We're happy to take something we already own.'

'Girls, don't worry, it's all in hand.' Mum's frown disappears. 'Bimpé has sorted us out. Remember, she's been before, so she knows the drill.' Mum sighs happily. 'Apparently, Saiyan Hedge Farm has the *best* food. I can't wait for this break. I really need it. We all do . . .'

Mum settles on my bed just as we hear a crash from the living room followed by an 'Oops' from Banks. Mum groans and puts her head in her hands.

'I'll go,' Willow says, hurrying out.

I sit next to Mum, resting my head on her shoulder. A second later, she kisses my forehead.

'It will be fun, Tia. I really am sorry that you're missing Mike's party, though.'

'It's okay,' I lie. 'And just for the record, if you're planning a family horse-riding session, count me right out.'

Mum laughs and uses my leg to hoist herself up. 'I'll keep that in mind. Oh, and don't forget to pack swimwear. There's a pool or hot tub. I can't remember which one.'

I pull a face. As if I'm going swimming in winter!

Mum tuts. 'It's heated, Tia. I'm not sending you to your death. Right, let's see what trouble that little madam has caused.'

I wait a few seconds after Mum's gone before I grab the white dress from my wardrobe. It's short and tight with long sleeves and a low scoop back. It's the sexiest dress I've ever owned, and I know Mike is going to love it. There's no way he'll want to break up once he sees me in this. I carefully fold it and hide it under my jumpers.

10th December

We spend all of Sunday packing and re-packing, or, in Banks' case, trying on everything she can find. Mum tells us to be ready by eight a.m. tomorrow. I call Mike before I go to bed, wanting to talk to him about the rules of our time apart, but it rings through, so I shoot him a text and wait for a response.

11th December

I wake up to Mum singing my name, and squint as I open my eyes. Mum's face is smiling down at me. My curtains are open, and the winter sun is pouring through. 'You've got an hour until we leave. Up you get!'

I groan and turn over, and see that Willow's bed is empty. My phone buzzes next to me and I immediately think of Mike, but it's just Remi checking how I am. Nothing from Mike. My stomach starts to twist.

'Tia! Move it!' Mum shouts from the other room.

When I've showered and dressed, I find Paul with Mum in the living room, helping Banks with her shoes.

'Tia!' Paul grins widely when he spots me.

He's cut his brown hair since I last saw him so it's less

nineties boyband flopping over his face. The new style is shorter, which suits him better, making his blue eyes more obvious. He's pushed the sleeves of his jumper up, so I can see his tattoos. Looking at Paul, with his neat and wholesome appearance, you wouldn't think he was inked up but he even has Mum's name tattooed on his bicep!

'Excited?' he asks.

'I guess,' I say. 'How come you're not staying with us?'

'Tia!' Mum snaps.

'I'm going up to Edinburgh to spend Christmas with my dad,' Paul says regretfully. 'It would have been great to have spent it with you guys.' He glances at Mum, who takes a long sip of her tea, raising the cup high so you can't see her face.

'I'm just going to finish getting ready,' I say.

Willow looks up from packing her handbag when I walk into our room. 'Did you know Paul was driving us?'

'Yeah, Mum said the other day. They're not getting back together, though, before you ask,' I reply.

'I wish they would. Paul's so lovely,' Willow says. 'Have you got any space left in your case? I want to pack a few more things.'

I nod towards the suitcase next to my bed and watch Willow carefully as she goes over to it. Even though my white dress is hidden under my jumpers, I'm still panicking a bit. Willow piles a couple of extra clothes on top of mine and then zips the suitcase back up. Thank God!

Once we're all ready, Paul takes my heavy suitcase from me and puts it in the boot of his BMW parked outside before glancing down at my trainers. 'You sure you want to wear those? They might get muddy.'

I don't own that much footwear so my options are limited, but white Air Forces go with most outfits. They're still pretty clean, considering they're over a year old. 'Yeah, they'll be fine. I'm not planning to go on any country walks.'

Once we're buckled in, Paul asks for music suggestions, but I don't respond because I'm looking at my phone wondering why Mike still hasn't messaged me back.

'Tia?' Paul asks. 'Music?'

'I don't mind,' I reply. Music is the last thing I care about right now.

Paul settles on an R&B playlist and taps his hands to the beat as he drives. The buildings thin out as we join the motorway and leave London behind. Every few minutes I check my phone. Nothing from Mike.

ELEVEN

Quincy

11th December

I linger in bed longer than usual, listening to the Monday-morning hustle and bustle of downstairs. Eliza texted me yesterday telling me to meet her in the college common room when I head in later today. I hope it's because she's found me a date.

Cam barges into my room, making me jump.

'Hey!' I say. He would go ape if I barged into his room without knocking. I'm about to cuss him out, but then I catch sight of his expression: he looks rattled.

'I fucked up, Q,' he says with his head in his hands.

I sit up. 'What happened?'

'I messed up a booking. All the holiday cottages are taken but a family have just arrived to check in.'

'What?' I jump out of bed, pulling on the hoodie and tracksuit bottoms that are on my bedroom floor without thinking. 'How have you managed that?' Cam groans in response.

I don't know why I'm surprised. Cam's barely been on reception lately and all of us have been chipping in here and there. No wonder there's been a mix-up. I understand that he wants to focus more on his gigs, but a mess like this affects all of us.

'Where's Mum?' I ask.

'She went to a meeting about the ball. Dad's doing the food shop, and I don't know where Drew is. I've texted her bare, but I think she's still mad at me for not helping out the other day.' Cam hits his forehead. 'How did this happen? Where the hell are they going to stay?'

'Calm down, Cam,' I say. 'Let's see if we can sort it before Mum gets back. Are they pissed?'

'I haven't exactly told them yet . . .'

Typical. We hurry down the stairs and I quickly fire off a text to Drew.

> CALL ME ASAP. Cam double booked.
> No room at the inn!!!

As we enter the reception, I see a fairly tall white man with two very pretty Black women next to him. The older one has dark hair and the younger one's hair is pink. A small mixed-race girl with big blue eyes stands in between them. The man has his arms crossed and a deep frown on his face, and the two women are talking animatedly to each other.

'Hi!' I smile brightly at them, and the older woman smiles back, but it looks strained. I can see her taking in my clothes. *Shit.* I should have dressed more smartly knowing I was about to greet guests. 'I'm Quincy Parker.' I hold out my hand, and she shakes it.

'I'm Tope,' she says in a strong London accent. 'This is Paul and these are my daughters Willow and Banks.'

Daughters? This woman looks pretty young and she's hot too. Willow gives me a more friendly smile. I wave at Banks, but she hides behind Willow's leg.

'It's nice to meet you. My brother said you have a booking?' I ask politely.

'Yes. Here's the confirmation email.' Tope shows me her phone and there's no denying they've booked to stay at Saiyan Hedge Farm.

The reception phone rings.

'Let me just double check this for you, Mrs Solanké,' I say, pronouncing her surname So-lan-key.

'It's pronounced Sho-lan-kay,' Tope corrects. 'And I'm Ms not Mrs.'

'I'm sorry about that. Will you excuse me for one moment?' I pick up the phone. 'Hello, Saiyan Hedge Farm.'

'Are they in front of you?' Drew asks. 'If so, act like I'm a customer.'

'Yes, that's right,' I respond, pretending to be busy on the computer. 'How can I help?'

'You can punch Cam in the face! Honestly, what a

bonehead,' she replies.

'Yes, I know which horse you mean. You're right, it's not the smartest in the stable.'

Cam gives me a quizzical look, and I bite my lip to stop myself from laughing.

'Are you arriving soon?' I ask.

'I'll be five minutes. Be charming,' Drew says before the line goes dead.

'Okay, no problem. I'll see you soon.' I hang up the phone. 'Sorry about that, Ms Solanké. The booking is for the four of you, yes?'

'Please call me Tope, and, no, Paul's not staying,' Tope says, and she steps away from the man as if to emphasize her point. 'The booking's for me and my girls. Wait, where's ... ?' She looks left to right before walking to the door and shouting outside. 'Can you come here, please?'

'There's no signal!' a girl's voice responds. 'What kind of place is this?'

Tope looks back at me embarrassed. 'Sorry about that. As I was saying, there should be two—'

The front door opens, and a Black teenage girl wearing this very cool forest green coat with a leather collar walks in. The women all resemble each other, but this girl is shorter with glossy shoulder-length black hair and the most perfect face I've ever seen. We catch each other's eyes, and my heart starts to race. *Who* is *she?*

TWELVE

Tia

11th December

How can there be no signal outside? What if Mike's tried to contact me? I'm already over this stupid place. It felt like we were in the car for ages. We stopped twice at service stations because Banks had to pee. Mum wouldn't even let me buy a hot breakfast and instead gave me a dry croissant to eat. I'm starving!

The further we got into the countryside, the more I noticed how narrow and bendy the roads were becoming, and how old-fashioned the houses were. I didn't spot any Black people once we entered White Oak, and it gave me serious *Get Out* vibes.

I open the door to the main house and walk into a spacious white reception area decked out with a Christmas tree, decorations and a bowl of candy canes on top of the front desk. 'Silent Night' plays in the background. Behind the desk is a very cute guy with shoulder-length locs tied up into a bun, sharp cheekbones and . . . Oh shit, it's the boy from Instagram! Quincy Parker. I can't lie, he looks even better in person, and he's so tall. Much taller than Mike. *Why am I comparing them?*

Quincy is staring at me with those intense eyes I noticed in the picture, like he's looking deep inside me. Butterflies start to flutter in my stomach, and a second later I feel guilty for even letting myself feel that when I have a boyfriend, but I can't help wiping my tongue over my teeth hoping the croissant I ate in the car isn't stuck between them.

The boy beside him with the long waist-length locs, who I think must be his brother because they look alike, glances from Quincy to me before nudging him. Quincy blinks and shakes his head before looking back at the computer screen.

'There you are,' Mum says, frowning at me. 'This is my daughter, Tia. There should be two double rooms for the four of us, please.' Even on holiday, I still have to share with Willow.

Quincy doesn't look up when Mum says my name. Instead, he taps away on the computer. His brother leans forward and points at something, and Quincy grimaces in response.

'Is there a problem?' Paul asks kindly.

'Erm . . . well . . .' Quincy looks at his brother. 'I'm really sorry, but we've overbooked.'

What? That can't be right. Mum's mouth drops open, and she looks from her phone to Quincy.

'But the booking confirmation is right here.' Mum shows him her phone. 'We drove all the way from London!'

'I'm so sorry,' Quincy says, and, to give him credit, he looks it. 'There's been an error on our end which meant your booking wasn't logged properly, and unfortunately all the holiday cottages have guests in them until after Christmas.'

'But ...' Mum looks like she's on the verge of tears. Paul puts an arm around her, and she doesn't push him away. Even though I never wanted to be here, I hate seeing Mum upset. She's had a lot of setbacks, and I've witnessed enough of them to last me a lifetime. She's been so excited about this trip too.

'This isn't cool,' I snap, and everyone looks at me, including Quincy, who raises his eyebrows. 'So *you* messed up our booking?'

'Well, you see—' Quincy begins, but I cut him off.

'We drove all the way here just for you to tell us we can't stay, even though we have a booking?' I don't care how hot Quincy is, this situation is fucked up. 'Where's the manager? I want to speak to them right now.'

The brothers look at each other, and then the one with long hair sighs. He whips out his phone and holds up a finger. 'I'll be right back,' he says. 'Please, take a seat.'

Paul leads Mum over to the sofas, and Willow takes Banks' hand and follows behind them, but, for some reason, I stay where I am.

'It might take a while,' Quincy says to me.

'I'm cool,' I respond curtly.

'Suit yourself.' He goes back to typing on the computer before his phone rings. How does *he* have signal when I don't? 'Hey ... Yeah?' he says, and laughs, and to my surprise I feel a twinge of envy. I bet he's talking to his girlfriend or something – a boy that hot is definitely taken. *But why do I even care?* 'Okay, in a bit,' he says and ends the call.

I'm about to query the phone service here when he looks up and out the front. I follow his gaze to see a black 4×4 pulling in. A dog with black, brown and white fur jumps out, followed by a tall, slender Black woman with curly dark hair, dressed in a navy coat and boots. She opens the front door and the dog runs in, panting. It looks around at us and immediately bustles over to me. Now, I do *not* like dogs. Big, small, whatever breed they are – keep them far away from me. I try to walk over to my family for safety, but the dog comes with me, close to my heel. I yelp and jerk my leg away from it.

'No, go away!' I say, squeezing my eyes shut and waiting for this monster to bite me.

'Sorry, he's just excited.' I open my eyes and Quincy's stepped out from behind the desk and is patting his thighs. 'Oreo! Come here, boy.'

Straight away, the dog runs over to him, and Quincy bends down to hug it.

'Doggy,' Banks says pointing at it and pulling on Willow's hand so she can say hi.

I shake my head at Willow, but she ignores me, and she and Banks go over to the dog and start stroking it. The dog licks Willow's hand and she laughs. *Ugh, disgusting.*

I look up, and now the woman standing at the door is glaring at Quincy with a deep frown on her face.

'Hello?' she says uncertainly to Mum before she walks

over with her hand outstretched. 'I'm Mel Parker, one of the owners here at Saiyan Hedge Farm.' She must be Quincy's mum, I realize. Mrs Parker shakes Mum's hand, then Paul's. 'How can I help?'

Mum goes on to explain the booking situation while Mrs Parker listens calmly. Quincy stands up, leaving the dog with my sisters, and comes to stand next to me. He has a woody, grassy smell about him.

'You scared of dogs?' he asks, watching our mothers go back and forth.

'They make me nervous,' I reply.

Quincy nods. 'Oreo's cool.'

'To *you*,' I respond, and Quincy frowns at me. 'Dog people always claim their dog is friendly, but what if that dog is only cool with its owner? A dog running up to me panting doesn't fill me with cheer.'

'Wow,' Quincy scoffs. 'Sorry I bothered.'

I can tell I've offended him. Pet owners are *way* too sensitive.

Mrs Parker is smiling at Mum, but then, when she walks over to Quincy, her smile disappears completely. She has that look on her face that Mum has when she really wants to cuss out Banks when she's acting up in public, but can't because other people are there. 'Where's Cam?' Mrs Parker says.

'Probably hiding,' Quincy responds, and his mum sighs. She does a double take when she notices me standing next to her son. 'I'm so sorry for the confusion, but I promise we'll get this all sorted out for you.'

'Thank you,' I reply, even though a really selfish part of me wants her to say we have to go home.

The sound of car tyres on gravel distracts us, and we all turn to look out of the window. I gasp as a black Rolls-Royce Ghost with tinted windows and blacked-out rims pulls up outside the reception. I've only ever seen that type of car in music videos.

'Wow,' Paul says, already on his feet admiring the vehicle.

The driver's door opens, and we all wait to see who climbs out. A slim, thigh-high boot comes into view first. The woman is wearing fitted jeans and a Fendi canvas ski jacket (that I would kill for). Sunglasses cover her eyes even though it's winter. She walks to the front door and pushes it open, whipping off her sunglasses at the same time.

I hear Willow gasp behind me. My brain is trying to form words to speak. It's Drew Parker!

THIRTEEN

Quincy

11th December

The Solanké family's reaction is exactly why I texted Drew. You see, there are two sides to my sister. Drew, the local farm girl, who lives in Timberlands and oversized shirts and is happy to drive around in Dad's dirty truck. And then there's the Drew Parker who only wears designer clothes, has her hair and make-up on point, and will drive through town in the most outrageous car.

'Hi, everyone,' Drew says cheerfully, placing the sunglasses on her head so they swipe back her long hair.

Tia looks like she's going to pass out. At least something has impressed her. The Drew effect strikes again.

'Hi, darling,' Mum says managing a tired smile. 'I'm in the middle of sorting out a booking issue.'

'Oh no,' Drew says playing innocent. She locks eyes with Tia first. 'Hi, I'm Drew. I love your jacket.'

Tia looks down at it and then back up at Drew as if she's not sure what jacket Drew is referring to. 'Th-thanks,' she eventually stammers, and Drew flashes her Hollywood smile before going to greet the rest of the family.

'That's Drew Parker,' Tia says breathlessly to herself. 'And she just complimented me.'

I'm about to tell her Drew just pointed out the obvious, because her coat is cool, but I doubt she cares what I think, so I just smile and stay quiet.

'Quincy?' Mum calls, and when I look towards her, she beckons me to follow.

We go into the dining room, where Cam is sitting at the table. He jumps to his feet when he sees us. 'I'm sorry,' he says quickly just as Mum goes to speak. 'I messed up, I know.'

'We do not need this stress!' Mum snaps. She glances back at the dining room door and lowers her voice. 'Cam, you're so lucky the guests are still there or I would have lost it.' Cam gulps in response. 'We have no choice but to move all the stuff for the ball out of the spare rooms and into the basement. The Solankés will have to stay here with us in the house.'

'Here?' I ask confused.

Mum tuts. 'Of course! Where else are they meant to go? An error like this is enough to give us a bad reputation. Thank God we have enough rooms. We can put the youngest one and the parents in the room by the storage cupboard, and the older sisters can have a room each. The least we can do is give them their own space. One can go opposite Drew and the other in the room next to Quincy.'

Great, now I'm going to have to see Little Miss Attitude every day. Tia may be nice to look at, but her personality is a joke.

'The man isn't staying,' Cam says.

'Good to know.' Mum glares at him. 'Now, this is your mess, Cam, so *you* can move everything out of their rooms.'

Cam's mouth drops open. 'But that will take me ages. Can't Quincy help?'

Now why am I in it?

'Quincy has college,' Mum says, and I smirk at Cam. 'And he's already stepped up a lot recently. It's about time you did the same.' She turns to me. 'Can you and Drew take the family on a tour of the grounds while we prepare the rooms? I think they may be fans of Drew.'

'Yeah, no worries. I've got a bit of time,' I reply.

Mum leaves the dining room, and Cam kicks the chair closest to him. I hurry after her and see her leaning against the corridor wall out of sight of the Solanké family. She looks up to the ceiling and lets out a long sigh. I instantly feel bad for her. Mum really doesn't need this extra stress. I put my arm around her and hug her tightly. It takes her a second to respond, but then she rests her head on my shoulder.

'It'll be okay, Mum. There won't be any more mess-ups,' I promise, even though I'm not the one who caused the problem.

'Thank you, darling.' Mum pulls back and cups my chin. 'You're such a good kid, Quincy.'

'Your best child,' I respond very seriously.

Mum laughs. 'Don't push it.'

Drew's still talking animatedly to the Solankés when we get back to reception, and they seem to be lapping up everything she's saying.

'Apologies for the interruption,' Mum says, and everyone turns to look at her. 'Once again, I'm so sorry for the confusion. As you know, all our holiday cottages are fully booked, but we have plenty of space here in the main house, and we'd be happy to host you for the entirety of your stay with us.'

'Really?' Tope asks, and Mum nods. 'Thank you, Mel. That sounds great.'

'I know you'd originally booked two rooms, but, to make up for our mistake, we're happy to give you three so your two older girls can have their own space. At no extra charge, of course.'

Tope puts a hand on her chest. 'That's wonderful.'

Everyone else looks pleased, apart from Tia, who has her arms crossed over her chest and is staring wistfully out of the window. What's her problem?

'Can I ask how long the rooms will take to get ready?' Tope enquires.

'A few hours, I'm afraid,' Mum replies. 'Drew and Quincy will show you around the grounds in the meantime, then you can have lunch in the dining room here. Unless you want to eat in town and have a look around?'

'What's in town?' Willow asks, stroking Oreo behind his ears.

'There's a Costa, a tearoom that serves really good sandwiches and cakes, a restaurant, two pubs – one of which also serves food, a supermarket, post office, hairdresser's, nail bar, gift shop, and then there's Everly Rose, where everyone gets their outfit for the ball.' Drew smiles.

Tope starts clapping like we've just told her she's won a free holiday to Turks and Caicos, but Willow and Tia look less than impressed. Tia checks her phone and lets out an exasperated sigh.

'Boyfriend problems,' Tope loud-whispers to us, and Tia's eyes grow wide.

'Mum!' she snaps. She quickly glances at me, but she doesn't deny it. Her boyfriend must have the patience of a saint to deal with her.

'What?' Tope asks innocently.

'Can you not tell everyone my business, please?' Tia huffs. 'I'm going to wait outside.' She storms out, letting the cold air in. Oreo lifts his head as if he's thinking about following her, but he decides against it and lies back down.

There's an awkward silence until Drew clears her throat to draw everyone's attention. 'Right, shall we start the tour?'

FOURTEEN

Tia

11th December

What is wrong with my mum? I don't want anyone knowing that Mike and I have problems, especially strangers. I glance at my phone and my data is definitely on, but there's still no signal. I need to get the Wi-Fi password ASAP.

When I walked into the house, I was in such a strop that I didn't even take it in. It's really something – three storeys high, with cream pillars out front, and pretty fairy lights. It wouldn't look out of place in *Bridgerton*. The Parkers are clearly rolling in it. It's a far cry from our council estate back in South London.

As I walk away from the main door, my phone buzzes in my hand. The signal is weak, but my phone is actually ringing! And it's Mike! Maybe he's calling to say that he regrets asking for space and of course he loves me.

'Hello?' I say, eagerly.

Mike's talking, but his voice sounds slow and robotic and keeps breaking up. I start to walk around, hoping the signal will get stronger if I move location.

'Mike? Hello?'

'Tia? Can you hear me?' he says faintly.

It's so good to hear his voice even though it's barely there. I'm gripping the phone hard, wishing he was here with me.

'Sorry, the signal here is shit. I was trying to get hold of you before I left . . . Hello? Are you there?'

Mike's still on the line, but I can't hear a thing. This is so annoying!

'Tia? T—'

The line goes dead. I look at my phone and there's no signal . . . again!

'Mike?' I say louder, even though he's clearly no longer on the call.

'Mike?' Quincy asks as he opens the front door and holds it for Drew and my family.

'Her boyfriend,' Banks sings before she bursts out laughing.

'Ah,' Quincy says.

'You got signal?' Willow asks.

I roll my eyes. 'I lost it.'

'Try the stables,' Drew says. 'The signal picks up there. Why don't we start at the stables and make our way back from there?' I pull a face at the thought of being near horses.

We begin to walk, and Quincy is in front of me with his hands in his pockets. I'm writing a text to Mike that I'm hoping

97

I'll be able to send, but I'm so distracted that I walk right into Quincy, who's bent down to tie his trainers.

'Shit! Sorry,' I say quickly.

He looks pointedly at my phone but doesn't say anything. The gesture really pisses me off.

'It's an important text,' I say defensively.

Quincy stands up. 'Wouldn't hurt to look up once in a while.'

Excuse me? Before I can retaliate, Mum catches up with us.

'I heard you're the horse whisperer,' she says to Quincy.

Quincy laughs, flashing his straight white teeth. 'Mum and her marketing. Do you like horses?'

'Yes, and Banks loves them.' Then Mum nods towards me. 'Tia's not so keen.'

'Why?' Quincy asks me, but this time his tone is softer. I bet it's because Mum's here now.

Where do I start? The Superman accident, the hooves, the big head, the teeth – the list is endless. He won't understand, though, so instead I say, 'They're not for me.'

'You're not a big animal lover, are you?' Quincy asks.

'Can't stand them,' I say, and Quincy's eyes widen.

'It's kind of weird that you hate animals and you're here . . . on a farm . . .'

'Yeah, well, it was my mum's idea,' I reply. 'Definitely not mine.'

'Give her a few days, Quincy, and I'm certain she'll love it here,' Mum says. I roll my eyes in response. 'Do you have ponies?' she asks.

'Yeah, a few,' Quincy says before he turns back to me. 'You

should watch a riding session. Who knows, you might fancy riding one yourself.'

I can hear Remi's voice in my head and her joke about riding Quincy instead, and before I can stop myself I snort. *Shit, did I just do that?* Cheeks burning, I cover my mouth with my hand.

Mum frowns at me, but Quincy bursts out laughing.

'Did you just snort?' he asks.

'No!' I deny. How fucking embarrassing.

'I can't believe you just snorted,' he says, chuckling to himself, and I want the ground to open up and swallow me whole.

It feels like we've been walking for ever, but finally we reach the stables. I smell it before I see it. It stinks of manure, and I try my best not to gag.

'Horsies!' Banks yells and runs off, with Paul chasing after her.

I look over and see a few horses grazing in the field. There's a huge black one that looks like it's ready to trample us. My family oohs and ahs over them, but what I instantly notice is that they're not tethered to anything. What if one decides to gallop towards me? I can't outrun a horse. I stay back to give myself the best possible chance of a head start.

Drew points and says something about the horses, but Quincy turns back to me.

'You good?' he asks, searching my face.

'I'm just gonna—' My phone buzzes in my hand, and it's like WhatsApp has resurrected from the dead, because now I'm getting back-to-back messages. Most are from Remi, but I see Mike's name pop up too. I quickly open the text.

What the fuck? Is that what he was calling me about?

'Tia, come and see!' Mum calls.

I sigh and take a few steps further forward, deleting the message I was planning to send to Mike. I'm so busy on my phone that I don't hear the 'Look out!' until it's too late and step my clean white Air Force into a pile of horse manure.

There's a stunned silence. Quincy looks frozen as he points down at my foot. I slowly glance down, and when I tell you my white trainer doesn't exist any more ... the manure has completely drowned it. And the smell! My belly churns and I feel nauseous.

'Breathe,' Quincy says, and I throw him a dark look.

'Breathe in the *shit*?' I snap. I throw my head back and let out the loudest I'm-so-pissed-off-I-hate-it-here scream.

Drew runs over. 'Tia! Are you ... Oh!' She covers her mouth when she sees my trainer.

Mum, Paul, Willow and Banks join us.

Drew laughs nervously. 'This doesn't usually happen.' She glances at Mum, who's staring at me, eyes wide.

Willow holds her nose and mumbles, 'Sorry, I can't ...' and takes several steps away from me.

My eyes start to burn and well up. I know this is a stupid thing to cry over, but I never wanted to come here and now my trainer is ruined.

'Everything okay here?' A muscular white guy with bright blue eyes comes over. Oh, great. More people to witness my humiliation.

'Hey, Ethan,' Drew says. 'She didn't see it.'

Ethan scratches his dark hair. 'You gave the horses quite a fright. Pop it off and I'll get it cleaned up for you.'

'That's so kind,' Mum says, smiling at him, and Ethan grins back at her. 'Come on, Tia.'

'Erm ... what?' Do they think I plan to put my foot back in this trainer ever again?

'Trust me, it will look as good as new once Ethan's worked his magic,' Quincy says. He steps closer to me, not looking the least bit bothered, and puts his arm round my waist. A jolt of electricity races through my body at his touch. *What the hell was that?* 'Lean on me and use the ground to help you take your trainer off.'

Everyone watches as I struggle to drag it off my foot, and after several attempts it works. My socked foot instantly feels cold. With Quincy's help, I hop away from the manure. Ethan picks up my trainer by the tongue and holds it high like a trophy.

'I'll let you know once it's clean,' he says.

'Thank you,' I respond, and Ethan nods his head as he walks back to the horses.

Quincy looks down at my socked foot. 'You got any more footwear?'

'I've got boots in my suitcase,' I say.

'You lot carry on. I'll help Tia back to the house,' Quincy says. 'Do you want to hop on?'

'What?' I splutter.

He points at his back. 'I'll give you a piggyback ride. Unless you want to walk shoeless in the mud?'

I lock eyes with Willow, who gives me an amused smile. A part of me thinks Quincy is taking the piss. It's a long walk back, but he looks completely serious.

'Oh ... okay,' I say.

He bends way down because he's ridiculously tall, and I place both hands on his shoulders before hoisting myself up and wrapping my legs round his torso. My jeans are super tight, and I'm praying they don't split. He holds my legs with his arms and I position my face on his shoulder so his locs don't block my view. Any time I sit on Mike's lap, he makes this exaggerated *oof* sound like I weigh a ton. I know he's joking, but there's a small part of me that thinks maybe I'm heavy. I hope Quincy isn't regretting his offer.

FIFTEEN

Quincy

11th December

Tia's wrapped her arms and legs round me so tightly it's as if she's afraid I'm going to drop her. Luckily, she barely weighs anything. I'm not someone who normally offers a piggyback ride to a complete stranger, but the look on her face when she stepped in the horse shit changed things. I legit thought she was going to burst out crying. It seemed almost cruel to make her walk back with only one trainer on.

'I can't believe everyone saw me step in shit!' Tia groans. 'You didn't have to do this, but thank you.'

'No problem,' I reply. 'Ethan is great at cleaning up after the horses. Your trainer will be fine.'

She lets out a small sigh, and because her head is resting on my shoulder, her breath tickles my ear. We fall into silence,

103

and I'm racking my brain for something to talk about but I'm coming up blank. The kind of people that usually come to Saiyan Hedge Farm have grown up in the countryside or want to be here. Tia doesn't fall into either of those categories.

'How long have you lived here?' she asks, breaking the silence.

'All my life. Which part of London do you live in?'

'South. Peckham to be precise. Have you ever been?' she asks in a tone that suggests she doesn't think I have.

I move my head to the side and lean back so I can see her face. 'Peckham? I've been there once with Drew and Cam. It's a cool area. So, city girl, what are your first thoughts about the countryside?'

'Honestly?' She raises her eyebrows at me. 'It stinks.'

I burst out laughing. To be fair, sometimes it feels like the smell of manure has seeped into my clothes. 'I hope *I* don't smell.' Suddenly I feel the tip of her nose and lips gently touch my neck. My heart starts racing, and it's not just because I haven't had time to shower yet and I'm worried that I smell, but because my neck is my soft spot.

'No, you smell good,' she says, moving her face away. My heart starts to calm down. 'For a horse whisperer.' She lets go of one arm and shuffles around in her coat pocket. 'Why is the signal so bad here?'

'That's the countryside for you. You can get the Wi-Fi code from reception.'

She groans as if reception is miles away. 'So, what's happening here in the next couple of weeks?'

'We've got the Seven Days party,' I say.

'Party?' she asks, perking up in a way she hasn't before. 'What's the Seven Days party?'

'It's a party for all the teenagers and young adults in the town that happens seven days before Christmas Eve and it finishes when the sun comes up. It's been running for years. It's usually held at this big barn a few miles from here, but there was a fire there recently so we can't use it this year. This girl called Bunny has offered to host it at her family's massive house instead. We call it the White House because both the exterior and interior are pretty much completely white.'

'Wait, did you say Bunny?' Tia laughs. 'A girl with a name like that would be chased out of Peckham. Seven Days sounds pretty fun, though.' She seems surprised, which makes me laugh.

'What, you don't think we know how to party down here?' I ask.

'No, I didn't, to be honest,' she replies.

City people always underestimate the parties we throw in the countryside. I'll be surprised if Tia can keep up with us.

The house comes into view, and I drop Tia off at reception, where the Solankés have left their luggage.

'Thank you, Quincy,' she says gratefully as she jumps down and opens up her suitcase.

'No problem.' I glance at my phone. I need to leave soon to get to college – and I still need to shower. 'Just walk straight back down to the stables when you're ready.'

She pauses, forcing her feet into a pair of heeled boots. 'Are you not staying with us?'

'No, I've got college,' I reply.

'Oh,' she says sounding disappointed, which throws me. I didn't get the vibe she was enjoying my company. I'm not sure how I feel about her either.

'I'll see you later. Enjoy the tour,' I say, leaving her at reception and taking the stairs two at a time. I surprise myself by glancing back at her before she disappears from view.

I take the last parking spot before making my way into college. I smile at various people as I walk down the hall. Everyone knows me. It's hard not to stand out, being one of the three Black people here. I pass the huge white banner covered in snowflakes hanging in the middle of the hallway. Every day the number on it changes as it counts down to the Winter Ball. Thirteen days to go!

'Q!' Eliza calls, running up to me.

We hug in greeting, and when we pull away, I study her.

'Nice hair,' I say.

Eliza pats her turquoise hair that's tied in some fancy-looking plait. 'It's a fishtail,' she explains. 'I needed two mirrors behind me to see what I was doing.'

Based on appearances only, you wouldn't put me and Eliza together. Eliza's wearing her trademark black skinny jeans, with rips that show her pale white skin, her black Timberlands, black leather jacket and a black hoodie underneath. Her ears are decorated with silver piercings, and last year she got her septum pierced. Two weeks ago, she dyed her black hair turquoise, so now she looks like a goth mermaid.

We start to walk, and she pulls out her phone, typing into it with her long pointy nails, painted black, of course. 'What do you think?' she says, showing me a picture of a hand with black nails covered in gold zodiac symbols.

'Very witchy. Is that the vibe?' I ask.

She shrugs. 'Might look cool for the ball.'

At this I laugh, and Eliza smiles knowingly.

Eliza lives to piss off her mum, especially when it comes to dressing up for the ball. Every year it's something else from thick eyelashes so you could barely see her eyes, a deep-cut lacy dress, that definitely wasn't ball attire and had all the guys staring at her tits and a fake dragon tattoo on her neck. Her mum is very conservative. She's all smart tops, sensible skirts, pearls and perfect bouncy hair. Whenever Eliza is in a bitchy mood, she refers to her as Bree Van de Kamp from *Desperate Housewives*. She says they have the same Stepford Wife energy.

'Have you got your dress yet?' I ask.

'Mum put one on hold.' Eliza makes a face. 'I already know I'm going to hate it. What day are you getting your suit?'

'I'm not sure. I think this week, though. You wanna go together?'

Eliza nods and opens the common-room door. It's surprisingly empty today. 'Okay,' she says seriously, 'before people come, I've got something to tell you.'

I sit down on the sofa, and Eliza sits opposite me.

'I saw Kali this weekend,' she says.

'Oh?' I say, surprised. 'Where?'

'She came to get her hair done. Anyway, she was asking about you, trying to find out more about this date of yours for the ball.' Eliza suddenly smiles and swats my arm. 'So you found one after you texted me? Who is she? Kali was so pissed. She was trying to get all the details.'

'Wait – what?' I frown. 'Who said I had a date?'

'Cam! He said you were bringing a mystery girl. I think he thought I already knew. Why didn't you tell me?'

Fucking Cam.

'You know Kali's got a date, right?' Eliza raises her eyebrows at me.

My stomach flips. 'With who?'

Eliza shrugs. 'She wouldn't say.'

I rack my brain, trying to think who she would have agreed to go with, but there's only one name on my mind: Simon. He wouldn't, would he? The idea of the two of them together makes me feel sick and pissed off at the same time.

'Q?' Eliza waves her hand in my face, and I focus back on her. 'Tell me all about this girl. What's her name? Where did you meet?'

I glance round the common room even though I know it's empty. If there's one person I can trust with this secret, it's Eliza, so I say: 'I lied. I don't have a date!'

Her face drops.

'I made it up. My family kept asking me about the ball and bringing up Kali and I just wanted them to stop.' I rub my face. Why did I ever think this was a good idea? 'Now I don't know what to do.'

'Oh shit.' Eliza pulls a face. 'Everyone I can think of already has a date or isn't going to be around for the ball.'

I throw back my head and groan. 'Fuck!' How can everyone be coupled up? There must be someone, anyone! I glance at Eliza, who's tapping her long fingers on the table. Cam said she has a date, but she hasn't told me, and now I'm curious. 'Who are you going with?'

At this Eliza blushes a deep red, which is very unusual behaviour for her. I've never seen her blush, *ever*. Smiling, I lean forward in my chair. 'Who is it?'

'It's still very fresh,' she mumbles.

I wait for her to say more but she doesn't. She can barely look at me.

I tap her forehead. 'I don't know who you are, but can I have Eliza Bennett back, please?'

Eliza thumps my knee in response, and I automatically rub it. 'You'll see him at the ball. Now, what are you going to do about this mess?'

Good question.

SIXTEEN

Tia

11th December

So. Much. Walking! Drew showed us around the whole of Saiyan Hedge Farm, which even I have to admit is gorgeous, but the tour went on for ages and my feet soon started to kill in my heeled boots.

Mum wanted to eat out for lunch, so now we've driven ten minutes into town.

'How picturesque is this place!' Mum takes out her phone and starts snapping away.

The town is busy with shoppers, some of whom I assume are buying Christmas gifts. Luckily, I've already sorted out presents for my family, using the last bit of my money.

We walk down the road and I take in the sights of White Oak. It's almost like a high street, but smaller, more rural, with half-timbered buildings and fewer people than I'm used to. I immediately spot the Costa and wander over to try to log into the Wi-Fi, but it's password-protected. Damn it. Apart from the coffee shop, I can see a couple of pubs, a small supermarket and one or two other shops.

'Oh, look at the post office!' Mum points at the small white building that looks like a miniature house. 'Can you imagine if the one in Peckham looked like that?' Mum's staring at all the pretty buildings in wonder. She's already brightened up so much since leaving London.

Willow and I hold Banks' hands as we wander from shop to shop. We pause by Everly Rose and peer in through the window at the racks upon racks of gorgeous gowns in all different colours.

'Can we go in?' I ask Mum.

'Not today, but we'll come back in a few days and try some dresses on.' Mum turns aways and gasps. 'Look at that!'

We walk over to where a Christmas display sits in the middle of a circular grassy area covered in fake snow. It's brilliant! There are fake reindeer pulling a red sleigh with presents stacked up high inside it. It's flanked by two huge Christmas trees covered in gold and red baubles, giant red bows, gold tinsel and fairy lights. Banks bends down to throw the snow up in the air, and she giggles as it falls back on her.

'Do that again, Banksy,' I say, filming the perfect video that I plan to post on my TikTok later.

'Shall we sit?' Paul points to a table by the display

that's covered by a deep red cloth. We squeeze up on the white benches.

'Quick pic,' Mum instructs, and we flash our best smiles for the camera. 'I'm so glad we're here. What do you girls think?'

'It's nice,' Willow says. 'Even better than the pictures, and the Parker family seem lovely.'

'Pity there was a mix-up over the booking.' Paul frowns.

'Oh, it's fine now.' Mum gently nudges him. 'We get to stay in the main house, we've all got our own rooms, and Banks has her first riding lesson thrown in for free as an apology. It's a win in my eyes. Tia, what do you think?'

'It's cool,' I say, trying to stay upbeat. 'So, what's the plan for the next two weeks?'

'That's the beauty of this trip,' Mum says. 'We can do whatever we want. I know how hard everyone has been working, and being here will help to recharge our batteries so we can go into next year feeling fresh. We can sleep late, eat whatever we want and have a good time – that's the most important thing.'

Willow laughs. 'I say cheers to that! Can we get a drink?'

'Yes, and let's get some food while we're at it,' Paul says. 'We passed the tearoom a little way back.'

I imagined the tearoom as being bright and feminine. It's not. It's painted a sombre blue and has bizarrely low ceilings, so Paul has to bend to get to our table next to the fireplace. Everyone glances at us as we settle in, like they've never seen a mixed family before. Once we're sat down, I look at Mum and can tell she's disappointed by the decor because she doesn't comment or take any pictures, but when I catch her eye, she smiles at me.

I can't remember the last time we ate out, especially with Paul there too. My stomach rumbles loudly. We're handed menus by one of the staff and my mouth salivates at the options – a full English, pancakes, cheese toasties with caramelized onions, different types of cakes. But it's the price that takes me out the most.

'This can't be right,' I say. 'How is their food only a fiver?'

'Can you even get a McDonald's meal for that price?' Willow asks.

We order a range of dishes so we can try everything, and thankfully the food makes up for the uninspiring decor. It's all *so* good. I love the little floral teacups and matching teapot. I make a mental note to come back to the tearoom as soon as possible.

'I'm stuffed,' Willow says, leaning back in her chair.

I am too, but I'm already looking at the dessert options, and I know Mum is as well.

'Same, but I want to try— Excuse me?' Mum waves at the middle-aged man who's just finished serving another table. He does a double take when he sees Mum, which is the usual reaction she gets from men. She doesn't seem to notice, but the rest of us do. 'I'm torn between the vanilla, carrot or red velvet cake.'

'How about I bring you a small slice of all of them to sample?' the man says, not bothering to pay any attention to the rest of us.

'Really? You're so kind.' Mum smiles. 'That would be great.'

The man comes back with not only the three cake options, but what looks like a sample of every dessert on the menu. 'Here you are,' he says. 'See if you like any of these.'

At least this day is getting better. Banks claps her hands as she gazes at the cake stand. Paul is frowning, probably wondering if this is all actually free. Mum's gushing, telling the man how lovely he is. And Willow and I? We give each other a knowing look. Typical Mum!

SEVENTEEN

Quincy

11th December

My phone buzzes in my pocket during geography. Luckily, our teacher Ray always has his head buried in a book, expecting us to get on with our work ourselves. It's a message from Dad.

> We've booked Ms Solanké's youngest daughter in for a riding lesson. It's her first time on a pony. All okay?

'Cute,' I say as I send back a thumbs up.

'What is?' Eliza asks, looking up from her work.

'A new family from London arrived this morning and the youngest daughter, Banks, is going to have her first-ever riding lesson.'

'That is cute. You going to put her on Legend?' Eliza grins.

'You're so funny,' I say, deadpan. 'Maybe I can convince Tia to get on a horse. She might warm up to animals if she enjoys it.'

Eliza frowns. 'Who's Tia?'

'She's one of the other sisters staying. There are three of them.' I explain.

'Really? How old is Tia?' Eliza questions intently.

I shrug. 'Around our age I guess.'

Eliza puts down her pen. 'Is she pretty?'

'Yeah, she's really hot.' I reach over for my textbook and Eliza slaps my hand. 'Ow! What was that for?'

'Sometimes you're so stupid,' she says.

I frown. 'I haven't done anything!'

'Exactly!' she hisses. She leans in closer to me. 'You don't have a date for the ball, you told your family you do, and you have a hot girl staying at the farm for Christmas.' I continue to stare at her, and Eliza taps my forehead. 'So ask this Tia girl out.'

I scoff. 'No way. One, she's a full-on princess. Two, we have nothing in common. And three, she has a boyfriend.'

Eliza looks dramatically around the room, where students either have their heads buried in their work or are on their phones. 'I'm sorry, are you planning on marrying her or something? You don't need her to be your date for her conversational skills. Plus, the rules of the ball still apply to townies. She'll need a date too if she wants to come.'

Despite how annoying Eliza's being right now, she does have a point. Tia and I both need a date, so it would make sense for us to go together, as friends. Although 'friends' is a massive reach. I barely know her, and what I've seen so far hasn't exactly won me over, but she's fit, and that will piss off Kali for sure. I could say my mystery girl cancelled.

'You're welcome,' Eliza sings.

I shake my head. 'I didn't say thank you.'

She looks at me knowingly. 'No, but you will when Tia says yes.'

'Whatever. You going to the twins' thing tonight?' I ask, wanting to change the subject.

Eliza shakes her head, avoiding my eyes. 'I've got plans.'

'Plans?' I question, but she doesn't elaborate. I want to push for more, but the bell rings and Eliza says she has to shoot off to her next lesson. Convenient.

I only had one lesson today, and usually I would have met up with Simon in the common room as we have similar timetables, but instead I head back to the car park. I see someone leaning on my car. They're wearing a beanie and a khaki winter jacket and, as I get closer, I can see the blond hair peeking out. Simon looks up at me. He waves tentatively as I march over.

'Why are you leaning on my car?' I snap, and Simon flinches at my tone.

'Sorry.' He stands up straight. 'I need to ask you something.'

'What?' I say bluntly.

'My mum was asking me about the ball yesterday, and I realized I don't actually know if you're cool with me coming. I get it if you want me to stay away, but you know how people talk around here . . .'

117

The last people I want at the ball are Simon and Kali, but if they don't come, people will definitely ask me where they are, and that's sure to ruin my mood on the night.

'Do you have a date already?' I ask, avoiding his question.

Simon shakes his head. *So he's not going with Kali after all* ... 'I heard everyone's taken,' he says. 'Maybe I'll do a Finn James and get my mum to come with me.'

I can't help chuckling at this. Finn's a guy from a college who brought his mum to the ball a couple of years ago. For months everyone talked about them slow dancing. When I notice Simon smiling at me, I instantly make my face blank again.

He hesitates. 'What about you? Have you got a date?'

'Why? So you can sleep with her too?' I bark back.

'Quincy, I'm so sorry, man.' Simon clasps his hands together like he's praying. 'I wish it never happened.'

'Yeah ... you and me both. Excuse me.'

He sighs but moves to the side so I can get into my car. He watches me with his hands in his pockets, and I deliberately turn up the music to block him out. He gets the hint and walks away with his head down. I watch him go, realizing I didn't confirm whether he could come to the ball or not. I don't know how I can say no without my parents questioning why. But now all I can think about is who Kali's date is.

EIGHTEEN

Tia

11th December

Cam opens the bedroom door for me, holding my suitcase in his other hand, and I take it all in. It's bigger than mine and Willow's room back home and is painted a pretty jade green. There's a double bed in the centre with white and emerald bedding, and a headboard that goes all the way up to the ceiling. Two side tables, a mirrored wardrobe, a chest of drawers, a desk and a chair fill up the rest of the space and an ensuite juts off from the side of the room. The window looks out over the fields. It's cute, homely and all mine.

'Do you like it?' Cam asks.

'It's great. Thank you!' I plop myself down on the soft bed. 'So, what do you do for fun around here?'

'I'm a DJ,' Cam replies.

'No way! Have you got any gigs coming up?' I ask.

'I'm pretty booked up with private parties because of the holiday season, but Seven Days is always fun and that's coming up soon,' Cam says.

'Oh, yeah. Quincy told me about that. Sounds fun,' I reply.

Cam leaves me to settle in and I lie down on the double bed, exhaustion creeping into my bones. I take my phone out and find the picture I took of the Wi-Fi code in reception. I silently cheer once I'm connected to the internet. The first thing I do is check to see if Mike has tried to contact me, but there's nothing to show. Then I bring up Google maps and look at the route back to London. Mum wasn't lying: there are no train stations nearby. Damn it. A WhatsApp from Dad comes through asking if we arrived okay, and I shoot off a reply. I look through Instagram stories to see what I've missed out on, but none of my friends have posted anything interesting and I remember they're all still at college this week. Mike hasn't posted anything either. I voice-note Remi, letting her know what's happened so far, and I'm just about to message Mike when someone knocks on the door.

I sit up as Paul pokes his head round. 'I'm heading off.'

'No, stay!' I protest. 'Spend Christmas with us.'

'I wish I could. Try to have a good time, okay? I know this isn't your idea of fun, but you never know, you might really take to it.'

'I doubt it. How about you take me back to London with you and we'll tell Mum when we get back?' I put on my best puppy-dog eyes.

Paul laughs, even though I'm not joking, and opens his arms for a hug.

'Merry Christmas, Tia,' he says.

'Merry Christmas, Paul.'

12th December
2.47 a.m.

I'm staring up at the ceiling and I can't sleep. Maybe it's because I took a nap earlier after Paul left. I was feeling so tired then, but I'm wide awake now. I was looking forward to a peaceful sleep in my own room, but the countryside has turned out to be anything but quiet. I can hear dogs barking, trees rustling, strange whooping noises – owls? It's like an out-of-tune choir singing outside my window.

I reach for my phone, re-reading the text I sent Mike earlier.

> Hey! First day done and I'm surviving :) You okay?
> The 18th sign should be at your house tomorrow.
> I want to chat about the space you asked for.
> It would be good to clarify what that means
> and for how long. Can we talk later? x

He still hasn't texted back. Frustrated, I get out of bed and put my slippers on. Maybe if I sneak down to the kitchen and make myself a hot chocolate I'll be able to fall asleep. I creep downstairs and, as I pass through reception, I notice that the front door is slightly open. I look out and see Quincy leaning

121

on a car with his hands in his pockets, his chin resting on his chest.

'Hey,' I call, walking over to him. The cold air instantly bites through my pyjamas, and I can see my breath in the air.

Quincy looks up surprised. 'Hey.' He smiles, and I notice how nice it is. 'What are you doing up?'

'Couldn't sleep.' Bizarrely, out here, it sounds super quiet. Maybe those animals are messing with me. 'You?'

'Oreo woke me up. He heard a noise outside and was determined to see what it was. It's probably just a fox,' he says.

'Ah, I see. Do you mind if I make myself a hot chocolate?' I ask.

'I can do it, if you're cool to wait a few minutes?' Quincy says.

To be honest, the cold air is making me alert not sleepy, but I nod and look at my phone to distract me from the bitter temperature, scrolling aimlessly through TikTok. Funnily enough, Drew Parker's latest video comes up and she's doing a ballgown clothes-haul edition.

'Wow.' Some of the gowns are stunning. I can't wait until we get to go to Everly Rose.

'What is it?' Quincy asks, looking up. I show him the video. 'Yeah, the Winter Ball is a massive deal around here. People go all-out. This year's extra special because it's the first time a Black family has been asked to host.'

My eyes widen in surprise. 'Oh, wow, I didn't know that. That's huge!'

Quincy nods. 'We can't afford to mess it up. If we pull this off, it will take everything my parents have worked so hard for to the next level.'

'I hear that. My family haven't had a great time recently, but after this break I have a feeling everything is going to start coming together,' I say.

I wait for Quincy to pry as most people do, but instead he nods and says, 'I'm glad your luck is changing,' before flashing me that smile again. This time I feel my stomach flip. Then he says, 'Have you ever seen stars this bright before?' He points up and I gasp.

The sky twinkles with thousands of stars scattered across the inky sky. You'd never see that in London with all the bright lights and pollution.

'So pretty,' I say. There's something about the stars that makes me feel so small, like all my problems are nothing compared to how huge the universe is. If this was my view every night, I guarantee I wouldn't be half as stressed. I could stare at this sky for ever.

'Yeah,' Quincy says, but when I glance at him he's not looking up. He's staring at me.

NINETEEN

Quincy

12th December

I quickly turn away, my face hot. Tia caught me staring at her.

'Oreo!' I click my tongue.

'It's pretty cold out here,' Tia says, hugging herself but making no move to go inside.

She looks wide awake, and I am too. Maybe we should hang out and watch a film together until we feel tired. A part of me wants to suggest it. I'm kind of intrigued by this London girl who's been dragged to a farm in the countryside. And I've got Eliza in my head telling me to ask Tia to be my date. But what if it's awkward? With Kali it was always so easy. We had a lot in common and would often find ourselves overlapping because we were on the same wavelength. With Tia, I feel like, with everything I say, she says the opposite.

Oreo bounds over to me and runs straight into my legs. Tia jumps away from us.

'Sorry,' I quickly say as Oreo licks my hand. 'Let's head inside and I'll make you that hot chocolate.'

I take Oreo with me to the kitchen to stop Tia from screaming her head off. I'm tempted to make myself a cup too, but decide against it. There's nothing more awkward than silence filled with drinking slurps. When I bring Tia her cup and tell her I'm going to head back to bed, I notice her shoulders slump. *Is she disappointed?*

'Oh, okay,' she says. 'I'll just finish this. Goodnight, Quincy.'

TWENTY

Tia

12th December

I'm woken up by a knock on my door and I drag myself out of bed, rubbing my eyes as I go to see who it is.

'Morning!' Drew says brightly, looking gorgeous in a white knit dress and thigh-high camel boots.

'Morning.' I step aside so she can enter, and quickly remove my hair bonnet, chucking it behind me on to the bed.

'Good sleep?' she asks.

'Erm, yeah, it was okay,' I say.

'Do you want any breakfast? Gia's still in the kitchen.'

I shake my head. 'No, thanks. I'm not a breakfast person.'

'Okay, no worries. I was talking to Willow, and she said you guys are fans of Regal. I'm going to meet her in town in a bit. Do you want to come?'

I gulp. 'Regal?'

Drew laughs. 'Honestly, she's the best. Nothing to be intimidated about. Is thirty minutes enough time for you to get ready?' I nod and she flashes me a smile before closing the door behind her.

I dress in a cream fitted turtleneck, patterned miniskirt and my boots, throwing my green coat on over the top. Once my make-up is perfect, I head to reception, where Willow is talking to Cam. He spots me and waves. Cam has a dangerous glint in his eye. I bet he's a terrible flirt.

'I was just telling your sister about the Seven Days party,' he says.

'It sounds fun, right?' Willow adds, and I nod. She turns back to Cam. 'Is there a dress code? I didn't really bring anything fancy.'

Cam looks her up and down appreciatively. 'You're not the kind of girl that has to try.'

I scoff. Knew it. I'm sure he's used that line with so many girls. Willow laughs and playfully pats his arm.

'All ready?' Drew asks, walking into reception and pulling a face when she sees how close Cam and Willow are leaning towards each other. 'I wouldn't get too close, Willow. Who knows what bed my brother crept out from last night.'

'Drew!' Cam shouts, as Willow abruptly moves back, but I laugh and Drew winks at me. Cam gives her the finger and stomps off.

'Does he flirt with everyone?' Willow asks, trying to sound like she's not bothered, but I know my sister, and she is.

Drew puts a hand on her shoulder. 'Cam's what you call . . . popular. Particularly around here and the surrounding area. You get what I'm saying?' Willow nods regretfully.

I put my arm round Willow's waist as we follow Drew outside. Willow's been single for over a year now, and the last boy she dated was a complete idiot. She deserves better than a guy who's an over-achiever in flirting.

Drew unlocks the Rolls-Royce Ghost and I look at her wide-eyed.

'We're going in that?' I ask stupidly. It's almost too perfect to drive.

Drew laughs. 'Yeah, unless you want to walk to town!'

'This car . . .' Willow says, stroking the exterior gently.

'It's epic, isn't it?' Drew says.

I get in first and slide across the cream leather seats with the famous double-R logo on the headrests. You could live in here, that's how spacious it is. When I look up, I notice that I'm sitting under a trail of stars. It reminds me of last night with Quincy.

'This is gorgeous,' I murmur, touching the ceiling, and the stars twinkle back at me.

'That's my favourite part,' Drew says.

My friends are going to completely freak when they see this! I start recording an Instagram story to show it off. It's not like I'm ever going to be in a Rolls again.

We set off, and the car moves super smoothly, but Drew drives a little bit too fast for me through the winding lanes. She catches my expression in the rear-view mirror and laughs.

'You think I'm bad? Don't get in a car with Cam. He drives like an absolute maniac.'

'I couldn't drive down here. Where are the wide roads with traffic lights and zebra crossings?' I ask.

'Everyone pretty much has to drive around here or you can't get about. The bus comes once in a blue moon.'

'Do you only come here for the holidays?' Willow asks Drew.

'I wish! Mum guilts-trips me into coming down at least every few months. I find White Oak a bit too slow for me. I'm definitely not a small-town person. Not that there's anything wrong with that if you are. Quincy loves it here. I can't see him moving to a city.'

'Can't you?' I ask. I'd die of boredom if I lived here. The Winter Ball seems like the highlight of the town's year. Back home, there's a party on every other week.

'I'm always telling him it's a big world out there and he should explore it, but he likes being here with the boys and girls he's known for ever. Quincy isn't keen on the idea of broadening his horizons.'

A part of me wants Drew to elaborate on exactly how many girls Quincy is friends with. I shake my head. *Why am I thinking like this?* I have a boyfriend. I glance at my phone, but there's still no reply from Mike even though I can see he's read my message now. I sigh and put my phone away as Drew expertly parks the car.

Now we're in town, there are more people milling about, but everyone is middle-aged and white, just like yesterday. I can't see one person that looks like us. Peckham is so diverse, with a prominent African and Caribbean community. Here I feel very aware of my race in a way that I've never felt before, and it makes me uncomfortable. At first, I think everyone is looking at the three Black girls in the expensive car, until I remember that the windows are tinted, so they must be looking at the car itself.

'I'm gonna grab a flat white. You girls want a drink?' Drew asks.

'Sure,' Willow says, and I agree.

We step out of the car, and I'm not exaggerating when I say people stare at us a little longer than is polite. I'm not sure if it's because we're new around here, or because we're with Drew. Either way, I don't like the attention.

'That's the tearoom.' Drew points at the unimpressive building.

'Yeah, we went there yesterday,' Willow says. 'The food was so good and cheap!'

Drew laughs. 'You notice how bumped you get in London, right? Did you try the cakes? They're amazing!'

'Yes, they were the best part,' I say.

'Your mum mentioned you love to bake, Tia. I need to try something of yours. She says you're the "best of the best".' Drew smiles at me.

Imagine Drew Parker eating something I made!

'Of course,' I say quickly.

We head into Costa and there's a short queue at the counter when we arrive, but there are a few empty tables dotted around. Again, everyone stares at us, but Drew flashes a pretty smile, and a few people wave back at her; some even take out their phones.

'Drew?' calls a white girl with long blonde hair and big blue eyes.

'Hey, Bunny!' Drew says, giving the girl a hug. 'How are you?'

This must be the Bunny hosting the Seven Days event, I think to myself, which Drew confirms when she says, 'Let me know if you need us to bring anything for the party.'

'Oh, thanks. That would be really helpful,' Bunny says. 'My dad doesn't actually know about the party, so the house needs to look perfect after everyone leaves.'

Drew and Bunny go back and forth, so I figure I might as well get in the queue to save time. I'm watching Remi's Instagram story, so I don't notice when the person in front of me moves aside.

'Hi? Can I help?' I look up and see a pretty white girl around my age looking at me enquiringly. She has wavy dark auburn hair and ice-blue eyes that almost look ghostly.

'Yeah ... sorry, one sec.' I look back, but Bunny is gone and Willow and Drew are sitting at a table. There's a small crowd gathered around Drew.

'Erm, I'll get three flat whites,' I say. I don't usually drink coffee, but I'm tired and need something strong to shake me awake.

The girl nods, but I notice she's looking over my shoulder at the crowd of people.

'Drew Parker's there,' I explain.

The girl's face instantly goes pale. 'Drew?' she repeats. I guess she's a fan. 'Did you come together?' she asks, and I nod. 'You're staying at Saiyan Hedge Farm?'

'Yeah, it's cool. I'm from London, so it's a bit different, you know?'

The girl smiles. 'So I guess you've met Cam and Quincy?'

I nod and glance at the coffee machine, hoping she gets the hint and starts making the drinks. What's with all the questions?

Instead, she asks, 'How is he? Quincy, I mean.'

'Erm ... what do you mean? I don't know him very well. We just arrived yesterday.'

'Oh, okay.'

I'm thinking the questioning is over, but then she asks, 'So you're staying for the ball?'

'Yep ... So, the coffees?'

For a moment, I think the girl's actually going to do her job, but instead she asks, 'Are you going with Quincy?'

Going where with Quincy?

'Huh?' I ask, confused.

'Tia!' Drew walks over to me, smiling, her adoring fans now back at their own tables. The girl quickly turns away and busies herself, finally, with making the drinks. 'Sorry, Tia, I didn't give you my card. Did you order?'

'Yeah, three flat whites. She's just making them now.'

Drew follows my gaze and instantly her face darkens. 'Kali!' she barks, and the girl freezes, a coffee cup in her hand. She doesn't turn round. 'Kali, you're not invisible. I can see you.'

The barista, Kali, keeps her head down and her shoulders drop, and I look from her to Drew and back again. What is happening?

'I didn't know you worked here.' Drew leans on the counter. 'Get someone else. I don't want you serving us.'

At that, Kali spins round, red in the face. 'Mason's busy in the back.'

'I'm sure he isn't. We both know how easily you lie,' Drew says.

Kali's jaw hardens, and for a second I think she's going to argue back, but instead she storms through the door to the back room.

What the hell was that? I look at Drew, who's glaring at the closed door like she's a moment away from following Kali. Who is this girl, anyway? And what has she done to make Drew so angry?

'Are you okay?' I ask.

'That girl is trouble,' Drew says with a finality to her tone. 'Let's sit down. Mason will bring our drinks over.'

She turns and walks away towards Willow, who's shooting me a confused look, and I shrug in response. What 'trouble' is Drew talking about? I glance back to the counter, but Kali doesn't return.

TWENTY-ONE

Quincy

12th December

I leave the car park, tapping the steering wheel as I drive in time to Wizkid and Ella Mai. 'Piece of Me' is one of my favourite songs on the 'Made in Lagos' album. I'm thinking again about Eliza's suggestion for the ball. I should have just asked Tia yesterday. She was definitely disappointed that I was going to bed, which makes me think she's warming to me and might have said yes. Now I need to find another time to ask. The song is just about to reach the best part when my phone rings, cutting off the music. It's Drew.

'Hey?' I say.

'Hey, you're on loudspeaker, by the way. Can you believe my car started acting up on the way to Regal's?'

'Oh shit, what happened?' I ask.

'It just kept cutting out as we were driving. I've called Rolls-Royce and they're going to come and pick it up to check it over. Can you collect us from Regal's later, though? I'm with Willow and Tia.'

I glance at the time. 'Cam has a gig and needs the car. His stuff is in the boot. Can't Regal drop you back?'

'Her mum borrowed her car,' Drew replies.

'Okay, why don't you call Cam and see if he can borrow Mum or Dad's car, meet us at Regal's and then we can swap?' I suggest.

'You're so smart, Q! I'll call him.'

'I'll just come now. I'm free anyway. See you soon.'

I hang up and do a U-turn. Regal bought her mum a mansion worth millions once she made it big, and whenever she's back in town she stays there. If I had that house, I'd never leave. It has a cinema room, sauna and steam room, a tennis court which no one uses, and just this summer they completed their man-made lake. Cam and I had the best time jet skiing on it. I always think Aunty Shola must get lonely when she's in that big house by herself. She retired this summer and now has a load of hobbies to keep herself busy. There's staff that live in, and I'm sure it's nice for her being waited on when she was a housekeeper most of her life, but those people are employees, not friends.

I drive off-road down a lane that feels like it goes on for ever until the four-storey house appears. It's not decorated for Christmas, because Aunty Shola thinks it's a waste of electricity having fairy lights on, even though Regal protests that they can afford it. I park up and I'm climbing out of the car as the front door opens. Belle, the Majekodunmis' housekeeper, appears.

'Hello, Quincy. Good to see you,' Belle says. She's a stocky white woman in her early fifties, with kind eyes and slicked brown hair in a tight bun. She's wearing a white shirt and smart black trousers.

'Hey, Belle. Where is everyone?' I say as I enter the house.

'In the formal living room.' She holds her hand out for my coat. Whenever I offer to hang it up myself, she always gets annoyed.

The formal living room is down the marble hall. In the corner, almost touching the ceiling, is a huge white Christmas tree covered in gold and silver baubles; the bannisters that wind up the staircase are wrapped in tinsel. Clearly Aunty Shola has no problem decorating the interior.

The smell of jollof rice wafts down the hall from the kitchen, and my stomach rumbles. I hope it's not too spicy.

'Hey,' I say as I walk into the living room, but I'm surprised to find only Regal and Drew curled up on the large sofa. 'Oh, I thought Willow and Tia were here, too.'

'They're checking out the house,' Regal says, getting up to greet me. She's in baggy jeans and a fitted crop top that shows off her toned stomach.

'Thanks for coming, Q,' Drew says. 'Cam's on his way. I was just telling Regal that I bumped into Bunny at Costa and told her we'd bring a few things for Seven Days. I was thinking I could ask Tia to make some cupcakes. She bakes.'

I shrug. 'It's worth asking.'

Regal scoffs. 'I can't believe Bunny is letting all these people come to her house. Is she actually crazy?'

'And her dad doesn't even know,' Drew adds. Regal's mouth drops open.

'How is she ever gonna keep that a secret from him?' Cam says, walking into the living room. 'I'm going to post that shit all over social, as will every single person that attends.'

To be honest, I'm glad Bunny stepped in to save the annual party, but I guarantee this year's Seven Days will be even more packed than usual. The Vauxs' white house is the most pristine, Instagram-worthy property around here, and hardly anyone's been inside before.

'Speaking of social media, my DMs are blowing up with people asking me to film the Winter Ball after I mentioned it online,' Regal says. 'It's a good idea, right? They want to see the decor and vibes, and, most importantly, what people are wearing. I was thinking I could tag Saiyan Hedge Farm. I'm sure you'll be flooded with loads of bookings.'

'That's a sick idea, Regal. You got a date yet?' Cam asks and she shakes her head.

'Nope, but I'll figure it out,' she replies with the air of someone who doesn't even have to try to secure a date, because she knows she will. I wish it was that easy for me.

'Q,' Drew says looking suddenly serious. 'I saw Kali today at Costa. She works there now.'

Just hearing her name makes my stomach tighten.

'And I kind of snapped at her,' Drew continues.

'Drew,' I groan. I'd rather everyone acted like Kali doesn't exist instead of causing a scene.

'I'm sorry,' she says. 'Just seeing her face pissed me right off.'

'I would have punched her,' Regal says with a shrug.

'Can we all agree that if any of us see Kali or Simon, we don't even acknowledge them?' I snap.

'Whatever you want,' Cam says, clapping me on the shoulder. He glances at Drew and Regal. 'Right?'

Drew tuts and eventually says, 'I guess.' But I know my sister. If she sees them again, she won't be keeping quiet.

TWENTY-TWO

Tia

12th December

Regal's house is like something out of a movie. Everything is cream and white, even down to the Christmas décor, and it's super clean. But because it's so insanely big, and almost everything looks untouched, it feels more like a show home than a lived-in house, which is kind of sad when you think about it. It's like there's no personality or soul here.

'I guess the countryside isn't so bad,' Willow says, taking a picture of the lake in Regal's back garden.

Yep, her back garden. There's a small boat and two jet skis tied up and bobbing in the water, as well as a table and chairs on the decking.

I'm connected to Regal's Wi-Fi and my DMs are blowing up because of the story I posted of the Rolls-Royce. I check to see who's viewed it, and Mike's profile appears. He still hasn't responded to my earlier text, which is really annoying and upsetting. There's a difference between asking for space and outright ghosting someone. Willow's busy taking selfies, so I click on Mike's page and spot he posted a picture an hour ago. Mike loves a 'natural' shot, which is code for him looking into the distance as his camera clicks away on the self-timer. The background looks like a hallway at college. Funny how he has time to post this but not reply to me.

'You okay?' Willow asks, looking over.

I force a smile. 'Yeah, course. Are you enjoying it here?'

Willow nods. 'The Parker family are cool, aren't they? And Cam's not too bad to look at.'

I roll my eyes. 'Didn't Drew say he's a ladies' man?'

'What's a little Christmas fling?' Willow laughs. 'Quincy's cute too, don't you think?'

'Quincy?' I shrug. 'He's okay, I guess.' Willow raises her eyebrows at me, and I laugh. 'What?'

'You should get to know him. He'd be a good distraction from Mike,' she responds.

'Mike and I haven't broken up,' I say forcefully, but it's more for my own benefit. 'And I'm not sure Quincy's my type.'

'Hot isn't your type?' Willow says in disbelief.

'He's not even that cute,' I lie.

'Didn't Mike ask for space?' she counters. 'You should be present in the moment, rather than checking Mike's socials, Tia.'

How did she know? I quickly close my phone and cross my arms over my chest, staring out at the lake.

Willow puts her arm round me. 'Like I said, there's nothing wrong with some harmless flirting. Shall we go find the others?'

I follow Willow through the maze that is Regal's house, thinking about what she said. Even if Mike and I have broken up, I don't think I'll be getting close to Quincy. It doesn't seem like we have much in common.

We walk into the living room, and the first person I see is Quincy. He's lounging on the sofa in jeans and a fitted blue top that shows off his toned physique. As before, his locs are pulled back into a top bun, accentuating his sharp cheekbones and full lips. We catch each other's eye. Okay, I've been kidding myself – Quincy's very cute.

'Did you enjoy the tour?' Regal asks.

'Your house is stunning,' I say, sitting down next to her. The familiar smell of jollof rice slinking into the room makes me think of home. 'Smells good – are you cooking something?'

'I got Belle to warm up the food my mum made earlier. You hungry?' Regal asks and I nod. All I've had today is a coffee.

'So, what's the dress code for Seven Days?' Willow asks, changing the subject. 'Is it a trainers or heels situation?'

'The girls are usually in heels,' Drew says. 'So definitely dress up.'

'Tia, you have the perfect dress!' Willow says and everyone looks at me. 'The white dress you were going to wear to Mike's party.'

I can't wear that dress. What if it gets dirty? Willow doesn't know I plan to sneak back to London . . .

'Nah, I didn't bring it,' I say quickly, and try to hide my relief when Willow looks disappointed. That means she hasn't seen it in my suitcase.

'It's so sexy. It would have been perfect,' Willow says.

'Sexy, huh?' Quincy looks at me with a smirk on his face, and I can feel myself suddenly getting hot.

'Let me check on the food.' Regal gets up and heads into the hallway.

'Tia, I was wondering if you could bake some cupcakes for Seven Days?' Drew asks. 'I told Bunny we'd help out. I'll pay you for it, of course.'

'Okay, sure,' I say with a smile.

'Food's ready!' Regal yells from the kitchen.

We walk down the long hallway to the kitchen, which is white and grey with black accents. Like the rest of the house, it's spotless. The table is heaving with a massive bowl of jollof rice, ayamase stew, akara, beef suya and plantain.

'This looks amazing,' Willow says, pulling out one of the white chairs.

'Mum cooked for an entire village as usual. I wish I could take the credit, but I can't cook to save my life,' Regal says. 'But I did fry the plantain.'

'Plan-*tin*.' Quincy grins.

Regal eyeballs him. 'Oh no, we're not having this argument again. In this house we pronounce it plan-*tayne*.'

'The right way,' I add, and Regal winks at me. She starts dishing the jollof onto everyone's plates.

'Is it really spicy?' Drew asks, looking at the rice nervously.

142

'It's normal,' Regal replies, and Drew, Cam and Quincy look at each other. 'What?'

'Last time, I almost coughed to death,' Cam says.

'You're so dramatic! Try a bit,' Regal says.

Quincy scoops up the smallest amount of rice, and I can't help laughing. He frowns at me.

'You can't handle spice?' I tease.

His jaw tenses before he puts the rice in his mouth, chews and swallows, keeping his eyes on me the whole time. We all watch him, and he shrugs like it's no big deal.

'That tasted f-f—' He can't even finish the word because he starts coughing. Drew slaps him hard on the back and passes him a glass of water. He glugs it down.

'It can't be that bad.' Regal puts a spoonful of rice in her mouth. 'Mum only put a few scotch bonnets in it.'

'A few?' Quincy asks, his voice strained.

Everyone in my household can handle spice, but Mum always tones it down for Banks' benefit. I scoop up a big portion of jollof and all eyes turn to me. The spices dance on my tongue, and there's a slight heat to it, but nothing dramatic.

'Hmm. It's mild,' I say and smile at Quincy, who glares back at me.

'Naija girl!' Regal claps her hands. 'We're the best.'

Willow, Regal and I eat with no issue, but the Parkers eat more slowly and cautiously. By the end of the meal, I'm scraping my plate to try to get every last morsel. The food was so good.

'Do you guys want to come out with me and Regal later?'

Drew asks. She wipes her mouth with a napkin, throwing it on her almost empty plate. 'We're going to Hollow Bar for some drinks.'

Willow and I glance at each other and nod. That's exactly what I need – a night out to forget that Mike's completely ignoring me.

'It's eighteen and over,' Drew continues, and everything in me deflates.

'Oh.' Willow looks at me. 'Tia won't be able to come, so don't worry about me either.'

'No, you should go, Willow,' I protest, even though I'm envious. 'You can tell me all about it tomorrow. I'll just hang out with Mum and Banks.'

'Quincy?' Regal asks.

'I said I'd pass by Jared and Lizzy's tonight. Plus, I've got an early-morning riding session with Banks tomorrow. I can't do it hung-over.'

'You're so dry,' Cam says.

'Whatever, man.' Quincy stands up, raising his arms and stretching so his top rides up and shows off his abs. I quickly look away before anyone can catch me staring. 'Shall we bounce?'

Quincy is a much better driver than Drew. He navigates carefully through the lanes and J Cole plays from the speakers. Back at the farm, everyone gets out. But as I go to walk towards the house, Quincy calls my name.

'Can I talk to you for a sec?'

'Oh . . . sure,' I respond.

Willow looks back at me and I shrug. I watch her as she walks into the house with Drew.

'So, the Winter Ball,' he says. 'I was thinking . . . you know, nothing serious . . . but would you maybe want to go together? As friends?'

I frown. Why would Quincy want to go to the ball with me? We don't even know each other.

'You want me to come with you to the Winter Ball?' I ask, just to make sure I heard him right.

'Yeah.' He waits a beat. 'Do you want to?'

Not really. To be honest, the only part of the ball I'm excited about is shopping for the dress beforehand. What if I say yes and then we're stuck on a table together, sitting in silence?

'Why me?' I eventually ask.

'I know you have a boyfriend,' Quincy continues, 'but the ball is very traditional. You need a date to attend. And because my family's hosting it this year, everyone will be watching us and . . .' He hesitates.

'What?' I press.

'My ex is most likely going to be there, and she has a date. She's heard that I have one too.'

'Oh, so what happened?'

Quincy raises his eyebrows at me, and I clock on. 'Wait, you don't have a date?'

Quincy sighs. 'I stupidly lied and said I had one. Everyone's up in everyone else's business here and I could tell my parents were stressing that I didn't have a date.' His shoulders sag and he looks so defeated. I didn't realize not having a date was that big a deal. That wasn't mentioned in the brochure. I guess that means I need one too.

'Well ... erm ...' I begin.

'And if you need anything in return, just let me know,' he says quickly.

'Anything?' I say, and he nods. This might be the answer to my problems. What if I can get Quincy to help me travel back to London for Mike's party without anyone else knowing? I'm sure, when Mike and I finally see each other after being apart, it will be just like old times. I still haven't figured out how I'm going to bake a cake and get it there, but I'll deal with that issue later.

'I need to go to my boyfriend's birthday party on the twenty-first, back in London. Just for a few hours. But I need to get there and back here without anyone knowing that I'm gone, especially my mum and Willow. Can you do that?'

'That's tricky,' Quincy says, rubbing his jaw.

'You said "anything",' I challenge.

Quincy stares at me, and for a moment we're just looking into each other's eyes. There's something about his eye contact that makes my stomach flip. I look away to break whatever that was.

'I want more,' Quincy says softly, and my head snaps back to him so quickly it makes my neck hurt. 'Having a date to the ball isn't enough. I've been ignoring my ex, but she hasn't got the hint that I've moved on. But if we were to pretend we're more than friends, and people saw us together ...' He trails off and shrugs.

'Me and you?' I point between us to emphasize the point. That is the stupidest thing I've heard. How would we pull that off?

'I know, it's mad. But if you help me with this, then I can get you to London and back. No problem.'

'Really?' I'm searching Quincy's face to see if he's joking, but he looks dead serious. He holds out his hand, and I'm tempted to shake it, but guilt floods me. I don't think pretending to be dating Quincy behind Mike's back is a good idea. 'Can I think about it?' I say instead.

I need to talk to someone about this. I need Remi.

TWENTY-THREE

Quincy

12th December

The four women that are staying in one of our holiday cottages for a 'girls' trip' get up from their table, leaving the dirty plates and half a bottle of wine. I'm standing beside our hostess, Emma, and we both wave as they leave.

'I'm just going to grab some juice for the Solankés,' Emma says.

'I'll do it,' I offer.

I've got time to kill until Jared and Lizzy's get-together, and maybe if I take the juice over to the table Tia will finally look at me. I'm not sure if I crossed a line asking her to pretend to date me, but does it mean something that she didn't turn me down? Maybe she and her man aren't in a good place, because I can't imagine even entertaining a request like that if I was in a happy relationship. And why did I say I could get her to London – especially without her family knowing? Maybe I can sneak off and drive her myself, but I'd need a pretty good excuse not to be working that night.

I grab the juice from the kitchen and place it on the dining table for the Solankés. 'Is everything all right?' I ask.

'It's delicious,' Tope replies. She takes a bite of Mum's famous oxtail. 'And these are all your mum's recipes?'

I nod. 'Our chef, Gia, cooks them following my mum's exact instructions. I can introduce you to Gia, if you'd like.'

'Oh, I'd love that!' Tope says.

Willow's already left for her night out with Drew and Regal. Banks is making a mess with the rice, but she's so cute it's more adorable than annoying. But Tia has only eaten part of her food.

'Is yours all right?' I ask, and Tia looks up at me. She opens her mouth like she's going to say something, but instead she just nods. I want to ask her if everything is okay between us, but it's not the right time, so instead I smile in response and head back to the kitchen.

There's no sign of Gia, but she's left our family's meals on the counter, wrapped individually. Next to the plates there's a white envelope with *The Parkers* written on it. Frowning, I pick it up and pull out the letter that's inside, skim through it and catch the odd phrase, like 'sorry to do this' and 'immediate effect' … *What the hell?*

I hurry out of the kitchen, through the dining room – ignoring the Solanké family, who all look up at me – and run to reception, but it's empty. I race up the stairs two at a time and knock on my parents' door.

'Come in,' Mum calls.

She's sitting on her bed studying the seating plan for the ball. The tap's running in their ensuite, and when it stops, Dad appears in the doorway, wiping his face with a towel.

He hesitates when he sees my face. 'What is it, Q? Everything okay?'

'You need to read this.' I hold out the letter and Mum and Dad look at each other. I hand the sheet of paper to Mum, and her face falls as she takes it in.

Now Dad's reading it over her shoulder and his eyes go wide. 'Gia's quit?'

'I just found it in the kitchen next to our dinner,' I explain.

'No, no, no!' Mum says, throwing the seating plan on the floor. 'She can't! Has her car already left?'

'I didn't even think to check ... I'm not sure.'

Mum stands up and hurries out of her bedroom. She races down the stairs, Dad and I following behind her. I can already see once we get to reception that Gia's red Mini isn't there any more. Nevertheless, Mum goes outside without a coat and looks around as if Gia's hiding somewhere in the dark.

'Mel,' Dad says softly, but Mum ignores him and takes out her phone.

'Pick up!' she snaps, but in the silence I can hear the ringing tone. Mum yells and throws her phone to the ground.

I've never seen her like this before and it scares me. 'Mum!'

I cry, running over to her. I pick up her phone, but I can't see if it's broken because of how dark it is out here.

'Gia knows how important this ball is to us,' Mum says, her voice breaking on every other word. 'How could she just leave like that?'

'I don't know,' I say, hugging her tightly.

Gia didn't even explain in her letter why she was quitting. All she said was that she had some personal stuff to figure out and that she was 'sorry'. 'Sorry' doesn't cut it! Mum has spent months planning every last detail of the event, from the invitations and marketing to the decorations and seating plan, not to mention all her new ideas for dishes which she's developed and practised over and over until she perfects them. Gia has always known that there's a lot of pressure on us, the first Black family to host the ball, to make it a success – yet she just ups and leaves a matter of weeks before.

'Oh, Mel,' Dad says and Mum transfers from me to him. She puts her head on his chest and begins to cry. Each heartbreaking sound feels like a knife to my gut.

'What are we going to do, Will?' Mum asks Dad, looking up at him. 'I won't be able to manage all the cooking by myself, and there's no way I'll be able to find someone to help cook for hundreds of people at this short notice, with Christmas round the corner.'

'Shh, shh, love. It's okay, it's okay,' Dad mumbles. He looks at me over her shoulder, and I shrug in response. What can we do?

'Is everything all right?'

We turn to see Tope, Tia and Banks gathered on the doorstep. Mum quickly stands up straight and wipes her eyes.

'Yes, we're fine,' she says, a fixed smile on her face. 'Did you need something?'

Tope and Tia glance at each other.

'No, we were just heading upstairs to put Banks to bed and heard someone crying,' Tope says gently. 'Is there anything we can do to help?'

At this Mum puts her head in her hands and starts to cry again. Tope hurries over to her, and Tia follows holding onto Banks.

'Mel, what's wrong?' Tope says, hugging Mum tightly like they're old friends.

Mum's response comes out muffled because she's crying, so it's hard to make out her words. Tope looks at me instead.

'Gia, our cook, quit,' I explain. 'She's meant to be cooking the food for the ball.'

Tope gasps. 'That's terrible! Why would she do that?'

'We don't fully know,' Dad says. 'Let's all go inside. It's too cold for the little one to be out here.'

But Banks, oblivious to it all, is looking up at the starry night sky. She doesn't seem the least bit bothered to be out in the cold. Tope still has her arm wrapped round Mum's waist, and Mum's tears have subsided into a sniffle.

'Mel –' Tope holds Mum's hands – 'I don't know if you know this, but I'm a chef by trade.'

No way! This could save everything.

'What?' Mum and Dad say at the same time.

'It's true,' Tia confirms. 'She's amazing.'

'Now, I may not be able to cook the dishes as well as Gia,' continues Tope, 'and I'm certainly not as good as you, but I'd be happy to help with the food for the ball and the cooking for the guests staying at the farm.'

'B-but this is your *holiday*!' Mum says shaking her head. 'I can't ask you to do that.'

'You're not asking,' Tope says gently. 'Honestly, it would be my pleasure to learn your recipes. I know what it's like to need a helping hand, so here's me offering you one.'

I can't believe Tope would be so kind as to do this for us. Mum's shaking her head, but this is a gift and she needs to accept. There's no one else we could ask.

'Thank you, Tope. Thank you so much,' Mum eventually says. 'And of course we'll pay you for your time.'

'I can help too,' Tia says, and we all look at her. 'I'm all right at baking.'

'She's *brilliant* at baking,' Tope says, smiling at Tia.

'We'll all help,' I chip in. 'Whatever you need, Mum. We'll make sure everything runs smoothly.'

Mum's eyes start to well up again, and I really don't want her to cry any more. Dad must think the same because he quickly says, 'Thank you. We accept.'

'Don't you worry. This is going to be great!' Tope says. 'Shall we talk in the morning about the menu? I've got to get Banks to bed now.'

Mum nods and smiles at Tope, her eyes still red and watery. Then Tope scoops Banks up and kisses her on the cheek before carrying her back into the house and up the stairs. Dad puts his arm round Mum, and she leans into him as they wander back inside too.

Then it's just Tia and me left outside.

'That was really kind of you guys,' I say.

'It's no problem,' she responds, avoiding my eyes.

Shit, I definitely crossed a line asking her to be my date. 'Sorry for earlier, by the way. I shouldn't have asked you . . . what I asked you.'

'No, it's fine,' she says, finally looking at me. 'I just need to sort something out. Honestly, I'm not—' but whatever Tia was about to say is interrupted by her phone ringing. She takes it out of her back pocket and her eyes widen when she sees who it is. 'Sorry, I've got to take this. I'll catch you in a bit?'

'Okay,' I respond.

She flashes me a smile before dashing towards the stairs. Oreo wanders out from wherever he's been and pushes his nose against my leg.

'Come on, boy. Let's get some food.'

At the word 'food', his tail wags. As I lead him back inside to the kitchen, I can't help but look up the stairs where Tia went a moment before. I really hope she decides to help me out.

TWENTY-FOUR

Tia

12th December

'Mike?' I jump onto my bed as I accept the FaceTime. He looks so fine in his baggy white T-shirt, his long hair hanging down over his shoulders. He's sitting on his beanbag chair, and I can see the light of the TV bouncing off the walls. I wish I was with him.

'Hey, what time is the DJ getting to my party again?' Mike asks.

I frown. *Is this what he called me for?* 'An hour before it starts so he has time to set up. Why?'

'Cool. He messaged me to confirm because he couldn't get through to you.' There's an accusing edge to his voice. 'I told him you're away and the signal is bad where you are.'

'Right.' I wait, but Mike doesn't say anything else. I'm expecting him to ask how I am, but instead we fall into an awkward silence. Mike's eyes keep looking at the TV screen, and I bet any money he's watching the football.

'But everything's okay?' I ask, drawing his attention back to me.

'Yeah, all good. Hey, whose car was that on your story?'

'Drew Parker's. You know, the actress?'

Mike's eyes go wide. 'No way! How come you're hanging out with her?'

I tell him about Drew and then Regal. He interrupts me constantly to find out more about them. 'Yesterday, Drew took us on a tour of the farm and I stepped in horse shit. I wanted to cry!' I wait for a reaction, but Mike's looking away from me again and so all I get is a distracted, 'Is it?'

I sigh impatiently. 'Did you hear what I said?'

Mike whips his head back to me. 'Sorry ... I'm just in the middle of something.'

I can't help feeling hurt by his lack of attention. How can I fix us if he can't even bother to listen to me?

'What did you say again?' he asks.

I repeat the story, and he reacts more animatedly, but it sounds forced. Usually, we're on the phone for hours, but this time it feels like he can't wait to end the call.

He confirms my worry when he says, 'Tia, can we talk later? I've got some work I need to finish.'

My heart sinks. 'Oh, right, okay ... But what about my text?'

Mike frowns. 'What text?'

'The one where I asked to talk more about the space you wanted. Maybe we should set some rules?'

156

Mike scoffs. 'Rules? What you talking about?'

I look up to the ceiling to avoid losing my temper. 'Rules, like are we still exclusive?'

Mike shrugs. 'I dunno . . . I feel like we should just see how it goes.' His words kick me in the gut.

'What?' I ask, searching his bored face. 'Cause you want to see other people?'

Mike hesitates. 'Look. We're taking this space to figure out if we're meant to be together, and I dunno where that will lead. If we're drawn to other people, maybe that's a sign.'

'Drawn to other people'? I thought the whole point of this space was so Mike could figure shit out for himself, but now suddenly he's open to meeting other people. Other girls, he means. Has he already met someone else? I take a deep breath in an attempt to calm my racing heart.

'Hello? Tia?' he says.

'What's happening to us, Mike?' I say quietly.

'Come on. I don't want to argue, okay?' he responds, even though I asked a basic question. 'I think we should commit to the space. Let's talk properly once my birthday's over, yeah?'

I look away, wishing I never answered this pointless FaceTime. 'Yeah, sure.'

'Say hi to the fam for me, yeah? And I'll tell people to email you instead of calling, if they need to get in touch about the party.'

'Okay. Bye.' I end the call, not waiting for him to say anything else. I dash my phone down, so it bounces on the soft carpet, before I lie on my back and look up at the ceiling.

My eyes start to water, and a second later tears are falling down my face onto the duvet. *Why doesn't he care about us any more?* The only thing this space is achieving is putting more distance between us, and I seem to be the only one that cares about that.

My phone rings and I rush to it, thinking it's Mike calling back to apologize, but Remi's name flashes on the screen.

'Remi!'

'Tia! I got your message about needing to talk, but I couldn't get through to you. How are you?'

'Sorry, the signal here isn't great.' I sniff and wipe my eyes with my jumper sleeve. 'I'm okay. You?'

'Missing my best friend!' she says.

'Miss you too.'

'Have you got a cold or something?'

'Oh no ... it's nothing,' I say, not ready to admit the truth about me and Mike.

'Have you sorted out how you're going to get back to London?' she asks.

'Well, I may have.' I sit back against the headboard. 'But tell me if you think it's mad, okay?' I catch her up on Quincy's idea. 'I said I'd get back to him, but I don't know what to say.'

'Erm, you say yes!' Remi says.

I pull a face. 'Isn't it weird, though? I don't even know the guy.'

'So what? He's hot, and he's currently your only way of getting back here. Unless you have another idea?'

I definitely don't, but how would we even pull off

fake-dating? We haven't got off to the best start. I'm sure everyone would immediately see through it.

'Just do what you gotta do and sneak back, okay?' Remi says. 'Who knows, you may even find it fun.'

I don't know if 'fun' is the right word, but my options are limited. Maybe it's not the end of the world, fake dating Quincy. If anything, it will be a distraction from this whole Mike mess. But only if Quincy and I establish some ground rules so I know exactly what he wants me to do. I say goodbye to Remi and head downstairs to find him.

Quincy is the only one in the dining room with Oreo sitting close by. Oreo gets up and trots over to me, his tongue hanging out, and instinctively I push myself up against a wall.

'Oreo, sit!' Quincy yells, and Oreo looks back at him and then at me, but then he does what Quincy says and sits obediently. Quincy clicks his tongue, and Oreo hurries back to him. 'I'm sorry. He seems to like you.'

'Mmm,' I respond. The feeling is not mutual. 'I was thinking about what you said earlier.'

'Yeah?' he says slowly.

'I'll do it,' I hear myself say, and his eyes light up. 'But how would it work?'

'Well, we just need to convince my friends we're seeing each other, so it gets back to my ex and she realizes I'm not interested in her any more,' Quincy says. 'These twins I'm friends with are having a get-together tonight. Why don't you come with me? All we have to do is pretend we're into each other.'

Quincy makes it sound so easy, but *how* exactly are we going to do that? 'Okay ... but we need some ground rules,' I say.

'What did you have in mind?' he asks.

'Well, obviously, no kissing,' I respond.

'Not even a bit?' he questions, and I eyeball him. 'Sorry – I'm joking, but we will need to hold hands and get close for it to look believable.'

'Yeah, I guess you're right. Okay, we can hold hands. Second rule – our families cannot know about this.'

'No, of course. If word gets back to any of them, I'll deny it. I did kind of tell my friend Eliza a bit about you, so she knows we're not actually dating, but she's cool and won't say anything.'

Quincy spoke to his friend about me? What does that mean?

'What did you say about me?' I ask.

Quincy shrugs. 'I said you were all right.'

It's not the biggest compliment, but I expected him to say I was a moody cow, so I'll take it.

'Fair enough. I'll have to check with my mum to see if I can come with you tonight,' I say.

Quincy looks at his phone. 'Okay, cool. It won't get going for at least another hour.'

The idea of hanging out here with just Quincy for an hour makes me nervous. What are we going to do until we set off? I don't really want to wait in my room. I glance at the kitchen door and point my thumb at it, an idea forming.

'Can I use your kitchen to do some baking while we wait?'

'Erm, sure.' Quincy stands and picks up his plate and glass. 'Come with me. Oreo, stay.' Oreo whines in response.

I follow Quincy into the kitchen, and I'm surprised by how pretty it is. One of the walls is exposed brick, while the others have been painted a dark cream. The cabinets are a rich blue with wooden worktops, and three gold pendant lights hang over the island in the middle.

'It's so nice in here,' I say.

'Is it?' Quincy asks, reaching inside a cabinet and pulling out a mixing bowl, whisk and cake tin. 'You're baking a cake?'

'Actually, I was thinking of making vanilla biscuits, if that's okay?'

'No problem. There should be everything you need in that cupboard.'

This kitchen has everything I need and more. I lay out all the ingredients on the counter.

'You want these?' Quincy pulls out star-shaped and Christmas tree cutters from a drawer.

'Perfect.' Instantly I feel calmer. I reach for the flour, expecting Quincy to leave, but instead he leans on the counter opposite me.

'How was your phone call?' he asks.

'It was okay.' I avoid his eyes as I mix the ingredients together in the bowl. 'It was my boyfriend ... I'm planning his eighteenth birthday.'

'Really? That's funny, my ex planned a surprise party for my eighteenth,' Quincy says in a weird tone.

I glance up at him. 'Did it go well?'

He laughs drily. 'I was in London when it happened.'

'London? So you missed your own party?' When he doesn't respond, I look up and catch him staring into space. 'Quincy?'

'Sorry. You're a good girlfriend. Organizing a party is a big deal.'

I don't miss the way he's changed the subject, but the need to be acknowledged for my efforts on Mike's behalf is important to me right now.

'Yes. I. Am,' I say through gritted teeth. Mike doesn't seem to think that, though. I take the dough out of the bowl and roll it out so aggressively that the rolling pin flies out of my hand onto the floor. 'Damn. Sorry.'

Quincy picks it up and hands me a new one from the drawer. 'You good?'

I sigh. Maybe it would be good to get his perspective on this. 'Why would a guy ask a girl for space?'

Quincy laughs. 'Because he wants to break up and doesn't have the balls to say it.'

My mouth drops open. *Mike wants to break up?* Have I been that naive? Is he just biding his time waiting for the right moment to end our relationship?

Quincy takes a sharp breath. 'Shit. Was that about you?'

'It's fine,' I say in a high voice that sounds nothing like my own.

'I'm so sorry,' he says quickly. 'Listen, I don't even know what I'm talking about.'

I ignore him and focus really hard on pushing the cutters into the dough. *Fuck*. My eyes are watering again. I blink quickly, praying the tears go away.

'Can I do one?' Quincy asks, pointing at the star cutter in my hand.

'Sure.' I pass it to him. I quickly wipe my eyes once he's looking down at the dough. I can't help but smile at how proud he looks when he lifts the cutter and a perfect star is left behind.

'Are we going to ice them?' he asks.

'Duh!' I say.

I place the biscuits on the tray and slide it into the oven before I grab a cloth and start to wipe down the surfaces. I start thinking about Mike again and my eyes begin to burn once more. Quincy places his hand on top of mine, forcing me to stop. I look up at him.

'I'm sure he really does need space just to think,' he says. 'I shouldn't have said anything about breaking up.'

'Maybe you're right, though.' I shrug like I'm not bothered, but my stupid tears betray me. 'He said he wants space to find himself, but now he's saying we shouldn't put any rules in place and just see how it goes. He even said if we're drawn to other people then it's a sign.'

'He said that?' Quincy pulls a face. 'Why are you still planning his party?'

'I dunno. I guess I thought after having a bit of space, we'd be able to get back to how we were, so I've been carrying on as normal.' I sniff, the tears now dry on my cheeks. 'I'm not ready to give up on us yet. Do you think I'm stupid?'

Quincy smiles. 'No ... I'm actually starting to think I was wrong about you.' I can't ignore the butterflies that start to flutter in my stomach at his words. 'This guy is lucky to have you.'

There's a whine outside the kitchen door, and Quincy rolls his eyes. 'Oreo! Let me just check on him – he might need to go out.'

I glance at my phone when he goes to Oreo, hoping to see a message from Mike, but, as usual, there's nothing. I lean on the counter, praying for a sign that will help me work out what I should do about my relationship. I scroll through my phone for a bit until the biscuits are ready. I've just taken them out when Quincy returns to the kitchen and eyes them greedily.

'They're hot,' I remind him, but he ignores me and fetches a spatula.

He scoops one up and blows on it before taking a bite. His eyes widen. 'These are amazing, and they don't even have icing on them yet! No lie – this is one of the best biscuits I've ever had.'

'Really?' I ask as Quincy finishes his biscuit and reaches for another. The compliment buzzes around me, filling me with warmth, and when Quincy smiles at me, I can't help but smile back.

TWENTY-FIVE

Quincy

12th December

Thankfully Tia cheered up after we started icing the biscuits. She made it look so easy. The ones I did were a mess, but we soon had a full tray of them decorated in red, green and white. I couldn't stop thinking about what I'd accidentally said about her boyfriend – even though what I said was true. But I didn't want her to feel shit about herself. When she first arrived at the farm, I thought she was a stuck-up princess, but I clearly read her wrong. She seems kind of sweet, and I can tell her boyfriend is stringing her along. She deserves way better.

We're in the car now heading to Jared and Lizzy's, and Tia is nodding her head in time to the music. I wasn't sure how her mum would feel about her coming out alone with me, but when

I said we were going to a campfire, Tope was more excited about it than Tia, who looked horrified.

We're onto the third Burna Boy track when Tia groans. 'Can you change it? I'm not the biggest Afrobeats fan.' *She what?*

Tia almost gets whiplash when I do an emergency stop. 'Quincy, what the hell?'

'How can you not like Afrobeats?' What kind of unseasoned person has a problem with that genre of music? Everything about it is perfection. 'You're Nigerian!'

'So?' Tia shrugs unbothered. 'It doesn't mean I want to listen to it all night. It starts to sound meh after a while.'

My eyes bulge. 'Burna Boy's "Love, Damini" album is far from "meh". It's amazing!'

Tia laughs. '"Amazing"? It's okay.'

I'm tempted to tell her to get out and walk home, but instead I re-start the car and I try to hold my tongue as she skips one of Cam's carefully curated playlists. Tia obviously has no taste.

As we approach Emberwood Forest, I start to see light glowing between the trees, clearly coming from the campfire. I turn onto the dirt road and drive towards my friends.

'This is so creepy,' Tia says, gazing out of the window.

She's not wrong. The forest is pitch black apart from the firelight ahead and the moon above.

'What do I talk about with your friends?' she asks. 'How shall I say we met?'

'Could say we met in London and you came down to see me for the holidays?'

166

Tia crosses her arms over her chest. 'With my family in tow? Who's gonna believe that?'

'Lots of people come here for the Winter Ball,' I explain.

People have actually *flown in* for the ball. It has a reputation, so it's not inconceivable that her family would want to come too. What might be harder to believe is why I'd date Tia when our personalities are so different. All the girls I've dated before have been from around here, and, like me, they've all loved life in the country, dogs, horses and riding. Kali was even looking into doing dressage, but she wasn't good enough to compete. I glance at Tia in her tight jeans, heeled boots and green fur coat . . .

'Maybe it's best if you follow my lead,' I say as we pull up beside the other cars, praying that this doesn't turn out to be the stupidest idea I've ever had.

TWENTY-SIX

Tia

12th December

I follow behind Quincy, walking slowly over the uneven ground. Suddenly, he stops, turns round and reaches his hand out to me. *What's he doing?*

'We're a couple now, remember?' he says.

'Oh, yeah, sorry.' I catch up with him and grab onto his hand. It sends a tingle through my body, but I quickly push the feeling away.

We continue walking down the dirt road, and my brain starts telling me someone is hiding in the trees and is going to jump out and attack me, so I completely miss what Quincy is saying.

'You okay with that?' he asks.

'Erm, yeah,' I say, not wanting to admit that I was thinking about serial killers instead of listening to him. He smiles, satisfied.

We reach the clearing, and my face starts heating up as everyone turns to look at us. Quincy squeezes my hand to reassure me, but it doesn't help. I assumed I'd find a bunch of teens sitting on some boulders, freezing their arses off as they hold marshmallows on sticks over a fire, but in fact it's much more cosy than that. A string of fairy lights hanging from low branches wraps its way around the clearing, camping chairs with red-and-black tartan blankets form a circle and in the very centre is the firepit. Music is playing from a speaker and drinks and snacks have been placed on a small table. Everyone looks like they're having a great time.

'You made it!' A bubbly white girl with blonde hair and a kind face comes over. She glances down at our joined hands. Quincy only lets go when she reaches in for a hug. She smiles politely at me once they're done. 'Hi, I'm Lizzy.'

'Tia,' I say, and Quincy grabs hold of my hand again. Lizzy and I both look at him.

'We met in London, and she's come to visit,' Quincy explains, and Lizzy's eyes widen, her mouth forming an O shape. 'A bit quiet tonight,' he says, glancing around the campfire.

'Yeah, I think some people are waiting for college to break up before they start coming out. I know Kali couldn't make it, but that's probably a good thing.' She nods towards me as if to emphasize her point.

I glance at Quincy, and he looks relieved.

'How are Drew and Cam?' Lizzy asks, leading us towards the chairs.

'They're cool. Drew's out with Regal tonight and Cam's got a gig,' Quincy explains.

'Ah, okay. And where's Eliza?' Lizzy adds.

'I think she had plans,' Quincy replies before turning towards the main group.

Some of the guys are standing round the drinks table where there are lots of flasks and bottles of alcohol, and the girls are sitting round the campfire. I smile nervously at his friends, who either smile back or look at me curiously. Quincy points at Jared, Lizzy's twin brother, and names the rest of the guys present, and I quickly realize we're the only Black people here. I wonder if that ever bothers Quincy.

'You want a drink?' he asks me, and I nod.

He heads over to where the guys are, greeting them all with a dap and a one-armed hug, and I take a seat on one of the chairs. The three girls, Lizzy, Sarah and Harley, who all have blonde hair and blue eyes, lean in towards me, and I wish Quincy would hurry back.

'So, Tia, where in London did you meet Q?' Sarah asks, sipping slowly from her flask.

Shit. Quincy told me to follow his lead, but how am I meant to do that if he's not here?

'Central London,' I say vaguely, and the girls nod at me, clearly wanting me to elaborate, so I add: 'At an event.'

'Like a party or something?' Harley asks before turning to Lizzy. 'Wasn't Q in London for his birthday?'

Sarah's eyes widen. 'Is that when you met?'

I shrug. 'Sure.'

She frowns, and I suddenly feel like I've said the wrong thing.

'Wasn't he still with Kali then?' Sarah asks, and Harley gasps.

Fuck.

'Sorry, I'm getting my dates messed up.' I force a laugh. 'I first noticed him at a party when he came to London for his birthday, but we didn't speak until I saw him again at another event a couple of weeks later.'

Sarah frowns. 'Where?'

What the hell is this girl's problem?

Lizzy claps her hands. 'Oh, was it the dressage event?'

Dressage? I have no idea what that even means, but I nod anyway and that seems to satisfy the girls. Quincy's laugh carries over from the other side of the forest. How can he not notice I'm being grilled?

'So you do dressage? That makes sense.' Harley smiles kindly at me, and I relax a little until she says, 'How long have you been doing it for?'

The smile that had been on my own face freezes. 'A while,' I say, non-committally.

Lizzy leans in closer. 'Dressage is so hard! Kali didn't qualify to compete,' she says, looking at the other girls. 'You must be really good, then?'

Compete?

'Oh, you know ... I don't really like to brag,' I say hoping it will shut down the conversation.

171

'I bet you've won loads of medals,' Harley says. 'Have you gone to Cheltenham? Or Ascot?'

I don't know where Cheltenham is. I've heard of Ascot, but the only thing I know about it is that people dress up in big hats to attend, so I shake my head, hoping they'll stop asking questions now.

'Oh. So, what type of horse do you ride?' Harley continues, and I sigh internally.

Did she say *horse*? What's the link between a horse and 'dressage'? Out of the corner of my eye, I spot Quincy grabbing a flask and two cups, and I quickly get to my feet.

'Sorry, I'm just going to help Quincy with the drinks. Anyone want something while I'm up?' I don't even wait for them to reply before I hurry over to Quincy.

'Hi. You okay?' he asks.

'They're asking me about dressage and Cheltenham and Ascot!' I hiss, not wanting the other boys to hear me. Luckily, they're too busy talking to each other to be paying any attention.

Quincy smiles. 'So they believed you. I knew they would.'

'Huh?'

'Remember when we first got out of the car, I told you to say you were into dressage.' He begins to pour what smells like hot chocolate into the cups.

'I don't even know what that means!' I reply.

Quincy slowly turns to look at me. 'What?'

'I've never even heard the word before. Has it got something to do with horses?'

'"Has it got something to do with horses?"' he repeats slowly, looking at me like I've grown two heads. I huff in irritation, still waiting for an answer.

'Tia.' Lizzy appears next to us. 'The girls and I wanted to know if you're on YouTube so we can see you competing?'

'Oh ... erm ... no, not any more.'

Lizzy frowns. 'Oh, right. How come?'

'Erm ...' I glance at Quincy, who has the audacity to stare back at me like he's waiting for my answer too. I have no idea what to say, so I go with the first thing that comes into my head. 'My horse died.'

Lizzy gasps and covers her mouth as Quincy's eyes widen.

I try to look as sad as possible. 'Yeah, he died suddenly, out of the blue. So if I'm being completely honest, this whole dressage conversation is kind of triggering me.'

'I'm so sorry, Tia.' Lizzy places a hand on my arm. 'I'll let the girls know to stop talking about it.'

I put on a brave smile. 'Thanks, Lizzy.'

Lizzy heads back to the campfire, and Quincy stands in front of me, blocking their view. 'What the fuck?'

'Oh, relax. At least now they'll back off.' I take one of the cups from him and sip the sweet hot chocolate. 'It's not like you helped me.'

'But why did you agree to the dressage lie if you didn't know what it was?' Quincy asks, confused.

I take another sip to delay responding.

'Tia?' he presses.

I sigh. 'I was convinced a serial killer was hidden in the

173

trees, so I was keeping an eye out for one and didn't hear what you said.'

Quincy's mouth twitches. 'What?'

'Oh, shut up, Quincy,' I say but his mouth twitch is now a full smile, and I can't help but mirror him. He bursts out laughing.

'You are . . .' He shakes his head, still chuckling, and I want to know what he's about to say, but he changes the topic. 'FYI, horse races happen at Cheltenham and Ascot. Shall we go join the others, Horse Killer?'

I grin and nudge him, and he almost drops his hot chocolate.

We sit down on two camp chairs next to each other, and Quincy spreads a blanket over the both of us. I find myself staring at him as the flicker of the fire lights up his face. He catches me looking, and I quickly turn away. His friends are talking about some girl I don't know, but I don't mind, because I'm actually enjoying sitting outside under the stars, with a hot chocolate in my hands and a blanket over my knees. Quincy finishes his drink and places his cup on the floor, and then, like it's the most natural gesture in the world, he puts his arm round my shoulders. To my surprise, it doesn't feel awkward at all, and I let myself snuggle into him.

I can see Sarah is watching us, and I'm convinced she's either really close to Kali or wants Quincy for herself. I reach up and hold Quincy's hand that's hanging over my shoulder, ignoring the way my heart starts to quicken, and she eventually looks away. But I can't work out whether I did it to convince the group that Quincy and I are dating, or because I wanted to . . .

TWENTY-SEVEN

Quincy

13th December

Last night was fun, and I actually enjoyed hanging out with Tia. It wasn't awkward like I thought it might be, and when we were sat down by the fire and she held my hand, an unexpected jolt went through my body. A girl hasn't made me feel like that since … Kali. At one point, Lizzy took a group photo, and Tia leaned in towards me just before the flash went off. Lizzy posted it on Instagram for everyone to see, and I thought Kali would message me, but surprisingly I haven't heard from her.

'These biscuits are amazing!' Drew is saying to Tia as I enter the kitchen. 'I can't believe you made them.'

'Thanks! Morning, Quincy.' Tia beams.

I frown at the empty biscuit plate. I'd been looking forward to another one today.

'Morning. How did you sleep?' I ask.

'Good,' she says. 'Banks is so excited for her first horse-riding lesson!'

'Are you going to attempt a ride while you're here, Miss Dressage?' I ask, smiling.

Drew looks at us strangely as Tia laughs and mouths, 'Shut up.'

At that moment, the door opens and Tope and Banks walk in, both dressed warmly in winter jackets, hats and scarves.

'There you are, Tia,' Tope says. 'I'm going food shopping with Mrs Parker. Do you want to come?'

'No, thanks,' Tia responds.

'Okay, but can you take Banks to her riding lesson?' At that, Banks drops her mum's hand and runs over to Tia. Tope looks at me and smiles. 'She can't wait, Quincy.'

I'm about to say something when Tia says, 'Why can't Willow take her?'

'Willow wants to come shopping with me.'

'And I'm coming too,' Drew chips in. She wipes her hands together to get rid of the biscuit crumbs.

'But, Mum!' Tia argues.

Tope glares at her. 'All you have to do is watch her lesson and take lots of pictures and videos, okay?' Her face softens when she looks at me. 'Thanks again, Quincy. Look after my baby, please.'

'Of course,' I say brightly.

Tope gives Banks a kiss before she and Drew walk out of the kitchen. Banks smiles shyly at me.

But Tia crosses her arms over her chest. 'How have I ended up being the one about to stand in the freezing cold surrounded by horses?'

'I bet you'll have more fun than you think,' I say, but Tia groans and narrows her eyes at me. 'Okay, I'm off to get ready. I'll see you out there, Banks.'

It's icy outside, and even though I'm wearing my thermal gear underneath my other layers, I'm still cold. Ethan has already saddled the horses, and he's standing behind the fence as he teaches Jack Owens, one of our regulars, who's currently trotting on Barbie, Drew's horse.

Barbie was the horse Kali always used to ride. We'd spend hours on horseback together, no matter the weather, she on Barbie, me on Legend, and usually after a good gallop we'd end up in the big fields, where we'd dismount, tie the horses up and within moments be kissing ... a lot. A wave of sadness washes over me at the memory, knowing I'll never experience that again, but I refuse to dwell on the past.

I walk over to the stables and go to Fairy's stall. Fairy is a brown Shetland pony with a white mane and tail. She's sweet and gentle, and not too big, so will be perfect for Banks. I spot a plastic bag on top of the bench and, when I peer inside, I see a clean white trainer. Well, that should make Tia happy. I go to grab a small helmet for Banks before tying Fairy to the fence. Fifteen minutes later, she arrives with Tia, who freezes when she sees the horses and ponies. I hurry over to them.

'She's not riding that, is she?' Tia asks, pointing behind me. I turn to see Legend.

'No, of course not! That's Legend, my horse, and she's only for experienced riders,' I explain.

Tia's eyes widen. 'That massive horse is yours?'

'Sure is.' I bend down so I'm level with Banks. Her blue eyes are darting to and fro, trying to watch all the horses at once. 'I have a lovely pony for you to ride. Her name's Fairy, and she's very excited to meet you. Shall we go see her together?'

Banks nods. I hold out my hand and she takes it. Tia follows reluctantly.

I can feel Banks tensing up the closer we get to the horses, so to distract her I say, 'I love your name, Banks. It's very cool.'

'It's from a hat,' she says.

I frown. 'A hat?'

Banks nods. 'Tia took it out of a hat.'

At this Tia laughs. 'She means we each chose a name, wrote it down and then put all of them in a hat. I wanted to call her Banks, and that's what was picked out. Paul wanted to call her Mary after his mum.'

'Oh, I think Banks suits you better,' I say, smiling at her.

When we reach the stables, Tia immediately pulls her phone out and starts taking pictures. I take off Banks' woolly hat and put it in my pocket. Then I place the helmet on her head, clipping it underneath her chin.

'Can you nod your head for me so I can see if it fits okay?' Banks does what I ask and the helmet seems secure. 'Okay, good. Just wait here while I fetch Fairy.'

I go over to Fairy's stall, untie her, and grab a brush from the bucket nearby. I lead her over to Banks and Tia, who immediately takes a step back. 'It's okay, Tia. She's a softie. Come on, Banks, let's brush her together.' I show Banks the brush and gently pull it through Fairy's mane. 'Do you want to try?'

Banks slowly nods, and I pass her the brush, guiding her with my own hand. She grins. 'Horsey.'

'Yes. She likes you,' I say.

We spend a bit of time grooming Fairy and Tia takes hundreds of pictures.

'Okay. Now let's get Fairy warmed up.' I hand Banks the reins. 'Hold them tight, okay? We're just going to walk over to there and back,' I say, pointing to a spot a little way off.

Banks, Tia, Fairy and I slowly walk, and Banks looks at the little pony in awe. For her first time properly near horses, she's doing a great job.

'Thanks for yesterday,' Tia suddenly says, talking over Banks' head. 'I felt less –' she glances down at her sister – 'S-H-I-T.'

I smile. 'No problem. I do have a question.' Tia looks at me. 'What do we do about social media? It would be weird if we didn't put anything up.'

'That's true,' she says.

'We can post on my account so it doesn't get back to anyone in London. It's private, so only my friends will be able see it – and my ex, of course, which is the whole point.'

'Okay, cool. Shall we shake on it?'

Tia stops and we lock eyes. She holds out her hand to

me over the top of Fairy and I grab it. Just like last night, a jolt goes through me when we touch. I drop her hand quickly, like it's on fire, trying to ignore the way my heart is thudding.

TWENTY-EIGHT

Tia

13th December

Quincy now has Banks sat on Fairy and I'm watching from the sidelines. I glance down at my hand, disappointment settling in my chest as I think of how quickly Quincy pulled his hand away from mine. I shake my head. *What am I doing?* I can't be looking at Quincy in any sort of romantic way. Taking a deep breath, I remind myself that the only reason I'm in this position is so I can get to London to see my *boyfriend*, nothing more and nothing less.

I take out my phone to record Banks when she suddenly bursts into tears. Quincy's trying to soothe her, but she's getting more and more worked up, shaking her head and turning red in the face.

'Banksy!' I call, running over to her, and she holds

her arms out to me. I pick her up and she wraps herself around me, her small body shuddering as she cries into my shoulder. 'What happened?' I ask Quincy, who looks just as surprised as me.

'Nothing. She was sat on Fairy and then she started to cry.'

'Oh, Banks.' I rub her back. 'Remember how excited you were about riding the horsey? Come on now, it's okay.'

'No,' she whimpers. 'I'm scared.'

'There's nothing to be scared of,' Quincy says, and Banks stares at him through her tears. 'Fairy is really friendly,' he says. 'And I'll make sure she's on her best behaviour. Do you want to get back on?'

Banks shakes her head in response.

'How about if Quincy gets on a horse and shows you how fun it is?' I suggest, and Quincy nods enthusiastically.

Banks sniffles, and I think I've won her over, when she says, 'Tia, you go on a horse.'

'Excuse me?' I ask, certain I didn't hear her right.

'Okay, Banks. If your sister goes on a horse, will you finish your lesson?' Quincy asks. Banks nods, and I just look at them, bewildered. Erm, excuse me? Have I agreed to that?

'No, sorry, I don't think so,' I say.

'Come on, Tia. All you have to do is sit on one; you don't actually have to ride it,' Quincy says, and Banks has the cheek to nod her head in agreement. 'Then Banks can finish her lesson on Fairy and everyone's happy,' he adds.

And what about me? I'm *not* happy! But now Banks is staring at me with her puppy-dog eyes. I don't want her to be afraid of horses, especially because she's loved them for ever. Oh, where's Willow when I need her?

'Wait here.' Quincy walks off, even though this situation is *not* resolved.

'You're a piece of work, you know that, missy?' I tell Banks as she rests her head on my shoulder. At least she's not crying any more. 'You know I don't like horses.'

'But you're brave,' Banks says.

I raise my eyebrows. 'You think I'm brave?'

She looks at me with her big blue eyes and nods. Maybe she's tired and is confusing me with Willow, because I'm the biggest scaredy-cat of the family.

'Tia!' Quincy waves us over, so I walk with Banks on my hip towards him, dreading each step. I see Quincy's big monster horse, and for a second I think he's going to put me on that, but instead he points to a white horse with black spots like a Dalmatian and a blonde mane. Ethan is holding the reins.

'You're going to be just fine,' Ethan says, handing me a helmet.

I put Banks down and reach out for the helmet, which I grip tightly in my hands as I look at this horse who's acting all cool, calm and collected, but who I bet is ready to attack the moment it gets a chance.

'This is Drew's horse, Barbie. Trust me, she's lovely,' Quincy says.

He takes the helmet from my hands and very gently brushes my hair away from my face, his fingers making my skin tingle. I catch my breath as he leans in close to secure the strap under my chin. He glances at me, and he's so close that our lips would touch if one of us made a move. *What is wrong with me?* It was only last night that I started warming to Quincy, and now I'm thinking about kissing him.

'Nod your head for me,' he instructs, pulling away, and I do as he says. 'Okay, you're good to go.'

There's a stool near Barbie that Quincy leads me to, but the closer I get, the slower I walk. My heart is thudding so hard it hurts. This horse is huge!

'You can do this, for Banks,' he whispers, and I try to tell myself it's true, even though I desperately want to run and hide.

'Go, Tia!' Banks cheers, clapping her hands.

It's an effort to smile back at her as my mouth isn't working properly. My hands are sweating, and I rub them on my jeans. *Those hooves!* I wince as I step onto the stool. I climb onto Barbie and take deep breaths as Quincy keeps telling Banks how brave I am. I'm so high up that I feel nauseous. The next second, a loud bang sounds somewhere nearby, making us all jump, including Barbie, who rears up, her front legs pawing the air. I scream as I feel myself falling backwards. This is it. I'm going to die. I quickly throw my arms round her huge neck and bury my face in her mane.

'Woah, girl,' Ethan says, tugging her reins and trying to calm her down.

'Get me off!' I scream.

Barbie is bucking underneath me, and somehow Ethan loses control of the reins. A second later, Barbie takes off, and my instinct screams at me to hold on for dear life.

TWENTY-NINE

Quincy

13th December

'Shit!' I shout as I watch Barbie gallop off across the fields with Tia barely clinging on. 'Watch Banks!' I yell to Ethan as I run to Legend and jump on her back. I hit my heels on her side and she charges after them.

Tia's scream pierces the air and I will Legend on. 'Faster, girl! Faster!' If anything happens to Tia I'll never forgive myself. Who knows where Barbie's heading, but I gasp and feel cold terror when I see the wooden fence a mile or so ahead of us and Barbie showing no sign of slowing down . . .

THIRTY

Tia

13th December

The cold air is whipping my face, making it hard to breathe. I never realized the wind would sound this loud travelling fast on horseback. My eyes are watering, and I can't even wipe them, because if I let go of this horse I'm screwed. I have no idea where we're going and I'm too scared to sit up and see. *Oh God, if this is how I'm going to die, please don't let it be too painful.*

'Tia!'

For a second I think God is talking back to me, but then the voice comes again: 'Tia, hold on! I'm coming!' and I know it's Quincy! I can't tell how close he is – no way am I looking behind – and I know I need to sit up so I can see ahead, but my body's frozen in fear.

Come on, girl – sit up and grab the reins! I will myself to move, but it's hopeless. Banks was wrong. I'm not brave, not one bit.

THIRTY-ONE

Quincy

13th December

'The reins!' I shout, but Tia can't hear me, because she doesn't move. Legend is closing in on Barbie, but I can see the fence getting closer and closer. I shift my weight forward and Legend picks up speed. I'm close enough now that I can reach Barbie's tail. 'Come on, come on!'

We're almost at the fence, and now we're racing alongside Barbie. Tia's practically lying down, her eyes squeezed shut. Barbie's reins are flying in the wind, and I reach out and grab them, yanking hard. She neighs loudly and starts to slow down. Legend runs in front of her and stands to the side, blocking her way, finally bringing her to a stop.

I let out a deep breath, suddenly aware that I was holding it. Tia slowly opens her eyes and they dart from left to right.

When she sees me, she bursts out crying, and a sea of guilt washes over me.

'It's okay,' I say gently, reaching forward and holding her shaking hand. 'You're okay.'

'That was so scary,' she says, finally sitting up. 'I want to get down.'

'Okay, I've got you.'

I climb off Legend, and Tia puts her hands on my shoulders, while I put mine on her waist. 'Jump and I'll catch you.'

Tia looks uncertain, but she does it anyway and falls into my arms. Now her whole body is shaking and she buries her face in my chest.

'It's all right,' I say, holding her tightly. 'Let's get you home.'

We walk slowly back towards the stables and I lead Legend and Barbie behind us by their reins. Tia stands some distance away, her arms wrapped round her body. I should never have encouraged her to get on a horse. I keep glancing at her to see if she's okay, but she's staring straight ahead, refusing to look at me.

'Tia!' Banks calls, running up to her when we reach the stables. Tia bends down and hugs her tightly.

'Is she okay?' Ethan whispers to me, and I shake my head. 'Here.' He hands me the plastic bag with Tia's trainer in it.

'Thanks. Do you mind taking them back to their stalls?' I hand both sets of reins to Ethan, patting Legend as she walks by. Barbie trots off without a care in the world.

'Tia,' I say gently. She looks up at me, and her eyes are red from crying. I give her the bag. 'It's your clean trainer. Do you want me to head back to the house with you?'

189

'No, it's okay.' She hands me her and Banks' helmets before they walk off hand in hand without another word.

I don't feel any better by the time I get back to the house. Logically, I know it's not my fault that Barbie bolted like that, but I still feel responsible. Cam is behind the reception desk typing on the computer. He looks up when he sees me.

'Where you been?' he asks.

When I tell him what happened, Cam's eyes widen.

'Shit!'

'I know. They're gonna have a list of complaints by the time they leave here,' I say. 'How was your gig last night?'

'Good.' Then Cam frowns. 'I saw Dora, though, and she said she does want to use the animals for the walking Nativity next week.'

I groan. 'Didn't we agree last year not to do that any more? It never works.'

Dora Russell has been in charge of the annual Nativity play since I can remember. And for some reason, there's drama every year. If it's not the animals shitting everywhere, it's the kids crying when they forget their lines, or the parents arguing about whose child gets what role. To make it even more tragic, the play travels! It starts at the church, where the choir sings, then it moves round the back to a small shed, which is meant to symbolize Nazareth where the Angel Gabriel speaks to Mary. There are various stops throughout the market square and high street until they reach the inn for the big scene, which always takes place at our farm. It doesn't help that Dora turns into Cruella de Vil during rehearsals and is so strict that all the kids cower in fear. It's pure chaos.

'She said the animals make it more festive,' Cam says. He waits a beat. 'So is your date coming up on the day of the ball?'

I'm just about to mention Tia's name when I remember my family still believe my earlier fake girl story. 'Yep, she'll be here.'

'What's her name again?' he asks.

'Leah,' I say quickly.

Leah ... Tia ... original. Thankfully, Cam doesn't catch on.

He leans on the reception desk. 'Where did you say you met her?'

'Oh, erm, in London when I stayed with Drew for my birthday. We spoke at a club ... about horses.' Cam frowns. 'Dressage,' I add, digging the hole even deeper.

'You met a girl in a club who does dressage?' Cam asks, and I nod.

Cam's quiet for a moment, and my heart starts to race. I shouldn't have mentioned horses and dressage. Me and my brain need to have a serious conversation. He finally nods and goes back to typing on the computer.

'We're going to Everly Rose later to get our outfits for the ball. The Solankés are coming too,' he says as he works. 'Want to meet us there after college?' I nod. 'Is Eliza coming?'

Eliza? Then I remember that she wanted me to see her dress. 'I'll let her know we're going and see if she wants to join.'

THIRTY-TWO

Tia

13th December

'I could have *died*!' I say hotly as Willow covers her mouth to stop herself laughing. She fails miserably.

'I'm sorry,' she says in between laughs, 'but I swear that would only happen to you.' She puts her arm round me, but I shrug her off. 'Tia! You're fine. Don't be like that.'

'Well, I wasn't fine,' I snap. 'After all that, Banks didn't even get back on the pony!'

Banks looks nervously at Willow, as if she thinks she's going to get into trouble, but all Willow does is tap Banks' nose gently and tickle her tummy. Banks laughs.

Mum's in the kitchen helping with the cooking so Willow busies herself changing Banks out of her pony-riding clothes and into her favourite Minnie Mouse tracksuit.

'It was very cool of you to face your fears and get on a horse for Banks' sake,' Willow says gently to me. 'And I'm sure she's appreciative. Did you say thank you to Tia, Banksy?'

Banks nods, even though she didn't.

'Don't you think there's something kind of romantic about Quincy racing after you?' Willow asks me.

'Romantic!' I scoff. 'I almost—'

'Died, I know,' Willow interrupts, sounding bored. 'But it's almost like a movie. Your horse runs off, he chases after you to come to your rescue, and then you kiss under the sun.'

What is Willow on? 'There was absolutely no kissing. If anything, I was angry at him.'

Willow frowns. 'For what?'

I huff. 'I don't know ... If he hadn't made me get on the stupid horse, it wouldn't have run off with me still on it.'

'Does he know you're scared of horses?' Willow probes.

'Well, no, but I told him I don't like them.'

Willow smiles. 'So you purposely didn't tell him your biggest fear is horses? Sounds like you were trying to impress him.'

'No, I wasn't,' I say quickly, but even I can hear the uncertainty in my voice.

Willow places Banks' legs across her own so she can tie the laces on her trainers. 'You can't be mad at him for a horse running off. I think Quincy's lovely. He rescued you today, *and* he helped you out when you stepped in that horse mess. You're just not used to a guy who's actually nice.'

'Mike is—' But I stop myself. What was I going to say?

'Mike is nice'? He hasn't been very nice recently and yet here I am about to defend him, which now I think about it, I do a lot, especially around Willow.

Willow smiles at me knowingly. 'You don't have to say anything. I know I'm right.'

Later that afternoon, Mrs Parker drives us to Everly Rose. It's bright and airy inside the shop, with shiny wooden floors and spotlights. Half of the store is lined with black tuxedos and suits, and the other has racks of rainbow dresses in every style imaginable. I'm practically drooling at all the options.

Mrs Parker smiles when she sees my expression. 'It's something, isn't it?'

She walks over to the men's section with Cam, while Mum, Willow and I start looking at the sequined dresses. Drew offered to look after Banks back at the house, which was a good shout. Too many tempting sparkles for her here.

When Mum isn't looking, I glance at a few price tags and sigh with relief. The dresses are pretty affordable. I know she said not to worry, but I've been religiously checking prices for a year now, and it's a habit that's hard to break.

'How are we doing?' A white middle-aged woman with auburn hair walks towards us in time with the upbeat Christmas music playing in the background. She's wearing high heels and a fitted black dress. 'I'm Kate. Welcome to Everly Rose.'

'Hello, Kate,' Mum says, shaking her hand. 'Your shop's gorgeous. We're looking for outfits for the ball. It's our first one.'

Kate smiles. 'There's nothing like your first Winter Ball. I'd suggest picking out four to five dresses, and then trying them on over there.' She points to the curtained area in the back. 'Call me if you need me.'

'Thank you,' Mum says. 'You heard her, girls.'

I had forgotten what it was like to shop without stressing out, and I enjoy taking my time looking at the dresses, holding each of them up to me in front of the mirror. I've just made my way over to a new rack when the bell over the door rings. I peer through the gap in the dresses and see Quincy walk in. My heart jumps. Willow's right. It wasn't his fault that the horse took off.

I'm just about to call him over when a very pretty girl with long turquoise hair comes in behind him and my stomach drops. They walk easily next to each other, smiling as they talk, and I can tell they're close. *Who is she?* They immediately go over to Mrs Parker and Cam, and the girl is clearly known to the family as she hugs them both. Quincy starts to walk around the store, and I busy myself looking at more dresses, pretending I haven't seen him, but I can feel him walking towards me and my body is on high alert.

'Tia.' He smiles warmly. 'Found anything nice?'

'Too many options!' I say. I brush my hair back nervously. 'Sorry about earlier, by the way, at the stables. I shouldn't have walked off like that.'

'No, I'm sorry. There's no need for you to apologize,' he says, but just then the girl with turquoise hair appears next to him. 'Oh, Tia – this is my best friend, Eliza. Eliza, meet Tia.'

Ah, best friend. I immediately relax. I mistook their easiness around each other for something more. I don't even know why I care. Up close, Eliza's even prettier, and her heavily ringed fingers, ripped jeans and bold eye make-up give off an effortlessly cool vibe. If I met her in Shoreditch or Camden and she told me she lived in a little place like White Oak, I wouldn't believe her.

'You're Tia!' she exclaims before hugging me tightly.

I'm caught off guard and look at Quincy over her shoulder. He shrugs in response.

'I love your hair,' I say when she lets go. 'My sister had hers that colour once.' I point at Willow, who's wearing a red wig today and holding up a navy ballgown. 'She makes wigs.'

'No way!' Eliza exclaims. 'My mum owns a hairdresser's but I dyed this myself. Excuse me, guys, I've found my people!' We watch as she bounces over to Willow, who at first looks confused, but they very quickly start admiring each other's hair.

'Eliza seems nice,' I say, watching them.

'Yeah, she's great.' Quincy's phone buzzes, and he reaches into his pocket to look at it. 'My friends are going ice skating on Friday, and they've asked if you want to join.'

'Ice skating?' I pull a face. Why do people like to be on ice when it's already cold?

Quincy raises his eyebrows at me. 'Let me guess ... you hate ice skating.'

'And I can't skate,' I add, and he groans. 'But we had a deal, and as long as I don't have to talk about dressage again, I can fake enthusiasm for ice skating.'

Quincy laughs. 'Cool. I won't leave your side this time.'

Butterflies flood my stomach at his words, and I quickly turn away, picking out the dresses I've been eyeing the most. 'I'm gonna try these ones. Are you going to choose a suit?'

'Yeah, but a suit's a suit. It's hardly a difficult decision,' he says easily, making me laugh. 'Can't wait to see what the dresses look like.'

We stare at each other, and Quincy quickly glances at my lips before returning his gaze to my eyes. I catch my breath.

'You found something?' Mum says, breaking the spell and making me jump. I drop one of the dresses. 'Tia! Be careful with that,' Mum scolds.

'I'll be back,' I say, walking quickly to the changing rooms, wishing Mum hadn't just interrupted whatever Quincy and I had going on.

THIRTY-THREE

Quincy

13th December

'It's really not bad,' I lie.

'It's bad,' Cam says.

We're standing in front of the big mirror by the changing room that Eliza has just come out of. Mum, Tope and Willow have already picked their dresses and are by the till, and Tia is still trying on options.

Cam and I are in matching black suits, white shirts, black bow ties and gold cufflinks. Mum's already taken a million pictures, gushing about how handsome we look. She's had the same suit put aside for Dad.

I turn my attention back to Eliza, who's wearing this ruffled baby-pink dress that swamps her and makes her look like a life-sized doll.

'Why does my mum hate me?' she groans. 'Who in their right mind would put this on hold?'

Kate comes over and quickly turns her startled face into a smile. 'Eliza, dear, you look ... Your mum really liked this one.'

'Then *she* can wear it!' Eliza snaps. 'I need something tight and sexy!'

'Try on the other one,' I say quickly, already sensing that Eliza is a second away from burning this place down if anyone tries to defend the ugly dress. She stomps back into the changing room. 'I'm good with this,' I say, taking one last look at my fitted suit.

Cam holds his phone up and takes a selfie of us. We look sharp.

I change back into my hoodie, jeans and Timbs, and when Cam and I come out of the changing room, Eliza shouts from behind the curtain, 'Okay, ready?'

'Ready,' we say together.

Cam's mouth drops open as Eliza steps out in a very tight grey silk dress with a deep V-neck and a long slit up one leg. She turns round and the back is made up of an elaborate criss-cross of straps, showing off the pattern of freckles that decorate her skin.

'Very nice,' I say. Her mum will hate how sexy it is, which means Eliza loves it.

'You sure?' she asks, studying herself in the mirror.

I nudge Cam, who looks like he's in a trance or something. 'What's up with you?' I ask.

'Nothing, man,' Cam mumbles.

'Tia, are you ready?' Willow calls, walking towards us by the changing rooms. She stops when she sees Eliza. 'Wow!'

'Too sexy?' Eliza asks.

'Very, but who cares?' Willow responds, and Eliza beams.

'Okay, okay, I'm coming,' Tia says from behind a curtain. 'I'm not sure if it suits me, though.'

'Let me see,' Willow replies.

The curtain is pulled back and Tia walks out in a red sequined dress that hits the light, making her twinkle like she's covered in stars. The straps wrap round her upper arms, and the front is tight and cleavage-hugging. It takes all my strength not to focus on her tits. Her waist looks tiny in the bodice, and the skirt floats out to the floor. I've never seen a more perfect dress on a more perfect girl.

'Well?' she says anxiously as we all stare at her.

'Wow,' Cam says first.

'Stunning,' Willow says.

'You have to get that one,' Eliza responds.

'Really?' Tia checks again in the mirror and then turns so she can view the back where the dress scoops down to the middle of her back.

I can't stop staring at her. She catches me gazing at her in the mirror and looks at me, questioningly, as if she's asking me what I think.

'You look beautiful,' I say, and her smile is so big that I suddenly feel lighter because it's directed at me.

*

As everyone heads out of Everly Rose, Tia catches my arm to hold me back.

'Should we take a pic for the 'gram?' she asks.

'Oh, good shout.' I pull out my phone as she nestles into me, wrapping her arm round my waist. I hold the phone up and snap a few photos before showing them to her. Growing up with Drew and Regal, I've learned that a picture isn't good unless a girl tells me it is.

'Cute,' she says. 'Post this one and tag me: at TiaSol, one word.'

'Don't you care if people back home see?' I ask as I open Instagram and click follow. She instantly requests to follow me back.

Tia shrugs. 'I changed my mind.' I'm guessing she and her boyfriend still aren't getting along.

I upload the photo and caption it:

Ball shopping with @TiaSol. You should see her dress 😵

I show it to Tia, and she laughs.

Tia, Willow, Cam, Eliza and I walk up the road to the Costa, while Mum and Tope head back to the house with our outfits. Tia's back in her normal clothes, but I can't stop thinking about her in that red dress.

'What?' Tia asks with a smile when she catches me staring at her again.

'Sorry,' I say quickly. My cheeks burn hot, and I scold myself for being caught out.

'I didn't ask you to stop,' she says in this flirty tone, which I haven't heard her use before but really like.

'I'll keep staring then,' I respond, and she grins.

I hold the door open for her and follow her in. Costa's pretty busy today, but Cam and Willow have managed to nab a table in the corner for us, while Eliza's queuing.

'What are you getting?' Eliza asks me, but I'm distracted for a second by a girl with auburn hair behind the counter who has her back to me.

Eliza follows my gaze and says, 'Kali?'

The girl turns round and there she is. Her ice-blue eyes widen when she sees Eliza and Tia, and then they land on me. Unlike Simon, who's looked rough every time I've bumped into him, this is the first time I've seen Kali since our break-up and she still looks beautiful. She's wearing a tight black jumper that suits her long, slender frame, and the heat of the coffee shop has brought out a flush in her cheeks.

My chest starts to feel tight, like someone is pressing down on it. I take a step backwards and the person behind says, 'Hey, watch it!'

'Quincy, are you okay?' Tia asks gently. She reaches for my hand and Kali notices. She looks from Tia to me and back to Tia.

'Maybe we should go somewhere else?' Eliza says, already leaving the line.

'No, wait, please! Quincy, can we talk?' Kali takes off her apron, and despite the long line, she comes out from behind the counter, her eyes pleading with me. 'Just five minutes.'

202

'Kali, leave it,' Eliza snaps.

'Please hear me out,' Kali says, ignoring her. Tia frowns, but Kali's only got eyes for me.

It feels too hot and too loud in here, and I can't hear myself think.

'I've got to go,' I say, and I hurry to the door, pushing through the crowds of people. I can't believe I forgot Drew told me that Kali works there now. Once I get outside into the cold air, I take a deep breath, but no matter how much I try to calm myself down, my mind still feels like it's racing one hundred miles per hour.

THIRTY-FOUR

Tia

13th December

Quincy looked like he'd seen a ghost, and he ran out of Costa before anyone could stop him. I glance back at Kali, whose bottom lip is trembling like she's a second away from bursting into tears. Okay, so this must be his ex. That would explain Quincy's and Drew's reaction and why her name was brought up at the campfire.

'Can we get some service?' a man in the line yells.

Kali quickly wipes her eyes and walks back behind the counter, retying her apron.

'Who is that?' I ask Eliza, just to be sure.

Her jaw tenses and she confirms what I suspect when she says, 'That's Kali. Quincy's ex.'

Now I really look at her, taking in her tall, slender frame

and pale skin. I thought Quincy was flirting with me earlier, but I'm clearly not his type.

'Why did they break up?' I ask Eliza.

She looks away awkwardly. 'It's … complicated. Quincy will have to tell you. Come on, we better go find him. Cam!' She waves him and Willow over.

It seems even busier in Costa now than it was a few minutes ago and, when we step outside, I understand why. It's pissing down with rain. I pull up my hood and we run to the car, the engine and wipers already on. Quincy's at the wheel, staring blankly through the windscreen, and barely registers us when we climb in. Cam lands a heavy wet hand on his shoulder.

'You okay, man?'

Quincy nods, and without a word, he checks his mirrors and pulls out into the traffic. I want to find out more about Kali and what happened between her and Quincy, but it's clear he doesn't want to talk. The car ride is completely silent, and I sit and watch the raindrops sliding down my window for the rest of the journey.

As soon as we get back to the house, Quincy disappears to his room. I take a step onto the staircase, and then pause, torn between going after him and not wanting to cross any boundaries.

'I'll go,' Cam says. 'There should be a fire lit in the living room if you guys want to sit and get yourselves warmed up.'

'I'm going up to my room to change,' Willow says before she too heads up the stairs.

'He'll be all right,' Eliza says, linking arms with me. 'Let's sit.'

Eliza and I head into the living room where the Christmas lights are switched on and a fire is crackling in the grate. I instantly feel cosy.

We sit by the fire and I hold my hands out towards the flames, sighing as the heat warms my body.

'So, what happened between them?' I finally ask.

'Tia . . . it's not my place . . .' Eliza begins, but then she says, 'Kali did something bad that led to them breaking up. Before that we were all really good friends.'

'Oh, wow. So you lost a friend too?'

'We still chat, but we're nowhere near as close. I've known Quincy much longer. He puts on a smile every day, but deep down I know he's still really hurting. Kali broke his heart.'

Hearing that makes me want to run upstairs and check on Quincy. I wear my heart on my sleeve and don't bother hiding my emotions, but Quincy has always seemed so upbeat that I never would have guessed he'd been through a terrible break-up.

'Do you think he still loves her?' I ask, not quite wanting to know the answer.

Eliza shrugs. 'He doesn't talk about her or Simon.' She shuts her eyes and mumbles, 'Shit.'

'Who's Simon?' I dig.

Eliza groans. 'Please don't tell anyone I said that.'

'Okay, but who is he?'

Eliza shakes her head. 'Sorry, Tia, I shouldn't have said

anything.' She reaches for the remote, switches on the TV and doesn't speak, leaving me with a load of unanswered questions.

Quincy doesn't come down for dinner, and his plate is left untouched in the kitchen. Seeing Kali must have really messed him up. Mum has done a great job with the meal – spiced honey-glazed roast goose and confit potatoes, followed by a pear-and-raspberry tart with crème anglaise. All the guests staying at the farm eat in tonight, eager to try the new chef's food, and each and every one of them tells Mum how much they loved it. Mum is beaming.

After dinner, everyone wanders off to do their own thing – Cam leaves for another gig, Willow heads out again with Drew, and I'm left alone. My go-to now would be to see what Quincy is up to, but I don't want to bother him, so instead I take Banks into the living room and we cuddle up on the sofa to watch *Encanto* for the hundredth time. I'm barely paying attention, even though I love belting out 'We Don't Talk about Bruno', because tonight my mind is elsewhere. I really hope Quincy is okay.

THIRTY-FIVE

Quincy

13th December

I'm on my bed, staring up at the ceiling. The curtains are drawn and the lights off. My belly rumbles again loudly over my Spotify playlist, but I ignore it. Oreo wakes up from his nap and looks at me. I just want to be left alone. I know Cam was trying to make me feel better earlier, but it didn't work. Seeing Kali again was weird. She's a stranger to me now, but a stranger who I've been intimate with, who I once loved and who knows my deepest fears. At one point, I thought she was the one. How am I meant to act around someone who I previously thought was my forever? My phone flashes with her name again, and my thumb hovers over the accept button. I sigh and switch it off completely, ending the music abruptly, then I turn on my side and close my eyes, praying that this shitty feeling doesn't last much longer.

THIRTY-SIX

Tia

14th December

Banks fell asleep last night halfway through the movie. Mum was talking with Mrs Parker, so I took Banks up to my room to sleep. I must have forgotten, because when I wake up, at first I'm confused by the small warm body next to mine. Banks is wide awake and is tracing the floral pattern on my pyjama top with her finger.

'Morning.' I yawn.

'Morning,' Banks sings.

I reach for my phone and realize it's only eight a.m. Ugh! I wanted to sleep in. But Banks must be hungry because this is when she usually eats. 'Do you want breakfast?' I ask her, and she nods, so I drag myself out of bed.

After we're both washed and dressed, we head downstairs.

A good smell is floating out of the kitchen, where Mum must be. Cam is on reception, and he looks surprisingly alert for someone who must have come in pretty late from a gig.

'Morning, Tia. Early for you,' he says, glancing at his watch.

'I know, but Banks needs cereal.' I wait a beat. 'How's Quincy?'

Cam shrugs. 'Haven't seen him today. I did try to check on him, but he's not opening his door. He'll be all right,' he adds when he sees my anxious face. 'He just needs a minute.'

'What happened with him and Kali?' I ask, desperate for someone to tell me. Banks tugs on my hand. 'One second, Banksy,' I say to her.

Like Eliza last night, Cam looks uncomfortable. 'Erm, you'll have to ask him.'

'Tia!' Banks grumbles. The last thing I need is a Banks tantrum this early in the morning.

'Well, I hope he's okay.'

Cam smiles. 'He will be. Enjoy breakfast.'

THIRTY-SEVEN

Quincy

14th December

'Darling, can I come in?' Mum calls from behind my closed door.

I sit up, running my hand over my head. I slept like shit, and I'm starving, but I still don't feel like facing anyone.

'Yeah,' I answer, hoping it won't be a long conversation.

She walks in and sits down on the edge of my bed. 'I saved you some food from last night. Tope cooked for the guests and it was unbelievably good.'

'Thanks, Mum. Fingers crossed we'll find someone as good as Tope when the Solankés leave.'

'Yes, fingers crossed.' Mum smiles sadly at me. 'So. Cam mentioned you saw Kali yesterday. You okay?'

I shrug. 'It was weird.'

'It's normal to feel that way when a relationship ends. Why don't you go hang out with Simon and Eliza? They'll cheer you up.'

Simon is the last person I want to see, and even though I'm not mad at Eliza, I know she'll be watching me closely, constantly asking me if I'm all right.

'I might chill at the stables today. Riding Legend should help me feel better.'

Mum taps my leg. 'Okay, baby. If you need me, I'm here.'

I smile. 'Thanks, Mum. I appreciate it.'

She winks at me before leaving the room. I glance at my phone and remember it's turned off. Last night I almost answered Kali's call in a moment of weakness, and I don't want to tempt myself again, especially in the state I'm in. I put the phone in my bedside drawer before heading for a shower.

THIRTY-EIGHT

Tia

14th December

I'm lying on my bed answering emails and messages about Mike's party. Everything is going to plan, and even though a few people have cancelled, it seems like the turnout will be good. I send a last email to the DJ before I glance out at the grey sky. What am I going to do with myself today? Mum's cooking and Willow's watching *Encanto* with Banks, *again*. I haven't seen Drew; Cam's on reception; which only leaves Quincy. I sit up, looking at the wall that separates us. No one seems that concerned that he's stayed in his room since last night. Should I check on him?

I knock gently on his door, but there's no response. 'Quincy? It's me, Tia,' I say, knocking again, when Mrs Parker comes along carrying a basket of towels.

'He's at the stables, Tia,' she says.

'Oh, right, thanks. I wanted to see how he's doing.'

Mrs Parker smiles. 'That's sweet of you. You're welcome to go down. I'm sure he'd appreciate some company.'

A flashback of Barbie galloping off with me comes to mind and I gulp. I do really want to see Quincy, but I don't think I can face being around the horses again.

THIRTY-NINE

Quincy

14th December

I jump down from Legend and already feel a million times better. I lead her back to the stables, grab a carrot from the bucket and feed it to her. She chomps it greedily and nuzzles my hand for more, making me laugh.

'Okay, but only one more,' I say. She eats the second one even faster than the first.

I grab the soft-bristle brush and gently start to smooth her coat.

'You always make me feel better, you know that, girl?' I say to her.

'Is that what you say to all the girls?' a voice calls out. I look past Legend and am surprised to see Tia by the stable door looking at the horses warily.

'Hi! What are you doing here?' I say.

She swipes one side of her long bob behind her ear. 'I wanted to see if you're okay.'

I wasn't expecting that. 'You came to the stables to check on me?' I ask, surprised.

'I'm already regretting it,' Tia says, taking one tentative step forward. Legend makes a huffing noise, and Tia yelps and quickly moves back.

'It's fine,' I say, trying not to laugh. 'She won't hurt you.' I hold out my hand. 'Trust me?'

Tia goes to take a step forward again but then stops. I can see her weighing up whether she does trust me, and I really hope she decides she can. I don't take my eyes off her, and even Legend stills, as if she knows how important this moment is. Tia inches a tiny bit closer, and when Legend doesn't move, she takes another step, and another, before practically running the last few towards me. She grabs my hand, and it's soft and warm, sending a tingle through my body.

'She's huge.' Tia looks Legend up and down.

'Here.' I hand her the brush. 'She likes it.'

'Oh, I don't know about this,' Tia says, and I gently put my hand on top of hers, guiding her towards Legend so the brush connects with her coat. Gently, I move Tia's hand from side to side. She looks at the hand brushing Legend and slowly starts to smile. 'I can't believe I'm actually doing this.'

'You're a pro, remember?' I tease, and she laughs.

I let go of her hand and pick up another brush, and we stand together in comfortable silence as we groom Legend. I'm watching Tia from the side of my eye, taking in the perfect flick of her eyeliner, the gold hoop in her cute nose and her glossy full lips. She really is something.

'Do you feel better?' she asks, looking at me, and I quickly avert my gaze so she doesn't clock I was blatantly checking her out.

'Yeah, a bit.' Even though I'm still rocked from seeing Kali, I do feel less shitty. And it means a lot that Tia has taken the time to check on me. 'Thank you for coming.'

'You're welcome.' She smiles. 'Seeing as we're going to be together in front of your friends again tomorrow, do you want to hang out today and get to know each other better?'

Before, the idea of spending one-on-one time with Tia would have filled me with dread, but the more I get to know her, the more I enjoy being around her. And I can't think of anything else I'd rather do today.

'I'd like that,' I reply.

After I put Legend in her stall and say goodbye to Ethan, Tia and I start off across the fields with no clear destination in mind.

'Okay. I think we should clarify how exactly we met,' Tia says. 'First at an event in London and then at a dressage competition, right?'

'Is that when your horse died?' I ask, and she playfully nudges me. 'By the way, what was the name of your horse?'

'Erm . . .' She frowns and glances down at her coat. 'Forest. We can even say I bought this coat in honour of her.'

'This story is getting even more depressing,' I say, and Tia laughs. 'Okay, what's my horse's name?'

'Lion?' she says hesitantly.

I freeze mid-step. 'Lion? Why would I call a horse Lion? Her name's Legend.'

'Right, sorry, Legend.' Tia takes out her phone. 'I'll make notes. Favourite colour?'

'Black,' I reply.

Tia looks at me deadpan. 'Black isn't a colour.'

'Of course it is, and it's the best one. What's yours?'

'Red,' she says, and now I'm thinking about her in that red dress again.

'I like you in red,' I reply with a grin.

'Really?' Tia asks, then she smiles. 'I'll bear that in mind.'

FORTY

Tia

15th December

My hands are covered in flour, and I'm smiling to myself as I grab the whisk. I can't believe I'm saying this, but I'm actually excited about going ice skating with Quincy later today. My phone is full of notes I jotted down during our conversation yesterday, and I keep glancing at them while I'm baking. I feel like I'm studying for an exam, but I know Quincy much better now. We're complete opposites, but when it comes to our families and how close we are to them, we have the exact same values. Despite our many differences, hanging out yesterday was fun, and there's something about him that pulls me in like a magnet. I barely thought of Mike at all. Quincy's going to pick me up after he's finished his last day at college before Christmas break.

'Tia!' Willow calls. She walks into the kitchen where I'm helping Mum make a lemon drizzle cake for dinner tonight. 'Dad's on the phone.'

I quickly rinse my hands and take the phone from her. 'Hey, Dad.'

'Tia!' Dad's deep voice booms, and I realize how much I've missed hearing it. 'How are you? It's a nightmare trying to get through to you lot. Are you enjoying yourself?'

'I'm good. It's pretty cool here actually,' I reply.

'Mum told me you went on a horse. I said, "No way, that's not my daughter."' Dad chuckles to himself but doesn't mention anything about the horse bolting. Mum and Willow must have kept that to themselves to spare me the embarrassment.

We chat for a few minutes more and I promise to send him pictures of the farm. After we say our goodbyes, I begin to whisk the cake mixture.

Mum comes into the kitchen. 'What's that?' she says, her eyes cast down. '"Legend, Virgo, loves chicken, hates liars",' she reels off.

I follow her gaze and she's looking at my notes on Quincy. *Shit.* 'Oh, erm . . . it's just a story I'm writing . . . for fun.'

Mum raises her eyebrows, clearly surprised, and I don't blame her. I've never written a story in my life.

'Yeah? What's it about?' Mum asks.

'Erm . . . it's about this girl . . . and guy . . . and—'

'A love story?' Mum interrupts.

'Yes! But I haven't worked out exactly what happens yet.' I giggle nervously.

Mum shrugs. 'It's good you're trying new things, Tia.'

My brain instantly thinks of Quincy, who's been on my mind all day. 'Maybe it is,' I respond.

We're in the car driving to the ice rink and Quincy's tapping the wheel in time with the radio that's playing old-skool hip-hop. I want to ask about Kali, but he's in a good mood and I don't want to ruin it. My hands feel clammy and I wipe them on my skirt. Why am I so nervous? I took my time getting ready, spending longer than usual on picking out a cute outfit and taking care with my make-up so it looks perfect, but I have to keep reminding myself that this is not a date. It's two people helping each other out.

Quincy points at the grand building in front of us, which I assume is where the ice rink is located. The car park is rammed, but he finds a tight space and manages to park easily. He turns off the engine and looks at me. 'Ready?'

'Just don't leave me alone with your friends again,' I warn.

Quincy smiles. 'I promise.'

We step out of the warm car into the freezing cold, and Quincy grabs my hand, interlocking our fingers. I look down at our hands in surprise.

'Might as well get into character now,' he says, even though there's no one in the car park but us.

'Smooth,' I reply, and he laughs out loud. I don't pull my hand away.

Inside the building, Christmas jingles are playing loudly over the speakers and there's a long line to pick up tickets and

221

skates. From where we're standing, I can see the ice rink is already full of people skating. It's lit up with blue and white lights, and a massive, richly decorated Christmas tree stands in the centre of it.

'Quincy!' someone calls, and he looks down the line to see the twins Jared and Lizzy and two other guys waving at us to come forward.

We join them and Lizzy gives us both a hug. 'I'm so glad you could come, Tia,' she says sweetly. 'Are you still enjoying your holiday?'

'Yeah, it's pretty good, thanks.'

'You already know Jared and Nic from the campfire night, but this is Dougie.' The new boy, Dougie, looks like Nic – white, slim, brown floppy hair and dark eyes.

'Nice to meet you, Tia,' Dougie says.

'Good to meet you,' I reply.

'Are you coming to Seven Days on Sunday?' Nic asks me and I nod.

'Where did you and Q meet again?' Jared asks.

'At an event in London.' I tell our rehearsed story, and everyone nods along. 'And then he invited me to the Winter Ball and I couldn't resist!'

'You do dressage?' Dougie asks. 'Nice! What's your favourite competition?'

'Oh ... erm ...' I glance at Quincy, who says with the most serious face, 'Tia's horse passed away, so she doesn't like to talk about it.'

'Shit.' Dougie covers his mouth. 'I'm so sorry.'

I smile bravely in response. 'But I've been able to spend time with Legend since being here. I know how much Quincy loves her, so it's sweet of him to share her with me.' Quincy squeezes my hand, and his boys smile approvingly at me.

Quincy handles the tickets and picks up the skates for me before we walk through the barriers. A girl with turquoise hair is facing away from us and watching the skaters, and I tug on Quincy's hand.

'Isn't that Eliza?'

'Eliza!' Quincy calls, and she turns towards us looking relieved.

'I've been calling you!' she says, grabbing him in a tight hug. 'Are you okay?'

'Sorry, I needed some time alone, and I left my phone at home,' Quincy says. He pulls away from her. 'But I'm feeling better.' He glances at me when he says this, and I feel my face go warm.

Eliza raises her eyebrows, a smug smile on her face, but it quickly darkens when she looks over Quincy's shoulder. 'What the actual fuck?'

I turn round and immediately see the blonde girl who was giving me weird vibes at the campfire – Sarah I think her name is. And she's standing right next to Kali.

FORTY-ONE

Quincy

15th December

For a moment I freeze. Kali looks right at me, her ice-blue eyes piercing mine, and I notice a shift in the air, like everyone is waiting with bated breath to see what happens next.

'Can you help me with my skates?' Tia says breaking the silence.

I blink and look at her. 'Huh?'

'Skates,' she says, and she grabs my arm, tearing me away from Kali and leading me to the nearest chair. 'Sorry, you looked like you didn't know what to do,' she adds, lowering her voice.

'Yeah, it's just . . . What's she doing here?' I glance over my shoulder and see Eliza and the rest of my friends surrounding Kali and Sarah, probably asking them the same thing.

'I knew that Sarah girl was messy,' Tia says. She pulls off her trainer and reaches for the skate, struggling to put it on.

'Here.' I bend down on one knee and gently push her foot into the skate before clipping it in place.

'They're looking at us now,' Tia mumbles. 'Ready to put on a show?'

I hesitate, not because I don't want to, but because being around Kali again when I hadn't prepared for it has thrown me.

Tia gently lifts my chin up with her hand. 'I know this is hard for you. Follow my lead, okay?'

'I'll try.' Once I've finished helping Tia with her skates, I sit beside her to do my own. I glance up and see my friends walking towards us. Kali's eyes are firmly on me, and at that very moment, Tia reaches over and kisses me on the cheek. My neck almost snaps when I whip round to face her. I can still feel her lips on my skin.

'In character, remember?' she whispers and holds out her hand.

God knows I'm thankful I've got Tia here with me tonight. I grab her hand. Her balance is terrible, and she can barely walk, but it's working in our favour, because it means she's leaning into me and my arm is around her.

'Sorry, Q, I didn't know Kali was coming,' Lizzy says, and I know she's telling the truth.

'It's okay,' I lie. 'We're gonna head onto the ice.' I catch Eliza's eye and gesture towards the rink.

When Tia takes a step onto the ice, she instantly almost slips over, but luckily I catch her. I'm preparing myself for her to say she's over it but instead she bursts out laughing.

'I'm so shit at this,' she says unapologetically.

I love seeing this side of her. 'You look like Bambi learning to walk,' I say, chuckling.

'Shut up,' she says playfully. 'I think I should hold on to the sides.'

'No way! We're going right into the middle where everyone can see you.'

'Don't you dare,' she warns, but her eyes are smiling.

I skate in front of her, holding both her hands. She looks down at the ice, watching her feet.

'Keep your eyes on me,' I say, and she looks up. 'You won't fall. Trust me?'

Tia nods. 'I trust you.'

I feel like we're dancing as she follows my lead, moving her legs forward, left then right, as I skate backwards. At first, I can see the worry on her face, but it doesn't take long for her to squeal when she realizes she's in safe hands.

'This is kind of fun,' she says.

Sarah and Kali expertly skate past us, shooting Tia a look as they go, but she misses it. I don't, and I glare back.

'I think I've got it,' Tia says. 'Let go.'

'Are you sure?' I ask uncertainly, but she releases her hands from mine, and for a moment she's doing it! I'm just about to cheer her on when she loses her balance and slips backwards onto her arse.

She shuts her eyes, seemingly about to cry because that

looked hella painful, but instead she bursts out laughing again. 'My bum is so cold,' she says in between gasps of laughter, and it's so infectious that I start laughing too.

'Tia, are you okay?' Lizzy asks, skating to a halt with Nic, Dougie and Eliza in tow.

'I'm good, don't worry,' Tia says, giggling.

'She's okay,' I reassure them, and apart from Eliza they all skate off.

Tia holds out her hands and I pull her up. She lands in my arms and slowly her laughter subsides. Her head reaches my chest, and when she looks up at me with her large eyes, I can't help wondering what it would be like to kiss her properly on the lips.

'Cute!' Eliza sings, her phone pointed at us. 'You two look so good together.'

Eliza shows us the picture, and she really has got the perfect shot. Blurred people are skating past us in the background, and in the centre of the photo Tia and I are staring into each other's eyes. We look great together, like we fit perfectly. I watch Tia carefully as she studies the picture, and for a second she looks elated, but then her face falls and suddenly she turns away. That's when I remember that even though I'm single, she's technically not.

FORTY-TWO

Tia

15th December

I fall onto my bed and groan. My muscles are in agony. I didn't realize how much of a workout skating is. We all grabbed a bite to eat after at a restaurant down the road, but luckily Kali and Sarah opted out. I did my best to wow Quincy's friends as his fake girlfriend, but the whole time I couldn't stop thinking about the picture Eliza took of us. We look like a real couple in it, and if I'm being honest with myself, I'm not having to fake feelings for him. Quincy's sweet, patient and fun to be around. My feelings are growing by the day, and Mike isn't constantly on my mind any more. This wasn't part of the plan, and I don't know what to do.

FORTY-THREE

Quincy

16th December

'The storm is heading towards the—'

Cam switches to another station so music fills the car, which we've piled high with items for the Winter Ball. With only a week to go, the countdown has begun and we're delivering all the stock to the Renaissance Ballroom. Mum and Dad are already there, beginning the set-up process with the help of some local volunteers.

The phone rings, cutting off Chris Rea, who's singing about 'driving home for Christmas', and Stacey's name flashes up.

Cam tuts. 'Not now,' he snaps, and cancels the call, and I can't be bothered to cuss him out for it.

We pull into the Tudor manor house car park, jump out

and open the boot so we can start unpacking. When we get inside, it's already super busy with people I know, some unstacking chairs, others unboxing items and one or two up ladders hanging decorations from the gilded columns. I see Eliza straight away, then spy Sophie, Simon's mum, laughing with Aunty Shola, but Simon and Regal are nowhere in sight.

The Renaissance Ballroom is really impressive. It's a large room, painted cream, with high ceilings covered in elaborate decorative plasterwork, gilded like the columns that stand at wide intervals around the room. In one wall are three beautiful stained-glass windows.

Mum waves us over. 'Is there lots more still in the car? I need one of you to help Dad.'

'Q can help Dad,' Cam says quickly. 'I'll get someone to help me bring in the rest of the stuff.' He looks around the room before calling Eliza over, who seems more than happy to oblige.

I turn to her, surprised. 'Really?' If I had asked her, she would have flashed her new set of nails at me and said, 'no chance'.

'I'm full of surprises,' she responds cryptically, and I watch her and Cam walk off.

I settle on one of the chairs, wiping my brow. We've been at this all day, but finally I can see the ballroom coming together for the event. We've decorated two enormous Christmas trees, set out the circular tables and chairs, hung sparkly ball lights from the ceiling, and now they're installing the dance floor. Mum also wants to decorate the room next door, where the little kids will have their own party.

'I can't do any more,' Eliza moans, leaning her head on my shoulder.

I'm starving and I want to go home, and – I can't lie – I also really want to see Tia. I haven't stopped thinking about her all day. Ice skating was fun, although she did seem a bit off when she saw the picture Eliza took of us, but she insisted she was fine, so maybe I'm overthinking it.

'Tia was perfect yesterday,' Eliza says as if reading my mind. 'Everyone loved her. They totally believe you two are the real deal.'

'Good. Did Kali say anything?'

'Not to me, but I saw she couldn't stop watching the two of you. Let's see how she is at Seven Days tomorrow.'

'Can I have a word, Quincy?' Sophie is walking towards me with a smile on her now-red face. She's been non-stop today. 'I've given Simon some bottles of wine for the Seven Days party.' Normally, Simon and I would go to Seven Days together. We'd agree on who was going to be the designated driver, and his mum would give us wine from the vineyard for us to take down. But now it will be different.

Eliza and I look at each other. Sophie's smile doesn't leave her face, and I don't know how to get out of this without sounding rude or telling her the truth.

'Aren't you meant to be helping Cam set up tomorrow, Q?' Eliza says quickly.

'Oh, yeah, right,' I say catching on. 'I did promise I'd help him with his decks.'

'Oh, no problem,' Sophie says kindly. 'I'll tell Simon to meet you there. Have a great time!' She smiles and wanders off.

'That was awkward,' Eliza says. 'Quincy, don't you think you should talk to Simon and Kali? I know they hurt you, but you're going to keep bumping into them. If you tell them exactly how you feel, you'll be able to move on.'

I rub my face. I know Eliza's right, but giving Kali and Simon the cold shoulder is the only way I feel I can reclaim some of my power. They obviously want to talk to me and clear the air, but why should I? They didn't think twice about hurting me. Sometimes the air is too thick to be cleared.

FORTY-FOUR

Tia

16th December

Sometimes I wish I kept my big mouth shut. I'm walking through the fields in this freezing cold weather all because I dared to tell Mum I had a headache, and she suggested fresh air would do me good. Suddenly it became a family affair and everyone else wanted fresh air too. Then Drew, who's on reception today, mentioned Oreo needed to be walked, so Mum offered to take him with us! Now here I am freezing my tits off, with Banks running around, living her best life, Oreo straining on his leash and Willow struggling to hold onto it, and Mum who keeps saying, 'Oh, girls! Isn't this lovely?'

It's not.

My eyes wander over to the horses on the other side of the field, and I instantly think of Quincy. He's been out all day setting up the ballroom, and I know I shouldn't be missing him but I am. Banks says she wants to see the sheep in the next field, which I'm fine with because everyone knows sheep are harmless.

'*Sheeeeep!*' Banks yells once we get close to them.

There are so many of them. Some look up when they hear us, others continue nibbling on the grass. I've never been this close to sheep before, and I'm tempted to touch one to see if its wool is as soft as it looks, but I don't think I'm allowed. Instead, I snap some pictures on my phone. Banks, however, runs at one with her hands outstretched and the sheep speeds off.

'Stop, Banks!' I hurry towards her, grabbing her hand. 'No touching!' She tries to push me off, but I grip her firmly. She starts crying.

'Oh, come on, Banksy,' Mum says gently, picking her up. 'No touching the animals, okay?'

We've started walking back towards Mum and Willow when I notice something white out of the corner of my eye. I look down, and one of the sheep has its mouth attached to my fur coat!

'No!' I yank my coat away, but the sheep keeps chewing on it. This cannot be happening! 'Get off!' I pull again, harder, and hear a loud rip. Green fur is in the sheep's mouth! This stupid animal has completely ruined my favourite coat. I'm so angry I could cry.

'It ate my coat!' I yell.

Mum gasps. 'Oh, no!'

'Let me see,' Willow says, but I can still feel something

behind me. I twist round and the sheep is following us! It opens its mouth and goes to gobble my coat again.

'Stop it!' I hiss, walking faster. But the sheep trots faster too, eyeing my beautiful coat like it's a snack. I break into a jog and the sheep starts to run. 'Can somebody help?' I scream. I'm now fully running. The whole flock is staring at me like this is the best show they've ever seen, with the sheep behind me showing no signs of giving up. It keeps lunging forward, trying to catch my coat in its small teeth.

'One second, Tia!' Willow yells, and she lets Oreo off his leash.

Oreo goes quickly into sheepdog mode. He chases after the sheep who's chasing after me and somehow heads it off so it starts running back towards the rest of the flock. I slow down, breathing hard, while Oreo rounds up the mischievous sheep and gets them all to move further down the field, away from us.

Willow is covering her mouth and her shoulders are shaking. When she sees me staring, she presses her lips together and tries, but fails, to stop laughing.

'I'm so glad I could entertain you!' I snap.

'I'm sorry!' Willow laughs out loud. 'It's just this sort of thing really does only happen to you!'

I'm expecting Mum to come to my defence, but she has a smirk plastered on her face. I scowl at her and it instantly disappears.

'You think this is funny? Look at my coat!' The front of it is now two different lengths. I look ridiculous.

'Tia—' Mum begins.

I throw up my hands. 'No, it's fine! I'm glad you all think that me being assaulted by a sheep is so funny!'

'Not "assaulted",' Willow chuckles, and Mum bursts out laughing.

I turn on my heel and walk back across the field, away from them. I'm not going to stand here while they take the piss.

'Tia, we're just joking!' Mum calls after me, but I ignore her. I shiver and just want to get back to the house and out of this cold as quickly as possible. Small wet droplets fall on my face, and when I look up I see it's starting to snow. Great, just what I need!

The house comes into view, and I quicken my pace. There are white snowflakes in my hair and my feet are frozen. A black car is in parked on the lane leading up to the house. I walk past it, then stop as I recognize the driver.

'Kali?'

Kali's eyes widen when she sees me and she lowers the window. 'Hey. It's Tia, right?' I nod. 'Is Quincy around?' I notice that she blushes as she says his name. It's obvious she's still into him. I wish I knew what happened between them.

'He's setting up the Winter Ball,' I reply.

'Oh, good, because it's actually you I wanted to speak to.'

Kali gets out of the car before I can respond. She's much taller than me, almost as tall as Quincy, so when she stands in front of me with her hands on her hips, glaring down at me, I can't help taking a step back.

'When did you and Quincy start dating?' she demands, and

236

I'm taken aback by how aggressive she is. Who does this girl think she is?

I cross my arms over my chest. 'It's none of your business.'

Kali looks up, likes it's an effort for her to stay patient, and takes a deep breath. If I walk on towards the house, I wonder whether she'll follow me, but the expression on her face tells me she's not done talking.

'Look, Tia, you're not from around here so you don't know that Quincy and I have a long history. We dated for three years.' She pauses as if I'm meant to be impressed. 'We're on a break right now, but I can't fix our relationship if you're in the way.'

'A break? Or a break-up?' I say, and her jaw hardens. 'From what I've been told, Quincy wants nothing to do with you. He's moved on. He's with me.'

'We love each other!' Kali spits, her face turning bright red. 'Whatever you have with him is nothing more than a rebound.'

'Is that right? What about Simon?' I throw out his name to see how she reacts, even though I'm still in the dark about Simon's involvement. At this, her eyes go wide. She steps back, stumbling on the gravel.

'He told you?' she says quietly, barely a whisper.

'You should go,' I shoot back. 'I don't think Quincy will be impressed that you've turned into a stalker.'

'Tia!' Mum calls.

A long way down the lane I can see my family walking towards us and Mum's waving. Kali follows my gaze then climbs back into her car. She does a flawless U-turn and a moment later has disappeared round a bend.

FORTY-FIVE

Quincy

16th December

I'm exhausted. The guests have just finished eating when we arrive home, so Tope starts dishing up food for us – Mum's famous curry goat with rice and plantain. Mum and Dad go upstairs to change; Cam and I sit down next to Drew at the dining table. Tia, Willow and Banks sit opposite.

Cam sighs. 'I wish I could cancel the gig tonight, man.' He rubs his eyes. 'I'm mad tired. I don't think I can even drive.'

'I'll take you,' Drew offers. 'I've been stuck indoors all day.'

'Thanks, D,' Cam says.

Tia smiles at me, and I wish I'd had a chance to freshen up. 'How did it go today?' she asks.

'It went well. The ballroom already looks pretty good,' I

say. 'There's more work to be done, but it's getting there. How was your day?'

Willow goes to answer, and Tia glares at her. Willow presses her lips together as if she's holding back laughter.

'Banks wanted to see the sheep,' Tia says.

'Did you like them?' I ask, and Tia scoffs, which makes me laugh.

Tope serves dinner and the curry goat is on par with Mum's. Gia's didn't taste this good.

'Mmm, it just melts in your mouth,' Drew moans. 'I'm not even done and I want seconds already.'

After dinner we have what's left of Tia's lemon drizzle cake, and it's legit the best cake I've had. When I ask for another slice, Tia beams.

'I can't believe you live in a house with those two cooking and baking for you,' Cam says to Willow. 'You're one lucky girl.'

One by one everyone excuses themselves from the table, finally leaving just me and Tia alone.

'Any plans for tonight?' I ask, hoping she's not doing anything.

'I was actually thinking of trying out the hot tub.' She waits a beat. 'Do you want to join me?'

It takes everything in me not to shout *YES!*

'Sure,' I say, cool, calm and collected.

The hot tub is in our back garden. I pause when I see Tia in it, her arms draped on the side of the tub, her hair tied up into a top bun and her head resting back so I can see the top of her red bikini. Why does she look so good in red? It looks skimpy too, not leaving much to the imagination, and I can feel myself getting hot.

She must feel me staring because she suddenly leans forward and looks directly at me.

'Quincy!' She waves me over.

'Where's Willow?' I say, standing by the tub. I don't trust myself not to stare, especially being this close, so I put my hand in the hot water, moving it back and forth and watching the trail it leaves behind.

'She's in the living room with Banks. How do you feel about yesterday with Kali?'

'Still weird,' I say truthfully. 'It helped that you were there, though.'

Tia smiles. 'You coming in or what?' She stands up and reaches for her drink that's on the side. I catch my breath when I take in her body, from her full tits to her flat, soft stomach, and her hips that curve gently out. The bikini bottoms are caught in between her arse cheeks, and I feel my pulse quicken.

'Sure,' I say quickly. I start to strip off. The cold air makes me shiver, but I discard my T-shirt quickly.

I catch Tia looking at me, from my face all the way down to my feet. I try not to smile when I notice that she likes what she sees. She quickly takes a sip of her drink, averting her eyes.

The water splashes over the side as I get in and sit opposite her, sighing as the heat warms me up. Tia is looking everywhere but at me.

'How are things with your boyfriend?' I ask, and no, I don't know why I'm bringing him up.

'Not great. I haven't spoken to him much since I've been here, and our last call didn't end so well. Maybe it's a sign.'

'A sign to break up?' I ask, and she shrugs, her expression blank. I don't know if that's a yes or a no; I hope it's leaning towards the former. 'Do you miss him?' I press.

Tia sighs. 'Yeah, I did at first, but I haven't recently. I was so angry when he first suggested having space, but it hasn't been as awful as I thought.'

'That's good. Remember when I first asked you what your thoughts were about the countryside? What would you say now?'

Tia frowns. 'I'd say "unexpected".'

'How so?'

'I think I just assumed it would be boring, but it isn't. If you told me at the start of this trip that I'd be getting on a horse, I'd have laughed in your face.' She giggles and her eyes light up. 'I've hung out with Drew Parker, been in a Rolls-Royce and gone to Regal Majekodunmi's house!' At this I chuckle. 'Tried on fancy dresses and . . .' She stares at me so seriously that for a second I think she's going to say something bad. 'And I met you. I've really enjoyed the last week.'

Slowly she starts to make her way closer to me. My heart starts thudding so hard I'm sure she can hear it. Tia floats next to me, but there's a small gap between us, and I wonder if she's waiting for me to make a move. I want her to know that I'm interested, so I close the space between us. I can hear her breathing. Fast.

'I've enjoyed it too,' I say softly. 'That bikini is making it really hard to focus right now.'

Tia laughs under her breath. 'I'm glad you like it.' She glances down at my lips then back to my eyes.

Is she about to do what I think she is? I gulp.

Her face continues to draw closer and closer . . .

I don't care that she has a boyfriend or a relationship she's trying to resolve, or that we're only pretending. I close my eyes and lean forward. Our mouths gently touch and I kiss her full lips softly before searching her face, making sure she's okay with this. She puts her hand behind my head and pulls me aggressively forward so her lips reconnect with mine. I pull her on top of me and her legs wrap round my waist. Then I forget about everything except her.

FORTY-SIX

Tia

17th December

I sit up and look out of my window at the grey and cloudy sky, then pull the duvet tighter around me. Flashbacks of last night appear in my mind. We were in the hot tub for ages, kissing and cuddling, and it felt good. Really good. After a while, Quincy pointed out that our families might see, so we quickly jumped out, laughing at how freezing the air was, ran past the living room, where Willow and Banks were watching a film, and up the stairs, dripping water all over the carpet. He grabbed me outside my room, and we kissed again. When we pulled away, he held my hand, gently stroking it.

'You're perfect,' he said softly, and his words made me feel like I was floating.

He kissed my hand before I went into my room. Even

though I was soaking wet, I jumped into my bed and squealed into my pillow, full of so much happiness I could burst. Now, though, looking out at this miserable day, I'm drowning in a wave of guilt and all I can think about is Mike. Was last night cheating if we're on a break?

'Oh fuck,' I mumble, putting my head in my hands.

A knock sounds at my door.

'Come in,' I call, looking up as Willow peeks her head round.

'Hey, I didn't see you after dinner. How was the hot tub?' She wanders in and settles down on the bed next to me.

'Good,' I say quickly. Willow stares at me intently. 'What?' My heart starts racing. Did she see us last night?

Willow frowns and leans in closer, gently touching the side of my neck. 'What is *that*?' Suddenly her eyes widen, and she gasps. 'Is that ... a love bite?'

What? I jump out of bed and race to the mirror. *Shit!* There's a dark red bruise there. I remember Quincy biting my neck yesterday and I loved it then, but not today. Mum is going to lose it.

'Tia? Who gave that to you?' Willow asks bluntly.

'Right ... erm ...' How am I meant to explain this?

'Tia?' Willow presses.

I turn round and face her. 'Okay, okay, I'll tell you, but you can't tell anyone, especially not Mum.'

'Okay,' Willow says slowly.

'I'm serious. Promise me.'

Willow holds up her hand, crossing her fingers. 'I promise.'

'So, last night, Quincy and I were in the hot tub . . . and we sort of . . .' I gulp and Willow's eyes widen. 'Kissed.'

Willow's mouth drops open. She closes it and opens it again, lost for more words.

'Please say something,' I beg.

'Sorry, I'm still processing.' Willow shakes her head. 'You kissed *Quincy*? In the *hot tub*?'

I groan and cover my face. 'I know! I'm a terrible person.'

'No, you're not,' she replies softly.

'Yes, I am!' My eyes start to water. 'What about Mike?'

'Tia, sit down.' Willow reaches out her hand and I go to her, grabbing hold of it. 'You're not a terrible person. And Mike asked you for space, remember?'

'I know we're not "together" together, but we haven't officially broken up. That means I cheated, Willow.' I take deep breaths.

'Tia, can you calm down?' Willow says firmly. 'What was the last thing Mike said to you about your relationship?' I tell her about our FaceTime, and Willow's eyes are slits by the time I'm done. 'He really is a piece of shit.'

'But I still love him,' I wail.

Willow sighs. 'I understand you may love Mike, but do you actually want to be with him? You've been so tunnel-visioned since you two got together, as if you think you can't live without him. But you can. You're amazing, Tia, and you don't have to settle down with the first guy that pays you attention. He asked you for space via text. That's a real dick move. And he said if either of you are drawn to someone else, you should see it as a sign. It's not your fault that you've found Quincy.'

They say the truth hurts, and they're right – Willow's words sting. I didn't settle for Mike because he was the first guy that paid me any attention. He was kind to me when I was at one of my lowest points. And I liked him way before he even showed an interest in me.

I rub my temples to soothe the headache I feel coming on. Willow makes it sound so easy, like I can forget about Mike in an instant. But there's a battle raging inside me and I'm being torn in so many directions. One part of me wants to let Mike go completely, but another still believes that if I show up to his party, he'll realize how much he's missed me and we'll go back to how we were. And then there's Quincy, the sweetest guy I've ever met. But we were only ever meant to be faking feelings for each other and now the lines have blurred. What future is there with Quincy when we live so far apart? But a future with Mike ... is that worth fighting for?

'It was a mistake, Willow,' I say firmly, and she frowns. 'With Quincy,' I clarify.

I turn my head away, because lying to my sister is really hard. *I spent a year with Mike*, I tell myself, *I love him* – and if there's even a small chance that we can make our relationship work again, I want to try.

'Right,' she says slowly. 'So what are you going to do about Quincy? You can't avoid him in his own house.'

'We're friends,' I say easily. 'It was nothing.'

'Really?' Willow crosses her arms over her chest. 'Tell that to the love bite on your neck.'

FORTY-SEVEN

Quincy

17th December

I haven't been able to stop thinking about Tia since last night. Remembering her kisses and the way she felt in my arms kept me awake all night, and yet I still have so much energy this morning. Kissing someone new for the first time after a break-up always feels slightly strange, but kissing Tia felt right. And now I can't wipe this stupid grin off my face. Kali who?

Cam, Drew, Eliza and I are still decorating the ballroom today. I can't wait for Seven Days tonight so I can dance with Tia until the sun rises.

I can see Cam looking at me, trying to figure something out. 'Is it a girl?' he asks.

I shrug. 'Maybe.'

He points at me. 'Leah, right?'

'Leah?' I grab an empty box and remember the story I told him. 'Oh ... yeah ... Leah. I was talking to her last night.'

'She must be something.' Cam unpacks a box. 'Cause you've been in the most annoying mood all day.'

'Cam, can you hold the ladder for me?' Drew calls from across the room.

When Cam goes, Eliza asks, 'Did something happen with Tia?'

I can't lie, I'm bursting to tell somebody. 'We kissed yesterday.'

Eliza gasps. 'No way!'

'In the hot tub!'

'You had sex in the hot tub?'

I scoff. 'I said "kissed"! What's wrong with you?'

'Sorry, just checking!' She laughs. 'She broke up with her boyfriend, then?'

'Well ...' I pause.

'Quincy!' Eliza scolds.

'I don't really know,' I finish.

Eliza rolls her eyes. 'Well, that wasn't smart, was it?'

She's right. Kissing Tia without knowing what's going on between her and her boyfriend wasn't a good move, but I couldn't think straight last night, especially not with her in that bikini. I wonder if Tia is regretting it. The idea of that sends a sharp pain through me.

Drew treats us to lunch in town before we head back home.

'Q, can you text Tia and ask her to only make vanilla

248

cupcakes for tonight? Bunny has sworn off chocolate,' Drew says.

I relay the message to Tia adding a kiss at the end. I'm hoping she'll message back, but nothing comes in. *I'll see her in a bit*, I tell myself, but there's this niggling thought in the back of my mind that she might be regretting last night.

Once we get home, I head straight to the kitchen. I spot Tia immediately, looking intently at the tray of cupcakes as she decorates them with snowflakes made out of frosting. It's boiling hot in here yet she's wearing a black turtleneck.

'Hey!' I gesture to her top. 'Aren't you hot in that?'

She glances up without a smile and goes back to the cupcakes. 'Didn't have any choice when I realized you left a love bite on my neck.'

I frown at her weird tone. I don't remember her complaining when I was nibbling on her neck.

'You okay?' I ask.

Tia stops and stares at me. 'We kissed. It was a mistake. Let's forget it happened.'

I stare at her, dumbfounded. Even though my whole body's gone cold like I've been drenched with icy water, I tell myself I've misheard her. We've been drawn to each other for days and that kiss was definitely not a mistake.

'Don't say that,' I say quietly. I take a step towards her, and she takes one back, like we're performing a choreographed dance. It reminds me of us ice skating and how much fun we had. 'Last night meant something.'

'Don't. I have to sort things out with Mike,' Tia says. She

wipes her forehead with the back of her hand leaving a trail of frosting on her skin.

'Here.' I grab the nearest cloth and stand next to her.

She catches her breath and, in that moment, I know she's lying to herself. Last night wasn't a mistake. I gently wipe her forehead. She bites her bottom lip and finally looks at me. We're staring directly into each other's eyes, and I want to kiss her again. Badly.

Tia turns her head sharply, focusing again on the cupcakes. 'I have to finish these,' she says, avoiding my eyes.

A barrier's gone up between us and Tia's trying to convince herself that she doesn't want me to cross it, but I'm desperate to get back to how we were with each other last night.

'Tia,' I say softly, but she shakes her head.

How can she act like our kisses didn't matter? Defeated, I drop the cloth on the counter and leave the kitchen.

FORTY-EIGHT

Tia

17th December

I'm leaning against the kitchen counter, scrolling through Mike's Instagram as Mum peels potatoes. Dinner is in a couple of hours. There's nothing interesting on Mike's page, and all I can think about is Quincy.

Before I can stop myself, I've clicked on his Instagram. I smile when his face floods my feed. The top picture is the one he took of us in Everly Rose and I think back to how he looked at me in that red dress. He'll probably never look at me like that again, not after the way I just was with him. Scrolling through, I realize I've met most of his friends. I wonder if Simon is on here. Quincy doesn't post a lot, so it doesn't take me long to see there are no pictures of Kali or anyone by the name of Simon. I haven't told Quincy about Kali coming to the farm yesterday afternoon.

I check Quincy's followers and find a Simon Rogers, but Quincy doesn't follow him back. Clearly something went down between Quincy, Kali and Simon.

'I hope this snow doesn't get much heavier,' Mum says looking out of the window. It's been snowing on and off for hours now.

The kitchen door swings open, and Quincy walks in in his dark winter jacket, looking so cute in a matching woolly hat. I wonder where he went. He catches my eye and I quickly look away. If I don't look at him, I won't follow through on this overwhelming urge to kiss him. It's hard, but it's working so far. Well, working in the sense that I haven't kissed him again, not that I haven't stopped wanting to.

'Tia,' Quincy says.

Reluctantly I look at him, and his eyes are harder than usual.

'We're leaving in an hour to help set up Seven Days.' He doesn't wait for a response before he leaves the kitchen.

Mum frowns at me. 'Are you okay? You seem quiet.'

'I'm fine,' I say quickly. 'I'll go and get ready.'

I head upstairs and knock on Willow's door. She's sitting cross-legged on her bed with white hair strewn across her legs. Regal asked her to make her a wig for the Winter Ball and she's been working on it ever since. The exposure my sister is going to get from this will elevate her business tenfold, and I can't wait to see the results.

'Hi, how's it going?' I ask from the doorway.

'Getting there,' she says. 'What are you wearing tonight?'

'I don't know. I wanted to see if you had anything.'

Willow laughs. 'Sorry, nothing. I raided Mum's wardrobe and I'm wearing her black dress. It's the only dressy thing she brought.'

Damn. I thought Willow would have options. I can't ask Drew because she's so tall. I head back to my room and go through my wardrobe, but everything in there is cosy wear. The only dress that will do for tonight is the one I brought for Mike's party. I guess I don't have much choice. I take my time getting ready, hiding the love bite with foundation. I slip my feet into the white heels and study myself in the mirror, smiling at my reflection.

As I walk downstairs, I can hear the others' voices coming from the reception area. There's a draught of cold air, and I see the retreating backs of Cam and Willow as they head outside towards the car. Quincy is looking at his watch, but then he glances up at me and our eyes lock. My cheeks feel warm under his gaze and I watch his eyes travel down the length of my body.

'Wow! Tia, you look . . . wow.'

'Thank you. You look good too.'

Quincy's wearing dark jeans and a black shirt that shows off his lean, toned physique. His hair, which he usually ties up, has been taken down and is framing his chiselled face. And those lips! A shiver travels through me.

'Quincy, I'm sorry for being so weird earlier. The kiss . . .'

He shakes his head. 'It's okay. Let's just have fun tonight.'

'And make your ex jealous,' I say, even though it feels like we're way past that. Quincy nods.

253

'When Kali sees you . . .' He mimes a head explosion.

I laugh, but it sounds hollow to my ears.

A door opens and Mum comes through from the kitchen with a Tupperware, her phone camera poised. 'Here, Tia, don't forget your cupcakes. Where's Willow?'

'She's already in the car. Please, Mum, no pictures,' I beg, but she ignores me as she pushes me and Quincy together.

She pauses and looks me over. 'Is that the dress you bought for Mike's party?' she asks, and Quincy tenses beside me.

'Yeah. Might as well get some use out of it,' I say quickly.

Quincy puts his hand round my waist and gently squeezes my side, leaving a trail of sparks on my skin. I take a deep breath, pleading with my heart to calm down.

'Say cheese,' Mum says. She doesn't stop taking pictures until I insist. Mum rolls her eyes. 'I've sent them to you. Have fun! See you in the morning.'

Quincy holds the car door open for me as I get in carefully. As he comes round to the other door and settles in next to me, his leg brushes against mine and my heart jumps.

'You look cute!' Willow says from the front seat. 'I thought you didn't bring that dress?'

'Forgot I packed it,' I lie. 'Love your hair!'

Willow is wearing a short black wig that's giving nineties Halle Berry vibes. It shows off her long, elegant neck and sharp cheekbones, and really suits her. Her face is beat to perfection and the gold highlight glistens even in the dark.

Cam starts the car, and Drew wasn't lying – he drives like a maniac! We speed through the country lanes with Giggs

254

blasting through the speakers. 'Talkin' da Hardest' plays at every party I go to and it's always one of the songs that gets everyone rapping along, or at the very least saying, 'Jheeze!'

'Cam, slow down!' Quincy shouts, but who knows if Cam can hear over the loud bass.

'I thought you'd like Giggs,' Cam says looking at Willow, lowering the music only slightly. 'He's from Peckham.'

'I like my eardrums more,' Willow says. 'I'm not really a fan.'

'Not a fan!' Cam looks so horrified it's comical. 'Giggs is a national treasure.'

Holding the container of cupcakes on my lap I don't have my hands free to grip the seat and Cam's driving is anything but smooth. When he turns to the right, not bothering to slow down, I slide towards Quincy until I'm practically sitting on his lap. I'm aware of that woody, grassy smell of his more than usual, but this time I inhale it, making my stomach flip. He puts his arm round my shoulders to steady me.

'You all right?' he asks, and I nod.

I try to move back to my seat, but my dress is so tight that it takes me ages, and every time Cam swerves, which is *all* the time, Quincy and I bump into each other.

'I'm sorry,' I say to Quincy.

'I don't mind,' he says with a smile playing on his lips.

Eventually we get to Bunny's and pull up outside the White House, and I lean forward so I can get a better view. The house is not a house. It's a mansion with a circular driveway, torch lights at the front and a huge wreath on the door.

Quincy and Cam take his decks out of the boot. I don't have

a coat on because the green one ruined by the sheep is the only one I brought, so I walk up the gravel path quickly and try to stop my teeth from chattering. Thankfully it's stopped snowing, but traces of white linger on the ground.

The front door is slightly open and I push it with my hip.

'Quincy! Cam!' The blonde girl we met at Costa hurries over. She's wearing a T-shirt and skinny jeans.

'Hey, Bunny!' Quincy hugs her. 'This is Willow and Tia. They're staying with us. Tia made cupcakes for tonight.'

'You did?' Bunny says. 'Oh, thank you! That's so lovely of you.' She gives me a one-armed hug and I get a whiff of peppermint.

'You're welcome,' I say as I look around. 'Your house is so cool.'

We're standing in a massive open-plan living area, and everything – from the walls to the paintings to the Christmas tree – is white. There's a huge TV mounted on the wall and a fireplace that's crackling away. Most of the furniture has been removed apart from one table at the far end that I assume is where Cam will set up and another covered with drinks and plastic red cups.

'Let me take these from you,' Bunny says, reaching for the cupcakes. 'Feel free to check outside.'

We all walk to the other side of room, where there's a huge floor-to-ceiling window that looks out on a perfectly manicured garden with a pool.

'This is my first time in the White House,' Quincy says. 'It's a mythical property in White Oak.' I can see why.

We wander back over to Bunny and help her put out some snacks on the table to accompany the alcohol, while Cam sorts the decks.

'One-two; one-two – King Cam on the decks,' Cam says into the microphone, testing the volume.

'King Cam? I like that,' I say, and Cam grins.

Bunny gives us the Wi-Fi password and I log in and see a missed FaceTime from Mike. For the first time ever, I don't feel the need to immediately call him back. I text him instead:

> Can't talk. At a party

My phone pings straight away.

> Party?! I thought you were at a farm or something

I ignore him. I click on my last message with Remi and see she's online, so I take a picture of the house and send it to her.

> Damn! Whose sexy-ass house is that?

I laugh at her response.

'What's so funny?' Quincy asks.

'Just something my friend said,' I say.

'Y'all ready to see how us country folk party?' he says in a spot-on Texan accent.

I laugh. 'Let's see if you can keep up with me.'

Quincy smiles and lowers his voice. 'Oh, I can keep up with you. Trust.'

Now it's me smiling, like a Cheshire cat.

The party gets packed quickly. Unlike back home where it's an unspoken rule to arrive at least two hours after the party starts, these guys come bang on time at seven p.m. I try to keep an eye on Quincy, but there are so many people milling around that I quickly lose track of him. Everyone looks at me and Willow when they enter. I'm sure it's because we've almost doubled the Black population of the town. They all greet us and ask us how we've found the trip so far, and lots of girls ask about my relationship with Quincy. I see what he means. People here do talk.

Drew and Regal arrive together. Drew's wearing a very short green velvet dress and her long hair hangs in sexy beach waves down her back. Regal is in sparkly silver shorts with a silver feather-banded bra and six-inch heels. Her dark brown hair is tied tight in a high ponytail. She looks like she came straight off the catwalk.

The music is banging, the vibe is great and I'm dancing with Eliza, who arrived in a tight black jumpsuit. I'm filming us for my Instagram story, and as soon as I post, Mike comments.

> You look hot x

The flutter that usually fills my stomach when Mike compliments me doesn't come. If anything, I find it odd that he's now suddenly making an effort.

'You want some?' Eliza asks, offering me her bottle.

I take a sip, and it's crisp and sweet. Over her shoulder I spy Quincy talking to someone in the kitchen. I'm not sure when Kali arrived, but she's standing with a group of girls to the side, one of them being Sarah, the girl I met round the campfire, and she keeps staring at me. *Weirdo*.

Eliza glances over my shoulder. I follow her gaze and see Cam blatantly flirting with Willow. Eliza's got a weird look on her face when I turn back to her.

'You okay?' I shout over the music.

Eliza points. 'Is something going on between them?'

I shake my head, and quickly notice how relieved Eliza looks. Does she like Cam or something?

'Hey.' Strong hands touch my waist and I jump. I spin round and Quincy's behind me. 'You wanna dance?'

My heart jumps. 'Sounds good.'

FORTY-NINE

Quincy

17th December

I grab Tia's hand and lead her to the middle of the dance floor. Everyone's looking at us, and I catch 'Where's Kali?' a few times, which suggests she's somewhere here. Good. I want her to see us.

This party is sick. Everyone's turned up and brought good vibes with them. Simon must be about because Eliza was holding one of the cider bottles that his family sell in their shop. There are so many people here, so hopefully that means I won't bump into him.

'What's Luv?' fills the room, and I start to move to the iconic beat.

Tia raises her eyebrows at me. 'Oh, you can move!'

'Can you?' I challenge.

She laughs and starts to dance with me as Ashanti begins to sing the chorus.

'I love this song!' she yells over the music.

We dance to song after song, shouting the lyrics and laughing at each other when we mess up the words. Cam plays a few songs across different genres, trying to appeal to everyone, and it seems to work as the party is buzzing. Someone finds the dimmer and the lights go low, making the room suddenly feel intimate and sexy.

The vibe changes again once a dancehall track comes on, and with the lights dimmed it feels like I'm in a nightclub. Tia turns round and puts my hands on her hips before she starts to rotate them in a circular motion to the beat. I catch the whine, focusing on the way she's moving so we're in time with each other. The girls round here don't dance like this. Tia's hips don't lie, and I wrap my arms round her waist as she presses her back against my chest. We continue to move together. It's almost like we're alone at this party. I wish we were.

We stay like this until Cam moves onto hip-hop and everyone cheers when Drake comes on. Tia faces me, her hands on my chest and her face glistening. 'I need some air.'

'Let's go outside,' I say.

This time it's she who grabs my hand and it's warm and soft. People glance at us as we walk by, and that's when I see Kali in the corner with Sarah, Harley and Lisa. She's staring at us, her eyes narrowed as we walk by, and I can't help but smile.

The cold air hits me as soon as I step outside the front, but it's pleasant because I'm hot from dancing. I close the door behind us, muffling the music. We're alone out here. Tia looks up at the sky full of stars, but I'm only focused on her and how incredibly hot she looks in her white dress.

'I know you're staring at me,' she says, her head still tilted up.

I laugh. 'Sorry.'

She turns to me, her voice low and sultry, making my heart race. 'Don't be. I like it.' She rubs a hand along her arm.

'You cold? You wanna go back in?' I ask.

Tia shakes her head. 'I like it out here with you,' but she rubs her arms again and an idea hits me.

'Follow me.'

Tia links arms with me as we walk carefully over the gravel. I unlock the car and pull out a blanket from the boot, freshly washed, and wrap it over her shoulders, swaddling her in its warmth.

'Quincy.' She laughs, but she stops abruptly and stares at me instead. She looks from my lips to my eyes and back to my lips, and the butterflies in my stomach are in a frenzy. I want to kiss her so badly, but I don't want to deal with the fall-out of her regretting it again.

'Are you sure?' I ask.

FIFTY

Tia

17th December

I don't take my eyes off Quincy as I step closer.

'I'm sure,' I reply.

I'm dizzy with the anticipation. Deep down I know I've been waiting for this moment to happen again. I close my eyes as Quincy leans in.

FIFTY-ONE

Quincy

17th December

Tia's lips are soft, and they taste sweet and slightly of alcohol. An electric current shoots all the way through my body. I pull her closer and kiss her deeper, making her moan. I don't want this moment to ever end.

FIFTY-TWO

Tia

17th December

This kiss is even better than the first time. How is that possible? I unwrap the blanket, letting it fall to the ground so my arms are free, and I pull Quincy closer. He lifts me up and presses me against the car, our lips not leaving each other as fireworks explode in my head.

FIFTY-THREE

Quincy

17th December

All I want to do is leave this party, drive her home, take her to my room and show her how much I want her. My phone vibrates in my pocket, pulling me back to reality, and I groan. I place Tia on top of the car bonnet so she's sitting. She pulls away, wiping the lipstick she's left on my lips with her thumb.

'Thanks,' I say as I answer the call. 'Yeah?'

'We're doing shots! Where are you?' Drew shouts over the music.

'Outside. I don't wanna do shots.' I roll my eyes and Tia smiles.

'Q, get inside and get drunk with your family!' Drew demands then hangs up.

'We'd better go back in,' I say regretfully.

I help Tia down and throw the blanket back in the car.

'I'm not done kissing you, just so you know,' I say, wrapping my arm round her shoulders. There's a small part of me that worries she's going to tell me she regrets it again, but when she says, 'You better not be,' instead, I grin so hard my face hurts.

We walk back in, pushing through the crowd until we find Drew, Cam, Regal and Willow. Drew hands me two shots.

'Two?' I groan, and everyone laughs. 'Why aren't you guys doing shots?' I look at Cam and Regal.

'We're driving, babe,' Regal says. 'Drink up.'

'To Cam.' Drew lifts her shot glass and we all follow suit. 'For absolutely killing it tonight.'

'To Cam,' we chorus.

I down the shots and the alcohol burns my throat.

'I'm starving,' Willow says, looking ruefully at the nearly empty table. 'All the snacks are gone.'

'I'll tell Bunny,' Regal replies. 'Everyone loved your cupcakes, Tia.'

Tia grins. 'Oh nice! I'm getting another drink. Anyone want one?'

'Wait, I'll come with you,' Willow says, and the sisters head for the drinks table.

'So, I saw you and Tia grinding on the dance floor,' Drew says, nudging me.

'He deserves to have fun after what he's been through,' Cam jumps in, and I feel this rush of affection for my brother. 'I switched up the music just for you. Kali looked like she was gonna vomit.'

I dap Cam. 'My guy.'

'She better stay out of my way,' Drew mutters.

'Oh, Bunny!' Regal waves as Bunny pushes past us, red in the face. 'Oh ... you okay?'

'No, I just had to kick some people out of my bed! And I need to get more snacks and drinks because we've already run out.' She looks past us and groans. 'Why are people in the back garden? I locked the door.'

'I'll sort it,' I say quickly before Bunny's head explodes.

There are a few people outside that I recognize from college and a lot of empty bottles and other rubbish littering the ground.

'Guys, Bunny wants everyone in,' I announce to the group. They all groan but slowly make their way inside. I start picking up the empty bottles, placing them on the garden table, when a familiar voice calls my name. I turn round and see Kali.

She's wearing this black catsuit that hugs her in all the right places, and for a second I'm distracted by the way it fits her. I quickly remind myself of the reason we're not together any more.

'No one's meant to be outside,' I say, heading towards the French doors, but Kali suddenly grabs my arm.

'Please, can we talk?' Her ice-blue eyes, which I used to love staring into, plead with me. My head is saying no, but my heart is telling me to listen. I hesitate, not knowing what to do.

'I just need ten minutes,' she adds.

'Five.' I turn round and cross my arms.

She plays with her hands, clasping and unclasping them in

a way I know she only does when she's nervous. I keep my face blank, wanting her to get this over with.

'I'm so sorry for what happened. I hate myself every day, and I wish I could take it all back. You were such an amazing boyfriend, and I let my emotions about your birthday party ruin everything. It was a drunken mistake, and I haven't spoken to Simon since. I know you're not ready to forgive me, but can we at least be civil?'

'Civil?' I jerk my head back. 'You slept with my best friend because I didn't show up to a surprise party you planned, when you knew I was going to be in London, anyway!'

'I *didn't* know!' Kali protests. 'Drew wouldn't tell me anything about it, even though she knew about the party.'

A fiery heat starts to build in my stomach. If Kali continues to put this on Drew, I will lose it.

'Drew had been planning my eighteenth birthday trip to London for months. She did the same for Cam when he turned eighteen. I told you that, and you still asked me to keep the date free. I know Drew spoke to you and made it clear that I'd be away for my birthday, but you chose to ignore her, thinking I'd pick you over my sister who had already organized everything.'

Kali juts out her chin and doesn't say anything. She knows I'm right. And suddenly I realize that, throughout our entire relationship, she's always needed to be number one in my life, constantly putting me in the middle until she gets her way. The one time she didn't, she slept with my best friend.

'What's worse is that you didn't even tell me about Simon.

He told me because he was racked with guilt.' I bark out a laugh. 'For weeks you just acted like nothing happened!'

'We agreed to tell you together,' Kali argues, 'but Simon went ahead and did it, so that I looked like the villain.'

'Kali, it had nothing to do with trying to make you look like the villain. You should have owned up to what you did and allowed me to decide what I wanted to do with that information. You were happy to let me believe everything was cool between us.'

Kali runs her hands through her hair and takes a deep breath. 'I fucked up, Quincy. I know that. I feel sick every day when I think about it. I'm still so in love with you.' Her words hang in the air, and she stares at me, waiting. I notice her eyes start to well up and a part of me wants to comfort her; but another part of me is pissed off that she's just crying crocodile tears. She was in the wrong, and then she tried to cover it up.

'I can't do this.' I go to head inside, but she stands in front of me, blocking my way. She's only a little bit shorter than me, so we're practically eye to eye.

'If you don't love me any more, then I want you to tell me that,' she says.

'Kali, leave it.' I step to the side and she copies me.

'Because I love you, and I'd do anything to have another chance.' Tears start falling down her perfectly made-up face. 'Do you still love me?'

I stare at Kali, at the face I've avoided for months. I have such complicated feelings towards her, but we can't come back from what happened. It's too messy, and it's not something I can mentally deal with right now.

'No. I don't love you any more,' I say, and I can see the hurt in her eyes. 'We're done, Kali. Please leave me alone.'

'Quincy—' She starts to properly sob, and her hair falls forward over her face.

I hate seeing anyone cry and, without thinking, I put a hand on her shoulder to comfort her. She leans in, looks up at my face, and a second later, to my surprise, she kisses me.

FIFTY-FOUR

Tia

17th December

Willow grabs a Coke before heading back to the dance floor, but there are so many empty bottles of alcohol on the table that I'm struggling to make a drink. I'm lifting up a bottle of vodka and peering at it in the dim light, trying to see if there's anything inside it, when an attractive white boy with blond shoulder-length hair comes and stands next to me. He's got this LA skater boy look about him.

'Hey.' He's wearing a baggy green top that matches his eyes and a silver chain. 'Any luck?'

'Seems like they're all out.' I smile at him. 'I'm Tia.'

'Nice to meet you. I'm Simon.'

'Simon!' I say it much louder than I mean to, and he looks surprised.

'Sorry, have we met before?' he asks.

'No ... Eliza mentioned you. I'm staying at Saiyan Hedge Farm with the Parkers. You must know Quincy,' I add to test his reaction, and Simon visibly flinches. I'm just thinking about how I can get him to give me some insight into what went down when my phone buzzes in my bag. It's Mum. 'Sorry, I've just got to take this.' He gives me a thumbs up as I wander away.

I spy the garden lights on and decide to head out there so I can hear her. People are still dancing so I have to squeeze through. I close one of my ears with my finger and shout into the phone, 'One sec, Mum.'

I open the door and step out, and that's when I see them: a tall, auburn-haired girl in all black leaning forward, her lips on Quincy's. My heart hits my stomach. My phone falls from my hand and lands with a thud. Quincy jumps back and Kali looks at me, her mouth forming a smirk.

'This must be a joke, right?' I say, my voice hoarse.

'Tia—' Quincy begins, but I don't want to hear it. I pick up my phone and run back inside.

I'm pushing through the crowds of people, using my elbows to make room. My chest hurts so bad, making me feel like I can't breathe, and my eyes are hot as they fill with tears.

'You okay?' Simon asks as I rush past him, but I ignore him.

As soon as I get out the front, I lean against one of the pillars and start to cry. I'm *so* stupid. I let myself develop feelings for Quincy, prioritized him over Mike, kissed him at this very party – and then not even five minutes later he's kissing his ex. Did he lie to me? Does he actually want to get back with Kali?

'Tia? Are you there?' Mum calls from the phone. I completely forgot she was on the line, but I can't talk to her right now. I hang up and quickly text her.

> Too loud. Everything okay? x

She responds straight away:

> No problem. Just checking it was going well x

I slide down the pillar and sit on the ground, not caring how the cold seeps into my legs or that my new white dress might get dirty. There's a loud blast of music as the door behind me opens, then it's muffled by the door closing.

Simon sits down next to me. 'You okay?'

I wipe my eyes, ruining my eyeshadow and mascara. 'I saw Quincy kissing Kali.'

'What?' Simon frowns. 'No way.'

'It's true!'

'There must be some sort of explanation—' Simon tries.

I sniff. 'I don't care. I just want to go home.'

'Wait here a second, okay?' Simon doesn't even give me a chance to answer before he goes back into the house.

I stand up, brushing down the back of my dress. I need Willow. The door opens, and I turn thinking it's Simon again, but it's Regal, who smiles when she sees me.

'Hey, what are you doing out here? I was just heading to get more snacks.' Regal comes closer, and her eyes fill with concern as she takes me in. 'What's wrong, Tia?'

'Everything,' I whimper, and I start to cry all over again.

'Hey, it's all right.' She grabs me in a warm hug that instantly makes me feel calmer. 'You're freezing. Come back inside.'

I step away from her. 'No. I want to go home.'

She looks at me in concern, as if she's trying to read my thoughts and find out what's happened. But I really don't want to be grilled right now, and she must sense that because all she says is, 'Let's sit in the car for a bit.'

FIFTY-FIVE

Quincy

17th December

'Fuck!' I hurry towards the French doors and Kali runs after me.

'Where are you going?' she demands, trying to hold my hand, but I shake her off.

'To explain to Tia that she misunderstood the situation.'

'Misunderstood?' Kali looks me up and down. 'You kissed me.'

'You know I didn't,' I argue back. 'I was trying to be kind and comfort you because you were crying and then you kissed me. I don't want to be with you, Kali. Don't you get that? I want to be with Tia!'

And I do. More than anything. I *really* like the girl. But now all I can see is the shock on her face when she saw Kali kissing me. I can't believe I was stupid enough to let myself get into that situation.

Kali jerks her head back like I've slapped her. 'Tia?'

'Yes! I'm not going to lose her because of this shit.'

I turn my back on Kali and storm into the house. Couples are pressed tightly together, and the bass is making my whole body vibrate. I'm scanning the crowds, trying to find Tia, but she's nowhere to be seen. My heart starts to race and I'm praying I can fix this.

'Q!' I'm surprised to see Simon rush over to me. He points at the door. 'Tia's outside.'

'Is she okay?' I ask without thinking.

Simon's eyes go wide. 'She said you kissed Kali!'

'She kissed me!' I yell.

I haven't got time to talk to Simon. I move as quick as I can through the packed room and open the front door. Regal's car headlights are on and I can see Tia sitting in the passenger seat. I race over and bang on the window. Tia looks determinedly forward, her expression one of stone.

Regal lowers the window. 'What's up?'

'I need to talk to Tia,' I say quickly.

Tia turns her back on me in response.

Regal frowns and looks from Tia to me. 'Am I missing something?'

'Tia, please,' I beg.

'Go away,' Tia says, sharp and cold. Her make-up has run down her face, and her eyes are red and puffy. Realizing I've made her cry is like a punch to the gut.

'Just give her a moment,' Regal says gently.

Reluctantly I nod and walk back to the house, hoping and praying I can save this.

FIFTY-SIX

Tia

17th December

Regal rolls up the window. She keeps glancing at me, but I deliberately keep my focus forward. My phone buzzes with an Instagram notification from Mike.

How's your night going? Miss you x

The message doesn't land the way it used to. I close my eyes, wishing I could go back to when Quincy asked me to be his fake date so I could say no. All I've done is jump from one boy to another and I still feel like shit.

'Did Quincy upset you?' Regal asks.

I hesitate for a moment. 'I saw Quincy kissing Kali in the garden.'

'Kali!' Regal spits.

Regal's reaction is as strong as Quincy and Drew's. Whatever Kali did, I know it must have been really bad.

'Kali is a devious little shit,' Regal continues. 'You're sure Quincy kissed her? It doesn't make sense.'

Simon questioned it too. Why is it so weird that Quincy would be drawn back to his ex?

'What makes her devious?' I ask, hoping I'll finally find out.

Regal huffs. 'Where do I start? Everything always has to be about her. She manipulates situations to get her way. For example, she planned that stupid surprise party for him knowing he was in London that weekend – and the Simon thing? That is a whole other level of fucked-up.'

What Simon thing? I want to ask, but Regal shakes her head and takes a deep breath.

'Sorry. She really gets my back up. So why are you upse— Oh!' Regal's eyes widen. 'Wait, do you like Quincy?'

At this point, I don't care who knows about us.

'We kissed.'

Regal gasps. 'You kissed? But isn't he dating someone he met online?'

I shake my head, not caring to conceal the truth any longer. 'He made that girl up.'

'He made her up ... Right.' Regal says slowly. 'But don't you have an actual man back in London?'

'It's ... complicated,' I reply.

'So Quincy made up a fake girl, but the whole time he's actually been seeing you?' she questions.

'No, he made up a girl so people would stop asking him about his date to the Winter Ball,' I explain. 'When I arrived at the farm I agreed to be his date, so I became said girl. Does that make any sense?'

'Right, okay,' Regal says, but I can hear from the way she says it she's confused.

'But then he kissed Kali,' I say.

Regal shakes her head. 'I don't know what that kiss was you saw, but Quincy is a thousand per cent done with her. She crossed a major line.'

I can't help the way my heart leaps with hope, but I'm pissed off with myself for feeling that way.

'What line did Kali cross?' I press, and Regal's jaw hardens.

'I think you should ask Quincy. I'm sorry this happened tonight, but don't let it ruin your evening. Talk to him about it.'

As much as I want to believe Regal, I can't erase what I saw, and I'm not sure I can trust what Quincy says any more.

'Quincy's a good guy,' Regal adds. 'And I promise I don't say that about anyone.'

Yes, he is a good guy, and that's what makes this whole thing worse. I didn't expect it of him. But maybe I should give him a chance to explain. I sigh, not sure what to do.

Regal reaches into her bag and pulls out her make-up. 'I'll fix your face while you think about it.'

I can't help giggling. 'Who knew a few tears would get me a Regal Majekodunmi makeover?'

She laughs. 'I only use my make-up on my favourite people.'

My head's completely messed up. Going back to the party

probably isn't the right move, but I do know that despite being pissed off with Quincy, my heart hurts when I think about leaving without talking to him.

'And we're done,' Regal says a few minutes later. She searches my face and a smile spreads over hers. 'Beautiful.'

I look in the mirror and I swear my make-up has never looked this good, even on my best day.

'Thank you so much.'

'You're very welcome.' She throws her make-up bag onto the back seat. 'You walk back into that party with your head held high, okay?'

'Okay,' I reply, but my heart is thundering in my chest. 'I might chill upstairs for a bit first. Do you think Bunny will mind?'

'Nah, I'll let her know.' Regal gently squeezes my hand. I follow her into the house, trying to calm my nerves. Despite Regal being so sure that Quincy is done with Kali, I'm finding it hard to believe.

The party is still going strong, although some people are now leaning against the walls or sitting on the floor, tiredness catching up with them. I spot Willow dancing with some guy. She waves at me, and I force a smile back. I don't want my problems to ruin her night. I can't see Kali anywhere, but I spot Simon hanging out with Eliza.

'Tia.' Quincy appears next to us, and Regal eyeballs him. 'Can I please speak to you?'

'Not now,' I respond curtly.

I walk around the couples dancing and head up the stairs.

Willow catches my eye and mouths, 'Are you okay?' I nod. I'm hoping a few minutes alone will help me feel better.

I go into the first room on the landing and realize it's a library filled top to bottom with books. I run my hand over the leather spines and then turn my attention to the white sofa in the corner. I sit down, take off my heels and sigh deeply as I wiggle my toes, trying to get the feeling back into them.

I click on Instagram, and I've been tagged in a load of stories. Someone I don't know has taken a video of me and Quincy dancing. It feels like it happened forever ago. I hear the dancehall music filling the room, can remember the feel of our bodies pressed closely together, and it almost seems wrong that anyone else witnessed that intimate moment.

'Hey—'

I look up, and Quincy is hovering nervously by the door. 'Can we talk? Please?'

I'm tempted to tell him to go away, but he's peering at me with those piercing eyes of his, and I find myself nodding. He sits on the other side of the sofa so there's a huge gap between us.

'I swear I wasn't even going to talk to Kali, let alone—'

'Kiss her,' I finish in a hard voice.

Quincy gulps. 'Yeah.'

We fall into silence, and I keep my eyes on the wooden floor. It was a mistake to agree to talk to him. I already know he's going to go back to his ex, and I can't handle my heart hurting any more than it already does. I start to put my heels back on.

'Kali wants us to get back together,' Quincy says quickly,

and my fingers freeze on the buckle. 'She kissed me out of the blue, and I promise I wasn't expecting it – nor did I want it.'

My heart starts to thud so hard that it physically hurts my chest. Quincy jumps off the sofa and kneels in front of me so I'm forced to look at him.

'I don't want to be with her, Tia,' Quincy says. 'And I told her that.'

'You did?' I ask, and he nods. 'I didn't tell you this, but she came by the house the other day when you were decorating the ballroom.'

Quincy frowns. 'What did she say?'

'That you were on a break, and I was getting in the way.'

'Wow.' Quincy laughs with no humour to it.

'I want to believe you,' I say, and Quincy gazes at me hopefully. 'It's just hard because I saw you kissing her. But Regal and Simon defended you.'

'Simon?' Quincy's quiet for a moment, and I wish I knew what he was thinking. Suddenly he grabs both my hands. 'Tia, I mean it – I don't want Kali. I really like you.'

'You like me?' I say slowly.

Quincy nods. 'I know we haven't known each other long, but there's something special here, don't you think?'

My heart starts to swell with happiness. Quincy likes me back.

'And I feel good when I'm around you,' he continues. 'I'm really sorry about tonight.'

My heart starts screaming *Kiss him!*, but for once my brain is less excited. I need to decide what to do about Mike once and for all. But first I need Quincy to fill in the missing piece of the puzzle.

'There is something between us,' I begin, and hope builds in Quincy's eyes. 'But you wanted us to pretend to be together to get back at your ex, and you never told me why.'

Quincy looks away and takes a deep breath. 'Kali had sex with my best friend Simon on my birthday.'

What the fuck? My mouth drops open. Quincy sits on the floor, his long legs outstretched.

'I was in London celebrating my eighteenth, and I didn't know Kali had organized a surprise party at her house for me and invited all our friends. Drew found out and told her I wouldn't be around that weekend. Apparently, Kali asked Drew if she could come to London with me, and Drew said no because it was meant to be a weekend for me and her. Kali kept trying to make me stay here, but I was so excited to hang out in the city – Drew goes all-out for birthdays. Anyway, I got back from the trip, and everything seemed fine, but later that day Simon filled me in on the surprise party plan and told me Kali went ahead and got everyone round to hers and then acted like she didn't know I wasn't coming.'

Now I can see why Regal called her devious.

'Most of them stayed and hung out. They were all drinking, and Simon said he was drunk by the end of the evening so went upstairs to sleep it off. Kali joined him in bed some time later.'

'And was she drunk too?' I ask.

'She said she was. Simon admitted everything, but when I

gave Kali a chance to come clean, she didn't. That's when I ended it, there and then.'

'Quincy ... wow, that's ...' I don't even have words. I can't imagine how I'd feel if Remi and Mike slept together. The idea of it makes my stomach bubble with nausea. 'So how come people are still cool with them? What they did was disgusting.'

'I didn't tell anyone,' Quincy says. 'Obviously Drew, Cam, Regal and Eliza know, but a scandal like that in a place like this can really mess up not just your own rep but your family's too. I've known Simon's family all my life, and I love them. And I can't throw Kali under the bus without Simon getting dragged under it too. I know what it's like when people chat and stare. And despite the foul shit they pulled, Simon is like my brother. And Kali ...'

Despite everything Quincy's said about not wanting to get back together with Kali, I know he's about to tell me he still loves her. All I want to do is cover my ears and block his next words out.

'... was an important part of my life for years.'

He didn't say he loved her. Maybe he really is over her ...

Quincy sighs and turns his head from me, focusing on the books. 'Cam thinks I should burn them to the ground, but that's not me. It wouldn't change what happened.'

'You're a better person than I am. I wouldn't protect someone that made me feel shit.'

'Really?' Quincy says. 'Isn't that what you're doing with your boyfriend?'

His hard tone startles me. What is he talking about? 'No,' I say slowly.

'You said Mike asked for space and that he practically said you could date other people, but I don't hear you trashing his name. And you're still planning to go to his party, right? The one you're organizing from your holiday. Isn't that you protecting him?'

How can Quincy compare our situations? They're not the same at all.

'I'm not protecting Mike,' I argue back.

Am I? Is it that I haven't told anyone the truth about Mike because … I'm protecting him? Is Mike like Kali, manipulating me to get what he wants? He must know that our last call was a joke, but he didn't contact me for days afterwards, and he hasn't apologized once. Funny that today, the one day I've ignored him, he's been trying to get my attention. What if he has no intention of us getting back on track? Is his eighteenth party the only thing he wants from me?

Hundreds of questions flood my brain and I don't have an answer for any of them.

FIFTY-SEVEN

Quincy

17th December

Why can't my mouth and brain work together? We've gone from taking two steps forward to three steps back in a matter of minutes and I've managed to upset Tia all over again.

'Can you please leave?' Tia asks in a small voice.

'Tia—' I start.

'I need some time alone,' she adds.

I nod, but where does that leave us now? Tia didn't deny she was still planning to go to London for Mike's party, so does that mean she wants to fix things with him? I suddenly feel frustrated. I've been honest with her, but I don't feel like she's being honest with herself or me.

I don't say a word as I walk out of the library, closing the door behind me and resting my head against it on the other side. When I get downstairs, I notice people are starting to drift away. The whole point of Seven Days is to stay up until sunrise and we've still got a few hours left. Some are sitting chatting on the floor, and Cam's downing an energy drink behind the decks. Stacey is dancing seductively in his eyeline, and I don't know if he somehow can't see her or is choosing to ignore her. I spot Eliza leaning against a wall talking animatedly to ... I can't quite see ... then I realize she's talking with Simon.

I never thought Simon and I would be on opposite sides of the room, barely speaking to each other. But can I forgive him? I honestly don't know. The music slows down and K-Ci and JoJo sing over the melody. Someone taps me on the shoulder.

'Want to dance?' Regal asks. She holds out a hand towards me and I take it, needing the distraction.

Several people are watching us – well, watching Regal – as we find a space on the dance floor. She's taller than me in her heels, but I hold her hand and position my other on her waist. A few years ago, this would have been the highlight of my existence, but right now I wish it was Tia in my arms.

'Did you sort things out with Tia?'

I shrug. 'Not really.'

'Give her time.' Regal waits a beat. 'She told me you made up that girl you met online.'

Oh. Great. That's my rep gone, then.

'You could have told us you didn't have a date for the ball, Q,' Regal says kindly.

'I wasn't thinking. Everyone kept asking me about my

289

break-up with Kali and who I was taking to the ball, so I lied. Then Tia showed up and stepped in, but I never thought we'd actually fall for each other.'

'Oh, Quincy.' Regal shakes her head but she's smiling. 'You're meant to be the drama-free brother!'

'Please don't tell anybody.'

'I won't,' Regal promises. 'Tia likes you a lot – God knows why.'

'Ha ha,' I say in a flat voice.

'Have you told her now about Kali and Simon?' Regal asks and I nod. 'Good. And do you know what else I think?' Regal spins herself round, making me laugh because I'm still holding her hand. 'If she's the one, she'll come back. It doesn't matter the distance or the time.'

'You think?'

I want to believe that, really I do, but after what's happened tonight, I'm not so sure.

Everyone heads outside when the sun comes up. I'm exhausted by all the ups and downs of the evening, but the crisp weather and the pinks, purples and blues that paint the sky take my breath away. Drew links arms with me and Regal, and Cam stands on my other side.

'Just look at that,' Drew says, her breath coming out in puffs. 'It doesn't matter how many Seven Days I attend, ending the party with the sun rising is always magical.'

Cam looks at the groups of people who are slowly starting to disperse. 'Next stop, the Winter Ball!'

Tia and Willow are in front of us taking a selfie with the sunrise in the background. I don't know when Tia came back downstairs because she's avoided me since our chat. Willow says something that makes Tia laugh, and I wish I was the one doing that. Eliza waves at me as she catches a lift with Jared and Lizzy, but Simon is still here, looking up at the sky.

'Did you have fun, Q?' Drew asks, looking at me.

'It was a night,' I say, and she leans her head on my shoulder.

'Can we have a moment of appreciation for King Cam coming through with all the bangers?' Regal says.

'And no girl drama,' I add. Drew laughs, and Cam rolls his eyes, but he's smiling. Thankfully they didn't see *my* girl drama.

Drew, Cam and Regal go inside to grab their stuff and help Cam pack up his decks. Tia and Willow are chatting and my eyes wander back over to Simon. He puts a hand up, as if to say bye, and without thinking I walk up to him.

'Can we talk?' I say, and Simon nods, but I can see the anxiety on his face. 'I wanted to say thank you for earlier, with Tia. She told me you backed me up.'

Simon waves his hand. 'No problem. She okay now?'

'We had a chat,' I say. 'I told her about me, you and Kali.' Simon looks guiltily at the floor. 'You were the last person I thought would hurt me like that, Simon . . .' I trail off.

'I know,' he says, staring at me, 'I'm so sorry, Q. I really am.' This time I don't feel that rush of anger that normally fills me when Simon tries to apologize. 'I was mashed that night, but when I fully realized what I'd done, I felt sick with myself. I still do. You're my family, man, and I hate that I hurt and betrayed you.' Simon runs his hand through his hair. 'I hope one day we can be okay again.'

I swallow the lump in my throat. 'Maybe take it a day at a time?'

Simon's eyes light up. 'You mean if I say hi to you at college, you'll actually respond?'

I chuckle. 'Maybe.' From the corner of my eye, I see Tia looking at us. 'You got a date yet for the ball?'

Simon scoffs. 'You know James from college? Apparently he's got the flu or something. Maria asked if I'll go with her instead.'

'Maria's cute,' I say, and Simon nods in agreement. 'You know Regal hasn't mentioned a date . . .'

'Not even on my best day would *she* say yes!' Simon laughs. 'It's cool. Who's Eliza's date? Do you think it's that guy her mum brought last time?'

I laugh out loud. Mrs Bennett was so fed up with Eliza's stance of trying to attend the ball alone that she found this random guy from God knows where to be Eliza's date. He was a tall, thin, pale-faced boy with oily black hair and a sliver of a moustache. We took the piss out of Eliza for weeks.

'She won't tell me,' I say, 'but I've seen her dress.' I give Simon a knowing look, and he raises his eyebrows.

'Oh! She's doing all that?'

'She'll be the scandal of the season.'

Simon and I laugh, and it feels like old times. I've really

missed it. I can tell he has too. Every time I've seen Simon since my birthday, he's looked a wreck, but this morning, even though he must be as tired as me, he looks the most alive I've seen him in weeks.

FIFTY-EIGHT

Tia

18th December

I must have fallen asleep on the drive home because I'm nudged awake by Willow. I stretch out my crooked neck from side to side as I look out of the car window. In the distance I can see Mr Parker and Oreo in the fields. Quincy leads the way inside the house. I wonder what he and Simon spoke about.

Mum and Mrs Parker are in the dining hall.

'How was it?' Mum asks excitedly, putting her arms round me.

'It was good,' I say. 'So hungry, though.'

'There are waffles in the kitchen,' Mrs Parker says. 'This isn't my first Seven Days.'

Cam collapses into a chair. 'This level of tired is mad.'

'Cam was amazing,' Willow says, smiling at him. 'Non-stop vibes all night. Absolute legend.'

'Aw, look at my superstar,' says Mrs Parker, kissing him on the cheek.

'Mum!' Cam moans, making us all laugh.

I manage a bit of breakfast, but I'm too tired for any more conversation so I soon head upstairs. It's an effort to change into my pyjamas and take off all my make-up, but I sigh thankfully when I'm wrapped up in my duvet on the soft bed. My eyes feel heavy and my body is drained, and yet I can't stop thinking about what Quincy said about me protecting Mike. I can hear Willow's voice in my head too, questioning whether I just went with the first person that showed an interest. And why did Mike message me yesterday? Does he really miss me? I wonder if Remi spoke to him after our chat and pulled him up on his behaviour. It wouldn't surprise me – she checks everyone.

I grab my phone from the side table and see Remi online. She's an early riser – not something we have in common. I WhatsApp her.

> Hey, did you tell Mike I was upset with him by any chance?

Remi starts typing straight away.

> Yeah! Did he apologize?

So now I know. Mike had to be told he'd upset me, he hadn't realized for himself, and on top of all the doubts he's made me go through this last week, I feel another wave of disappointment in him. I always thought we were in sync, but maybe we never have been. Or maybe he just doesn't care any more. Is that the kind of guy I want to be with? I sigh, put down my phone and turn onto my side so I'm facing the wall that adjoins with Quincy.

FIFTY-NINE

Quincy

18th December

My eyes are so tired they're burning. I strip off my clothes, leaving only my boxers, and climb into bed. Sighing, I turn to the wall that's shared with Tia, hoping we'll talk later. I'm glad I told her how I feel. I don't know where we stand but bottling things up isn't healthy. Speaking to Kali and Simon has lifted a weight off my shoulders and it feels really good.

I've only just closed my eyes when there's a knock on my door. *Why, God? What now?*

I'm thinking about staying silent when I hear, 'Quincy?'
It's Tia!

'Come in,' I say, sitting up and rubbing my eyes. Tia walks in looking cute in a red pyjama set. Her eyes widen when she sees my bare chest.

'Erm,' she begins, shaking her head. 'Sorry to disturb you. I couldn't sleep and I wanted to talk, if that's okay?'

'Yeah.' I shift over on the bed so she can sit beside me.

'You were right,' she says, glancing at me. 'About me protecting Mike.'

I wait, wanting her to continue.

'Do you remember that first night, when I came outside because I couldn't sleep? I mentioned my family had gone through a hard time recently.'

'I remember,' I say.

Tia takes a deep breath. 'My mum lost her job about a year ago, and we got behind on the bills and had to move house. I found that really hard. Mike was a friend from college who I'd liked for a while, but he never seemed to notice me, until one day he did. He was so supportive during those first hard months, and he made everything feel less shitty. I thought we were good, so when I found out he didn't think the same I was determined to fix things. But the space and time apart has made me finally realize we're not on the same page.' Tia looks at me with her large eyes and I forget to breathe. 'Mike doesn't love me.'

'Are you sure?' I ask, and Tia sniffs as a lone tear falls down her face.

'He's never said it to me in the whole year we've been together. But because I was in love with him, I constantly defended him and made excuses for him. You said something earlier that really stuck with me.'

'I did? What?' I ask gently.

Tia smiles. 'You said I make you feel good. I never thought those were words I'd want to hear from a farm boy!'

I laugh and gently wipe the tear from her face with my thumb. 'I meant it. I haven't felt good for a while, and then you came along.'

'You make me feel good too,' Tia says, reaching for my hand and holding it. A perfect fit. 'And I don't have that with Mike. I know I can be bratty sometimes, but you take me as I am, and I know where I stand with you. And –' she rolls her eyes – 'you're not awful to look at either.'

I gaze at her. 'I think you're beautiful, Tia.'

Tia looks down at her hands. 'I'm not.'

I gently push her chin up forcing her to look at me. 'The first time you walked through the door, I remember thinking, *Who is that girl with the most perfect face?* I was drawn to you from the moment I laid eyes on you.'

'Really?' Tia says, sounding breathless.

'Really.' I stare at her lips that are calling to me. I'd kiss her all day if I could. I lean forward a bit, and Tia glances at me before coming closer. Her lips brush against mine and I can't hold back any longer.

When our lips meet, shooting stars burst inside me. Our tongues dance with each other and heat rises through my body as this overwhelming need to feel her, all of her, takes over. Tia's hand runs slowly down my chest, dropping to my stomach, and when I reach over and unbutton her top, she pushes my hand away and our lips break apart. I'm just about to apologize for crossing a line, but she smiles at me, her eyes never leaving mine.

'You're taking too long,' she says, her sultry gaze staring deep into my soul. I swear if you asked me my own name right now, I wouldn't be able to tell you. Tia takes off her top and I forget to breathe.

SIXTY

Tia

18th December

I wake up to squeals of joy from outside the window. Falling asleep in Quincy's arms was perfect. Actually, the whole experience was better than I could ever have imagined. I'm still tired and I'm tempted to go back to sleep, but whoever's outside is making a hell of a racket. I reach out to tap Quincy, but his side of the bed's empty. The clock by his bed says it's one p.m. and my stomach rumbles, so I get up, put my clothes back on and look out of the window. A blanket of snow covers the fields. Usually, snow puts me in the worst mood, but today I smile because it's beautiful, and Banks and Quincy are outside building a snowman.

Watching Quincy patiently playing with Banks confirms to me that I've made the right decision. I don't want to ruin

Mike's birthday, so I'll go to London, take him his cake and act like everything's normal, but I'll leave him a letter explaining how I feel for him to read after the party. That way I'll be able to say everything I want without getting tongue-tied. I'm ready to end things.

'Tia!' Quincy shouts and waves at me. 'Come join us.'

I hold my hand up to signal five minutes. I must really like this boy to be heading out to play in the damn snow. I walk out of his room in my pyjamas, close the door quietly behind me and turn towards my own room . . .

'Mum!' She's standing outside my room holding a cup of something hot, and her hand's poised in front of my door like she's about to knock. Her forehead creases. She looks past me at Quincy's door and then back at me.

'Did you just come out of Quincy's room?' she asks.

Fuck, fuck, fuck. I rub my sweaty hands on my pyjama bottoms. 'Oh . . . erm . . . yeah, I had to grab a charger.'

Mum's frown deepens. 'So where is it?'

Stupid, Tia! 'I couldn't find one.'

Mum continues to stare at me, taking in my pyjamas and my unkept hair because I didn't sleep with my bonnet on, not to mention that Quincy and I were rolling around on the bed. I try to clear my mind to stop her from reading my thoughts, but now all I can think about are Quincy's muscles, his tongue, his—

'Are you okay?' Mum asks, and I will myself to calm down.

'Is this for me?' I ask quickly, reaching for the cup. Mum slowly hands it to me. I take a quick sip, burning my tongue in the process, but grin and say, 'This is lovely. Thank you. I'm just gonna get ready.'

I have to turn sideways and slide past her because she doesn't move out of the way. I flash another smile before closing the door. I rest my back against the door, my heart racing. Does Mum know what happened in Quincy's room? She'll kill me if she finds out.

I dress quickly and head outside and it's so cold that my teeth immediately start to chatter. I've borrowed Willow's coat because I don't want to have to explain to Quincy why mine is half eaten. Banks is wrapped up in her pink puffer jacket and matching hat, scarf and gloves, which are soaking wet from patting the snowman. Quincy's on his knees helping to build it.

I stand to the side watching them. 'How did she drag you into this?' I ask him.

Quincy laughs. 'I came down to get us a drink and Banks asked if she could play outside. I couldn't say no to that face.' He leans back and rocks to his feet, surveying his handiwork. 'Mr Snowman looks great, don't you think?'

Banks has already lost interest and is picking up the snow and letting it fall from her hands. Quincy scoops up some too and starts to mould it into a ball. I'm thinking about whether I should take Banks inside when I'm hit by something hard.

'Ow!' I put a hand protectively on my torso and realize my jacket is damp. Oh no, he didn't! 'Are you for real?'

'Aw, come on!' Quincy picks up more snow. 'You've never had a snow fight?'

'Why would I have a snow fight?' I don't usually leave the house if it snows, let alone play in it for fun. Pushing my hair into my hat, I shout, 'Don't try that again or I'll—'

Quincy throws another one and I quickly pivot so it hits my back.

'Or you'll what?' he taunts.

Now he's done it. I quickly make a snowball of my own, ignoring how it numbs my fingers, and throw it at Quincy. I don't have anywhere near his power, so it doesn't hit him with the impact I wanted, but he still gasps. There's a moment where we're looking at each other waiting to see what the other's next move will be before Quincy gives me a sly look. I pick up more snow and throw it at him at the same time he lobs one at me. Before I know it, snowballs are firing back and forth, and Banks is watching wide-eyed as they fly through the air. A snowball hits me on my head and that's it for me.

'Quincy! I give up,' I shout.

'You give up?' He grabs me in a hug, lifting me up, but then he slips and we both fall over so I'm right on top of him. We start to laugh, and suddenly I can't stop. I roll onto my back, clutching my stomach as I laugh my head off. Banks starts clapping her hands like she's just witnessed the best show ever.

Quincy starts moving his arms and legs out and in. 'You ever made a snow angel before?' he asks.

I'm about to respond sarcastically (because why would I *lie* in the snow out of choice?), but I stop myself... *Oh, why not?* Quincy smiles slowly as I start copying him.

'You've got a different coat on,' he says suddenly. 'What happened to your green one?'

I'm just thinking how I'm going to explain that a sheep ate it without him taking the piss when Banks runs over and says, 'Sheep.'

'*Banks!*' I hiss.

Quincy props himself up on his elbows and peers over to look at her. 'Sheep?'

'*Baaa!*' Banks says for emphasis, and Quincy, thinking she's just being cute, laughs. It doesn't sound like she's going to say any more but then she blurts, 'The sheep ate Tia's coat.'

Can the ground swallow me up right now?

Quincy's quiet for a moment, and then, as if in slow motion, I see the corners of his mouth turn upwards. He closes his eyes and bursts out laughing.

'It's not funny!' I say, but it's a half-hearted protest because, being with Quincy, I can't be mad. I feel genuinely happy. I start giggling too, and Banks joins in, and soon all three of us are hugging our sides.

Quincy wipes the tears from his eyes. 'You're so funny.'

I've never thought of myself as funny. Someone who overthinks, who panics ... but funny?

He stands up, holding out a hand, and helps me to my feet. 'Let's look at what we made,' he says.

And there, at our feet, are the most perfect snow angels. They're so close together that they look like they're holding hands. I turn to Quincy with a wide smile on my face and he's already beaming back at me.

305

SIXTY-ONE

Quincy

18th December

It's still snowing so I drive slowly as I make my way into town to meet Eliza. I can't believe Christmas is next week and the Winter Ball is five days away. It feels like my family have been planning it for ever.

Eliza's sat at a table in the tearoom, and our cakes and coffee are already there when I arrive. She grins when I sit down opposite her. 'How good was Seven Days? And Cam!' She chef-kisses.

'Yeah, he was sick.' I take a sip of the hot coffee and instantly feel warmer. 'So, something happened at the party.' I tell her about what went down with Kali and Simon.

Eliza gasps. 'Kali kissed you? What was she thinking?'

'God knows,' I say. 'But I was clear with her that we're completely done.'

'Good, and I'm glad you and Simon cleared the air. How's it going with Tia?'

I can't help the cheesy grin that spreads over my face.

'What? Did you kiss again?' she says. I take a sip of my drink and Eliza gasps. 'So it was more than that?' I smile and she leans back in her chair with her eyebrows raised. 'Quincy Parker.'

'I like her a lot,' I say truthfully.

Eliza puts a hand on her heart. 'I love that for you. So the boyfriend is out of the picture now?'

'Well ...' I explain what Tia told me and Eliza frowns. It only gets deeper as I continue to speak.

'So she's still going to London with a cake for his birthday? And you're still helping her get there?' She shakes her head. 'That's weird.'

'That was her end of the deal.' I sigh. 'She says she has a plan and I trust her.' Eliza doesn't respond, which speaks volumes, but I know Tia will sort it out. 'There's another thing, though. I need to ask you a favour ...'

'What?' Eliza says with an edge to her voice.

'I can't sneak off and take Tia to London when we're in the middle of prepping for the ball, and I know you're going there to get your mum's Christmas present,' I mumble.

Eliza glares at me. 'You want Tia to hitch a ride with me to London?'

'And back.' I put my hands in a praying position.

'What if her mum finds out? I want no part of this,' she replies firmly.

'How would she find out?' I argue. 'We'll say Tia's hanging with you all day. She's only dropping in at the party, so you won't even have to be in London for long.'

Eliza purses her lips looking just like her mum, but I know better than to tell her that.

'Please?' I beg. 'I'd do it for you.'

She looks up to the ceiling and huffs. 'Fine, but you owe me!'

SIXTY-TWO

Tia

19th December

We're sitting in a church with beautiful stained-glass windows to watch the walking Nativity this morning. It's packed, like the whole village is here. Dora Russell, who organizes the play, asked Banks if she wanted to be an angel in it, and she looks too cute in her white costume. Her only job is to flap her arms like she has wings, which she's been doing perfectly.

'I think we're moving,' Mum whispers to me as Joseph and a pregnant Mary begin to head outside, and everyone in the church follows behind them.

'Chop chop, people!' Dora booms from the front. 'Mary needs to give birth in ten minutes!'

We're not far from Saiyan Hedge Farm, and en route we pass a youth choir singing Christmas carols, and various children tell Mary and Joseph there's no room at the inn. The Parkers' stables have been lined with straw with a few sheep gathered around, and Oreo is watching everyone excitedly.

'There's no room at the inn,' Mr Parker says loudly, 'but there's room in my stable!' and the crowd cheers. He gives a mock bow.

Banks is now holding a doll wrapped in white.

'Give the baby Jesus to Mary, dear,' Dora coaxes quietly, but Banks holds the doll tighter.

'No, it's mine!' she says.

Dora laughs nervously. 'Give it to me, then.'

'No!' Banks yells.

I know my sister and she's on the brink of a meltdown in three, two, one ...

Dora takes the doll from Banks and hands it to Mary, but Banks screams like she's legit lost her child and grabs the doll back then runs off into the field as fast as her little legs will take her.

'Banks!' Mum yells, and runs after her, but she's wearing heels and the field is wet with snow so she doesn't move very fast.

Everyone's laughing and Cam takes out his phone to record. Willow covers her face, and I'm torn between embarrassment and finding this the funniest thing I've ever seen. Dora's yelling something at Quincy, who snaps back, 'It's always a mess!'

I look out across the field and Mum, Banks and baby Jesus are so far away now that they're just dots against the snow. This could only happen to us!

SIXTY-THREE

Quincy

19th December

The Nativity didn't manage to get back on track after Banks went off script. Dad, bless him, led the round of applause and everyone left soon after that. Tope eventually returned, her mouth set in a line, holding onto Banks, who was hugging the doll tightly. Tope didn't say a word to anyone and took Banks straight back to the house and upstairs.

I decide to make dinner that evening to give Mum and Tope a break from cooking, and as we settle down to eat, Tope apologizes for the tenth time.

'Her dad thought the whole thing sounded hilarious, but I'm so embarrassed.' Tope looks at Banks, who is now pretending to feed her doll macaroni and cheese.

'Something goes wrong every year at the Nativity so I

wouldn't worry,' Cam says. 'And Banks was my highlight. It doesn't normally snow, though.'

I glance out the window. The snow hasn't stopped. If it keeps going like this, the roads will be affected. With the ball only days away, and Tia and Eliza travelling to London on Thursday, I'm praying it stops soon.

SIXTY-FOUR

Tia

20th December

Everyone is over at the ballroom putting up the final decorations for the Winter Ball, but I volunteered to stay home with Banks. Mike's party is tomorrow, and I need to bake his cake before then. Remi called me yesterday and squealed so loudly when I said I'm definitely coming back to London for it. She told me to come to hers to get ready and finish the cake. I've got a lot to fill her in on.

I hum as I mix the cake ingredients together, thankful that the Parkers' kitchen is so well stocked. Banks is distracted by a cartoon on my phone. I pour the cake mixture into a tin and place it in the oven. Wiping down the surfaces and cleaning up the evidence, I place an airtight container on the counter to pack the cake in later so I can hide it away in my room.

The buttercream and fondant will be right at the back of the fridge, out of sight.

While the cake is baking, I take Banks to the living room. She sits on the sofa and watches the TV and I wander over to the drawer where the Parkers keep their stationery. I settle back next to Banks, a pen poised in my hand, and think about everything I want to say to Mike. How do I sum up a year's worth of feelings in a letter? I have no idea, but I start to write anyway.

Dear Mike . . .

21st December

'Bye, Mum.' I quickly kiss her on the cheek as I head towards the kitchen door.

Mum's cooking lunch and luckily has her back to me so she can't see the bag I'm holding with the cake, buttercream and fondant inside. My white dress is in there too. I haven't managed to wash it after Seven Days, but I plan to drown it in perfume before this evening. Willow's at Regal's finishing off the wig. If everything goes to plan, I should be back in White Oak by nine p.m.

'Where are you going again?' Mum pauses cutting the potatoes.

'Eliza's taking me to this fair in the next town over, remember?' I say lightly.

'Here.' Mum pulls out a tenner from her pocket. 'Make sure you call me when you're on your way back.'

'Thanks, Mum. And I will. See you later.'

Mum looks over her shoulder and notices the bag in my hand, but I hurry out of the door. My heart starts racing, thinking she's about to follow me and ask to look inside, but she doesn't.

As I walk into the reception area, I spot Eliza leaning on the desk grinning at Cam, who's mirroring her. I watch them for a second and see Cam reach over and grab Eliza's hand, rubbing his thumb along her skin. Eliza bites her bottom lip, but as soon as she sees me, she quickly steps back.

'Tia,' she says, her voice a note higher. 'You ready?'

I love that she thinks I haven't clocked onto them. 'Yep.'

'See you, Cam,' Eliza says quickly. She holds the door open for me and I glance back over my shoulder at Cam, who now looks worried.

Cam and Eliza are a couple I did not see coming. They're obviously keeping it on the down-low and I bet it's because of Quincy. He's bound to find out sooner or later and I wonder how he'll feel about his brother and best friend seeing each other. Or are they already boyfriend and girlfriend ... ?

I climb into the car and put my bag on the floor in the back while Eliza types Remi's postcode into the satnav. She's dropping me off first before she goes to do her Christmas shopping.

'It should take a few hours, but the snow might slow us down a bit,' Eliza says.

She starts the car and the music turns on automatically. We drive in silence for a few minutes before she says, 'I know you want to ask me.'

'Only if you're comfortable answering,' I say back.

Eliza keeps her eyes on the road, showing off her flawless profile. Who can blame Cam? The girl is stunning. 'Ask away,' she says eventually.

'How long have you been seeing each other?'

'It's casual at the moment, but we've been on a few dates.'

'Oh, so you're not exclusive?' I ask.

Eliza shakes her head. 'I want to make sure he's serious before I commit.'

'Smart. Is he your date for the ball, then?' I probe.

Eliza nods. 'Yeah. It's been so hard to keep it secret.'

I frown. 'And Quincy doesn't know?'

Eliza groans as she joins the motorway. 'We don't know how to tell him we like each other. I know Quincy is going to lose his shit when he finds out.'

It's kind of mad that they think leaving the reveal until the ball is the best way to handle it, but who am I to judge? The track changes and I bop my head to the beat.

'Nice playlist,' I say.

'Cam made it for me.'

'He makes you playlists?' I put my hand to my chest because that's the cutest thing I've heard.

Eliza grins, her face coming alive. 'Cam communicates best via music. When he told me he liked me and I was wary because he has a rep, he sent me Jon B's "They Don't Know".' She glances at me. 'Do you know it?'

I shake my head. With one hand on the wheel, Eliza uses the other to skip through the music until she gets to the R&B track. I close my eyes and listen. The song's all about a guy telling a girl to ignore people when they tell her he's running game. He says it's in the past and all he wants now is her. It's so honest and so Cam, and if a guy sent me that, I'd be willing to give him a chance too.

'That's a co-sign from me,' I say, and Eliza laughs. 'Quincy will get on board with time.'

Her smile instantly disappears. 'I hope so. Okay, your turn. Tell me all about Mike.'

Maybe it's because I don't know Eliza that well, but I find it easy to share our entire relationship with her – the good, the bad and the ugly. She shakes her head when I'm done.

'He sounds like a complete idiot.' I don't disagree with her.

The journey passes quickly as we chat and listen to music, and before I know it, we're about ten minutes away from Remi's. It's weird seeing all the buildings squashed together and the hundreds of people walking down the streets. Bizarrely, and I never thought I'd think this, I yearn to be back in the countryside, surrounded by fields.

'What do you think Mike will say when he reads the letter?' Eliza asks, signalling left.

'To be honest, I'm not sure.' A part of me thinks he'll be surprised that I've got the courage to end things, but I don't think he'll fight me on it. He gave up on us the moment he asked for space.

We pull up outside Remi's house and Eliza turns off the engine and looks at me. 'Do you actually like Quincy?'

'Of course,' I say.

'No, I know. It's just ... Quincy's been through a lot, and I don't want him to get hurt again.'

I smile, because it's easy to do that when I think about Quincy. 'Trust me, he's the last person I want to hurt. Quincy's amazing.'

Eliza nods, satisfied. She reaches for my hand and squeezes it, and I look down surprised.

'I really hope tonight goes well. Mike doesn't deserve you. You're doing the right thing.' And I believe her. 'I'll be back just before eight, but call me if there are any problems, okay?'

I squeeze her hand back. 'Thank you, Eliza.'

Remi answers the door on the first ring and throws herself at me, gripping me hard. 'I've missed you so much! Bowling was so shit without you.'

'I've missed you too,' I reply, ecstatic to be reunited with my best friend. 'Girl, I've got so much to tell you.'

We enter the kitchen and the HAPPY BIRTHDAY MIKE cake topper is already on the counter with a few other bits and pieces.

'What's going on?' Remi asks, leaning on the counter.

I fill her in on everything from Quincy to Kali and my plan to break up with Mike tonight.

Remi's mouth drops open. 'Tia ...' is all she manages to say when I'm done.

'I know, but this is the right thing to do.' I pick up the packet of desiccated coconut that I asked Remi to get for me.

'Why did you want coconut, anyway? I thought Mike

didn't like it.' I slowly grin, and Remi bursts out laughing. 'You're bad!'

'Just a bit,' I shrug.

I glance up at the clock on the wall. Only three hours left until the party starts.

SIXTY-FIVE

Quincy

21st December

I keep glancing at my phone, checking there aren't any problems with their trip, but I haven't received any more messages since Eliza said she dropped Tia off at her friend's. The snow here has been getting heavier all afternoon. It's the only thing any of us are talking about. If it keeps going at this rate the roads will be closed and we'll have no choice but to cancel the ball.

I check the London forecast – light snow right now, but it's predicted to get heavier at six p.m. I really hope Tia and Eliza are able to get back okay.

'You all right?' Drew puts a hand on my shoulder, her voice tinged with concern.

'Yeah . . . just a bit worried about the snow.'

'I know! What a piss-take! And now this snowstorm—'

'Snow*storm*?' I practically shout. I haven't seen or heard anything about a snowstorm.

'Honestly! The amount you drive I'd have thought you'd listen to the news once in a while.' Drew tuts. 'They've been saying for a few days now that a snowstorm could be on its way.' She looks out of the window. 'And I think they're right.'

Shit! This can't be happening. If there's a snowstorm this evening, Eliza and Tia definitely won't be able to drive back. I have to get in touch with them.

'I've gotta do something quickly,' I say, walking away, but I don't miss the quizzical look Drew gives me.

SIXTY-SIX

Tia

21st December

I arrive at Rye Levels and walk in slowly in my white heels, holding out the cake carefully in front of me. The DJ is setting up and cling-filmed platters of food and bottles of drink have already been placed on the long tables covered in white tablecloths.

Quincy texted earlier to tell me the snow is coming down heavily there and a snowstorm might be on the way. In a panic I called Eliza, who was surprisingly chilled. According to her mum, the snowstorm isn't coming tonight, but she said she'd pick me up from Mike's earlier now that the drive back is likely to take longer. That means I have less time at the party, but as long as I can hang out with my friends for a bit and give Mike the letter it's fine.

'Tia!' Mike's sister Sarika kisses me on both cheeks and then Remi. She's wearing a short white strapless dress with silver heels. Her eyes light up when she spies the cake container. 'Can I see?'

I place the cake down on the table and carefully remove the lid.

Sarika gasps. 'Tia, it looks amazing!'

To be fair, it is kind of brilliant. It's a red Nike shoe box with a white Air Force One trainer on top of it. And it's all edible. Mike's going to be pissed when he tastes the coconut, but I won't be here to see his reaction, so who cares?

'He's gonna love it,' Sarika adds. 'Anything else we need to do?'

I glance around the space. Everything looks good, but where are the balloons? As if on cue, one of Mike's cousins walks in holding giant silver '18' balloons and two bin bags filled with smaller white balloons.

'I think we're good,' I say.

Sarika beams. 'Great! People should be arriving in the next thirty minutes, and Mike will be here after that to make his entrance. I'm just going to see if they need any help with the balloons.' She squeezes my arm as she walks off.

'Are you still going through with it?' Remi asks. She looks amazing in a white sequined romper.

I can't lie, it does feel weird being here at the party I've been organizing for months, talking to Sarika while knowing I'm about to break up with her brother. I take a deep breath, trying to calm my racing heart.

'Yeah, I am,' I say.

*

The party's in full swing and I've spent the past forty minutes dancing with my friends. They haven't stopped asking me questions about Regal and Drew. The DJ is decent, but he's not as good as Cam. I keep glancing at my phone . . . Half past seven now and Mike still isn't here yet, but Eliza is already on her way to pick me up. The letter feels like it's burning a hole in my bag. I look over at Remi, who's dancing with Aaron, while Ashleigh shoots them dirty looks. They were fighting over him weeks ago, but I can't be bothered to find out why that situation still hasn't been resolved.

The music abruptly cuts off and we all turn towards the DJ, who's holding a microphone. 'Can we give it up for the birthday boy? Everyone cheer for Mike!'

The whole room starts clapping and some people chant, 'Mike! Mike! Mike!' I catch Remi's eyes, and she rolls them.

Mike walks in with a massive grin on his face. He's wearing a white shirt and trousers, with a khaki bomber jacket in his hand, and his long hair has been pulled back into a tight bun. My stomach is in knots when I see him. I still think he's one of the hottest boys I know, but the pull I usually feel towards him isn't there any more. He dumps the jacket on a chair and everyone rushes over to wish him happy birthday as the music starts playing again. I hang back and a few people glance at me, obviously expecting me to be one of the first to greet him. Instead, I'm eyeing the jacket, wondering how I can slip my letter into a pocket without anyone noticing.

'Tia?'

I turn my head and Mike is staring at me. The party

separates as he walks up to me, his arms wide, looking genuinely excited to see me. I hesitate for a second before I remember I need to act like the Tia he knows.

'Happy birthday!' I say, wrapping my arms round his neck. He places his hands on my waist and we sway in time to the music. It feels both familiar and odd being in his arms again. I'm so used to Quincy's lean, tall frame and having to go up on my tiptoes to reach him, whereas Mike is the same height as me when I'm in heels.

'I've missed you,' he says, pulling back and staring at me with his dark eyes. 'I'm so glad you're here.'

These are the words I wanted to hear from him for weeks, but they don't land now. I will myself to say I've missed him too, but I can't get it out, so instead I ask, 'How was bowling earlier?'

Mike frowns. He clearly wanted me to say something else. 'Yeah, it was cool. But I ...' Mike shakes his head. 'Can we talk in a bit?'

'Oh ... what about?' I ask, trying to conceal my panic.

'Us,' he says simply.

I grip my bag tightly as if Mike has X-ray vision and can see the letter glowing inside. Maybe he's going to break up with me? A part of me wants this, so he can be the bad guy in this scenario.

'Okay, I'll come find you,' I say. 'Go have fun.'

He smiles. That smile used to floor me, but now all I'm thinking about is how he won't be smiling for much longer.

SIXTY-SEVEN

Quincy

21st December

My phone pings, and I quickly check the text from Eliza.

Ten mins from Tia x

Thank God! I'll feel better once I know they're on their way home. Tope walks into the living room clutching her phone.

'Hey, Quincy. Have you heard from Tia by any chance?' She holds up her phone. 'She's not picking up.'

'No, but I just heard from Eliza and they're leaving soon,' I say. The music must be so loud at the party that she can't hear it ringing.

Tope puts her hand on her chest, relieved, and I instantly feel guilty for not telling her the whole truth.

SIXTY-EIGHT

Tia

21st December

Almost there x

I text Eliza a thumbs up, ignoring the missed calls from Mum because I don't want her to hear the music. I'll ring her back when we're in the car. Hopefully Quincy can cover for me in the meantime. I glance at Mike's jacket, still hanging off the chair. He's talking to Winn and is swaying a little because everyone has been handing him drinks. Usually that would annoy me and I'd be following him around, encouraging him to drink some water, but instead I watch him as he trips over his own feet and almost falls flat on his face. Winn laughs and catches him.

The lights are dim and a lot of the adults are sitting down, talking and eating, but everyone else is dancing. Keeping my head down, I walk quickly towards the chair. No one's paying any attention as I quickly take the letter out of my bag and shove it into Mike's jacket pocket. The tightness in my chest suddenly loosens. I know Mike wants to talk, but everything I need to say is already in this letter. What I need to do now is meet Eliza outside.

I try to find Remi so I can say goodbye, but there are tons of people and she's so tiny that I can't see her. I jump as strong arms wrap round my waist from behind.

'There you are,' Mike whispers in my ear, and I pull a face at the strong smell of alcohol.

'Hey,' I say, turning to face him. I put my hands on his shoulders to keep him at a distance. 'Are you having fun?'

'So much fun! And that cake you made is sick.'

I smile. 'You're welcome. I was actually just about to head out.'

'What?' He frowns. 'You only just arrived.'

'I know, but my ride's here.'

I try to step away, but Mike pulls me back close to him.

'Give me two minutes. I want to talk to you,' he says, suddenly looking sober.

I nod even though my heart's thumping. He takes my hand, and we walk towards the exit. I almost scream when he picks up his jacket.

'Why do you need that?' I ask, trying to keep my voice light.

'Let's talk in the courtyard. It's too loud in here.'

I grab my coat and see that my letter is poking out of his

pocket as he leads us outside. *Shit.* I can't even reach it without him noticing.

'So ... erm ...' Mike begins, rubbing the back of his neck, avoiding my eyes like he's nervous. Mike's never nervous. Maybe he *is* going to break up with me. 'I've had some time to think, and I wanted to start by saying I'm sorry.'

What did he say? It takes me a moment to understand his words. 'You're sorry?' I question.

Mike nods. 'For the way I acted and the things I said. I haven't handled this whole thing very well and I've really missed you these past few days.'

You've missed me because I've been ignoring you, I want to say, but instead I force myself to smile.

Mike puts a hand in his pocket and frowns as he pulls out the letter. *No, no, no!* I wasn't planning on sticking around when he read that.

'What's this?' he says and opens the envelope.

'You can read that later,' I quickly say, but he ignores me.

He takes out the sheet of paper that's inside and his eyes widen when he sees my writing. My heart starts racing and I want to grab the letter and rip it into pieces, but I'm frozen. All I can do is watch as Mike's eyes race across the words, his expression changing from puzzled to hurt to shocked and now angry.

'What is this, Tia?' he snarls at me, waving the letter in my face. 'Are you breaking up with me?'

'Well ... I, erm, I—'

'"You don't make me feel good any more"?' he says,

pointing at my words. '"We're better off apart"?' He hits the letter, making me flinch.

'Mike, you were the one who asked for space,' I remind him, and he shakes his head aggressively. 'You said you weren't sure about us.'

'That's not true,' Mike argues. 'I said I needed time to think.'

My phone buzzes in my bag and I know it's Eliza calling to ask where I am.

'Do you know how fucked-up it is to write this letter and give it to me *on my birthday*?' Mike shouts. 'A happy birthday card too basic for you, is it?'

'You weren't meant to read it tonight,' I explain, and Mike scoffs. 'I wrote it because a lot of the time I can't get my words out around you. You always twist them and turn them into something else.'

But Mike isn't listening. He's pacing up and down, clutching my letter. My phone buzzes again, and I quickly take it out and answer it, accidentally pressing loudspeaker.

'I'm coming now,' I say.

'Okay, cool. Quincy is blowing up my phone,' Eliza says. 'I'm parked by the entrance.'

I hang up and turn to see Mike staring at me.

'Mike, I need to go. We can—'

'Who's Quincy?' he asks slowly.

My whole body goes cold and it's not because of the weather. Mike walks towards me, his eyes narrowed, like he knows I'm going to lie and he's ready to catch me out.

'Tia, who's Quincy?' His jaw is hard and tense.

'Quincy lives on the farm we're staying at,' I explain.

'So why's he blowing up that girl's phone?' he asks. 'He seems very concerned about where you are.'

'I-I dunno . . .' I stutter. I want to tell the truth, but the words are stuck in my throat.

'You don't know?' he echoes. Mike glances at my phone, and before I can stop him he grabs it from me.

'Mike! Give me back my phone,' I yell, reaching for it, but he turns his back, pushing me away with one hand.

Seconds later, he looks back at me, and I've never seen him so angry. *What's he seen? What's he seen?* I think desperately. He thrusts the phone in my face and lit up on screen is a picture Mum took of me and Quincy before Seven Days. Mike scrolls through my camera reel. In every one, Quincy's arm is round my waist and I'm leaning into him.

Mike crumples my letter in one hand and all the emotion that I poured into it is now nothing more than a tiny ball. 'So you're telling me this is a "family" trip? But this looks like a fucking prom picture!' he yells. 'Is that what you're doing? Out in these streets with other guys?'

'I'm not out in any streets,' I snap. 'You said you didn't want to be with me, Mike. You even said if I catch a vibe with someone else I should go for it.'

Mike scoffs and crosses his arms over his chest. 'I didn't say that.'

'Yes, you did!' I shout. 'Don't stand there and lie to me.'

'Have you fucked him?' Mike asks, and I laugh because

he legit didn't hear a word I just said. 'Oh, is this funny to you, Tia?'

'Why do you even care?' I yell. 'You don't even love me!'

'What?' Mike stammers, lowering his arms.

'You've never said it, Mike. Not once. Because the truth is, you don't love me.'

He doesn't respond, just like I knew he wouldn't. What Quincy and I have may not yet be love, but I already know he'll be honest with me about where we stand.

'I like you a lot, Tia,' Mike says gently. 'And I *feel* love for you—'

'But you're not *in* love with me,' I finish, and Mike sighs heavily. 'I loved you, Mike, and I was waiting for you to say it back to me for almost a year. And just when I thought you would, you asked me for space.' He closes his eyes and looks pained. 'I've never felt so hurt, worthless or embarrassed. Before I went away, I promised myself I wouldn't give up on us, but it soon became clear to me that you already had.'

Mike rubs his face. 'I hadn't given up on us. I just didn't know what I wanted. And now I do.' He closes the gap between us, grabs my hands and places them on his chest.

I gently pull my hands away and step back. 'I don't want this any more.'

'Are you for real?' Mike looks me up and down, an ugly snarl appearing on his face. 'After all I've done for you? You're gonna throw it away for this fool you met the other day?'

'Excuse me?' Heat is building in the pit of my stomach. 'All

I asked for was time and space to think about what I needed. And it took you, what, a couple of weeks to find someone else? Someone you're never going to see again once your holiday is over.'

'That's not true,' I say, but I can hear the wobble in my voice. I've deliberately not thought about what will happen to me and Quincy once I come back to London.

'Oh, you think he's a forever ting?' Mike smirks. 'You think *he* loves you?'

'Shut up, Mike!' The heat travels up to my chest.

He laughs. 'Well, fuck off back to him, then.'

'You could never be on Quincy's level,' I shout, and Mike glares at me. 'Fuck you, Mike.'

I turn on my heel and walk out of the building, trying to calm myself down. My eyes are burning, but I refuse to cry. I'll never waste another tear on Mike again. I run over to Eliza's car, open the door and sit down, breathing hard.

'What happened?' Eliza asks, her voice full of concern.

I sniff as I buckle myself in. 'I can't believe I was ever in love with that guy.'

'I'm sorry,' she says gently. 'I guess it didn't go well.'

'No, but we're officially done,' I say.

Eliza smiles. 'Well, I'm proud of you. It must have been really hard.'

I'm proud of me too. I never thought I'd be the one breaking up with Mike.

'You ready to go?' Eliza asks.

'Yeah.' I want nothing more than to be wrapped up in one

of Quincy's hugs. 'Did you get everything you wanted for your mum?'

Eliza rolls her eyes. 'Yeah, but the queues at Westfield were crazy so she better appreciate the effort I went to.'

As she starts the engine and pulls off, I take out my phone and text Quincy:

On our way x

SIXTY-NINE

Quincy

21st December

The snow is coming down heavier than before, covering everything in white, and despite the fireplace being on there's a chill in the air. I'm sitting here with Cam, Drew and Willow, watching the flames dancing over the logs. Mum and Dad are up in their bedroom trying to work out what we'll do if the ball gets cancelled.

'I just spoke to Tia,' Tope says, coming in. 'She said they're driving extra slow because of the snow but will be here soon.' She sighs in relief. 'I'm going up to put Banks to bed, but let me know if Tia arrives.'

As soon she's gone, Drew says, 'Quincy? I heard the fair ended early because of the weather.'

I gulp. 'It did?'

'Yeah, so what's taking them so long?'

I shrug and hurry into reception to call Tia. She answers on the first ring.

'Hey,' she says. Hearing her voice makes me feel warm inside.

'Hey,' I reply softly. 'You okay?'

'Yeah. I ended things with Mike.'

My stomach clenches. 'How did he take it?'

Tia sighs. 'Not great, but it is what it is. We should be home soon. Eliza's driving carefully because of the snow.'

'Ping me your location,' I say.

A second later I can see exactly where they are – a good twenty minutes away.

'Okay, so I'll see you—'

'*Shit!*' I hear Eliza yell, and then Tia screams. My knees buckle and my hand starts to sweat as it tightens round my phone.

'Tia! What is it? What's happened?'

'The car – it's spinning!' Tia yells. 'Eliza! Watch out—'

The line becomes just a crackle.

Now my head starts spinning. Have they had an accident? 'Hello? Tia?' I scream into the phone, but there's no answer. The phone cuts out.

'What's going on?' Cam asks from the living-room door. 'We heard shouting.'

'Tia said the car's spinning.'

Cam seems to lose all colour in his face.

'Quincy?' Drew joins us, Willow behind her. They look from me to Cam.

'What is it?' Willow says, but my heart's thudding so hard it feels like all the sound around me is muffled.

'I need to go,' I say. 'Quick, Cam, where are your keys?' He starts patting down his jeans.

'Go?' Drew frowns. 'Go where?'

'It's Tia and Eliza ... The car started spinning.'

Willow gasps and covers her mouth.

I take out my phone and show them the location. 'They're by Crombie Wells, just off the motorway.'

'Crombie Wells?' Drew says slowly. 'Why are they there? That's nowhere near the fair. Crombie Wells is on the way back from London.'

Slowly Willow lowers her hands and a deep crease appears in her forehead. 'London ... ?' Her eyes widen, and she looks at her phone. 'Shit. Twenty-first of December – it's Mike's party.'

'Mike?' Drew asks.

'Her boyfriend. I can't believe she snuck back to London for the party, especially when Mum told her she couldn't!' Willow looks at me regretfully. 'Sorry, Quincy, I thought she really liked you. Especially after you kissed.'

Drew's mouth drops open. 'You kissed Tia?'

'Kissed Tia?' Cam yells in surprise. 'I thought you were seeing some girl called Leah!'

Willow frowns. 'Who's Leah?'

They're firing questions at me so fast, but all I can think about is Tia and Eliza lying in a ditch somewhere.

'Guys!' I say over them, and they fall silent. 'I swear I'll explain everything later, but right now I need to go make sure the girls are all right.'

'I'm coming with you,' Willow says, but Drew holds her arm.

'No. How will you explain that to your mum? Let the boys go and we'll cover for them.'

Willow hesitates but eventually nods.

'The keys are upstairs. I'll grab our coats,' Cam says before he disappears.

I send up a silent prayer that Tia and Eliza are okay. They have to be . . .

SEVENTY

Tia

21st December

One second we're coming off the motorway onto one of the country lanes, and the next the car is skidding. Eliza grips the wheel tightly, trying to get the car under control, but the roads are so slippery that we start to spin. I drop the phone and grip the seat, my eyes squeezed shut. Then I feel a bump that jerks me forward, but the seatbelt catches me before I can go too far. I'm breathing hard and my hands are sweating. I slowly open my eyes and realize we've driven into some sort of ditch. There's snow, grass and hedge surrounding us. Eliza starts groaning and I can see she's holding her wrist.

'That was so scary,' I say, swallowing hard. I really thought we were going to die at one point.

'I know!' Eliza grimaces. 'You okay, Tia?'

I nod, but I'm still feeling shaky, especially as we can't see out the side windows and the front one is covered in snow. 'What about you? Are you hurt?'

She glances at her wrist, and it's clear she's in a lot of pain. 'I banged it on the wheel when we tipped forward. I just need to reverse and get us out of here,' she adds, but I shake my head.

'You can't drive in pain like that. We'll call a towing company.'

Defeated, Eliza nods.

A buzzing fills the car, and Eliza and I look at each other before I realize it's my phone. I unbuckle my seatbelt and reach down, searching the floor with my hand until I find it under my seat.

'Quincy?'

'Tia! Thank God! Are you both okay?' he says in one breath.

'We're in a ditch,' I say. 'The roads were slippery, and we lost control of the car. Eliza's hurt her wrist.'

'Shit. Can I talk to her?'

Eliza holds the phone between her ear and shoulder, to save her injured wrist.

'Hey ... yeah, I'm okay. We're at Crombie Wells ... I'll put my hazard lights on ... Really?' She glances at me, and I wonder what Quincy said on the other end. 'Okay, see you in a bit. Thanks, Q.' Eliza hangs up and hands me my phone. 'Quincy and Cam are on their way and are going to call a towing company.' Her face falls. 'Your sister knows you went to London.'

I groan. 'Is she mad?'

340

'He didn't say.' Eliza turns on her hazard lights.

What if Mum knows too? I think. My life will officially be over. I take a deep breath and dial Willow's number. She answers on the first ring.

'I've been going out of my mind!' she cries. 'Are you hurt?'

'No, I'm fine,' I reply. As soon as I start speaking, my eyes well up and, before I know it, I'm in floods of tears. The shock of the accident, breaking up with Mike and the shit I'm going to be in when I get home is too much to handle.

'Don't worry, Tia. We'll talk properly when you get back. Stay put – the boys will be with you soon,' Willow says softly.

I nod but remember she can't see me, so I say, 'Okay. Love you.'

'Love you too,' she replies before hanging up.

I turn to Eliza, tears still streaming down my face. 'I'm so sorry. This is all my fault. The only reason this happened is because I insisted on going to Mike's stupid party.'

'It's not your fault,' Eliza says gently. 'The roads were fucked, and this could have happened to anyone driving down here. I might cry when I see the damage to my car, though!' She chuckles, but I can see she's anxious. 'My mum is going to lose it.'

I wish I could say something to comfort Eliza, but the truth is, we're both in deep shit.

SEVENTY-ONE

Quincy

21st December

We're about ten minutes away and Cam's driving slowly through the lanes, something I very rarely see. Thankfully the car has an off-road ice and snow setting that makes driving in these conditions manageable. Tia seems okay. Eliza needs to go to hospital for her wrist and the car's a mess, but that can be sorted. They're alive, and that's the important thing.

'Did Eliza sound upset?' Cam asks once I'm off the phone.

I frown. Cam's known Eliza as long as I have, but I wouldn't say they were friends, so I'm not sure why he's asking about her in particular.

'She sounded okay, apart from her wrist, but we'll need someone to tow the car.'

'Let me ask my boy Louie. His dad owns a towing company and he might be able to give us a discount.'

I can't help feeling guilty. If it wasn't for me raising the fake-date idea, Tia wouldn't have asked me to help her sneak to London, and then none of this would have happened. What if the car had flipped over or, worse, crashed into another vehicle?

'Cam!' Louie's voice fills the car. 'What's good?'

'I need a favour, Lou. Eliza's car's in a ditch. We need a tow. Can you help?'

'Erm, have you seen the weather?' Then Louie laughs. 'But, yeah, all right, but only cause she's your girl.'

I whip my neck so fast to the right, but Cam keeps his eye on the road. *Cam's girl?*

'Thanks. They're at Crombie Wells. We'll be there in a bit.'

'Okay, give me fifteen and I'll see you there. Peace.'

Louie ends the call, and I notice Cam gripping the wheel tightly. I must have misheard Louie. Cam doesn't claim girls like that, and there's no way he and Eliza are together.

'What girl is he talking about, Cam?' I ask. A part of me thinks he's about to say Louie must be confused, but he sighs.

'Let's not get into it now.' He shuffles in his seat like he's uncomfortable.

I rack my brain, trying to work out if I missed something. The only thing that comes to mind is Cam's reaction to Eliza's dress at Everly Rose but, the way she looked, if Eliza wasn't like a sister to me I'd have reacted the same way. And now

I think about it, Cam did ask if Eliza was coming shopping that afternoon with us, and he's never singled her out like that before. But . . . Cam and Eliza? There's no way!

'You're not dating Eliza, are you?' I say in a playful manner, expecting him to shut me straight down.

But instead Cam checks his mirror, signals and turns left. Then he says, 'We were going to tell you together but never found the right time.'

The right time? What is he talking about? There's no way he's serious.

I laugh. 'You almost got me.'

Cam frowns and glances at me. 'I'm not joking, Q.'

He has to be joking. This is my brother we're talking about, and my best friend. There's no way anything is happening between them. Besides, I know Cam.

'You don't date,' I say matter-of-factly. 'You hook up and bounce.'

'I used to,' Cam says seriously. 'But I really like her.'

'No you don't,' I snap. 'You were fucking Stacey in the car a few weeks ago, and what about the girl you're bringing to the ball?'

'Eliza's my date for the ball,' he replies.

'She can't be, she's going with—' Then it dawns on me. Eliza never told me who she's going with because that person is my brother! 'When did this even happen?'

'At Bethany's eighteenth. Remember you were sick so didn't go? Eliza arrived early to do Bethany's hair and I was setting up my decks. We started to vibe that night.'

That party was in August. How did I not know this has been going on for four months?

Cam's jaw hardens. 'For your information, Eliza knows about everything, including Stacey. Are you really giving me shit, Q? You were meant to be taking Leah to the ball and yet you've been kissing Tia . . .' Cam trails off, and a moment later he barks out a laugh. 'Oh, wow!' He looks at me in disbelief. 'Leah . . . Tia . . . you think you're so smart. It was Tia this whole time, wasn't it?'

'No!' I say, but even to my ears it sounds untrue.

'Come on, it was. Why would you make up a girl? What kind of weirdo behaviour is that?'

'Why are you dating my best friend knowing you'll eventually screw it up?' I shout back. 'If you hurt her, I swear I'll never forgive you.'

Cam brakes and I jolt forward in surprise. He stares at me, and from the look in his eyes I can tell I've hurt his feelings

'Is that what you think of me?' he asks in disbelief.

I know I should say no, but his track record with girls is hardly a secret. What is Eliza thinking? This is a recipe for disaster. I don't respond and Cam nods his head sadly before driving off again. We fall into an awkward silence.

I spot Eliza's car thanks to her hazard lights. Apart from those it's pitch black round here. Cam parks up and we jump out and hurry over. The wind is blowing the snow sideways, so for a moment my vision is blurred. I walk carefully through the drifts and sense Cam following behind me. I wave, hoping they can see us.

The driver's side of the car has a deep scratch along it, and the front is face down in a ditch. Even though I can't see the full extent of the damage, I can tell it's bad. The front of the car is through a hedge, blocking the doors, and Cam and I pull the branches back on Eliza's side so her door can be opened. She breaks into a smile when she sees Cam and flings herself into her arms. He holds her tightly and she buries her head in his chest. It's weird seeing how close they are – especially when I didn't know. Eliza pulls away from him, and for a moment we stare at each other before she looks down, shyly.

Why didn't she tell me? I wonder. But then I think about how I just acted towards Cam. Eliza knows me well; she knew that's exactly how I'd react. I walk up to her and hug her, and she squeezes me back. I want to ask her a ton of questions, but now not's the right time.

We watch as Cam helps Tia climb over the gear stick and out of the car. She shields her eyes from the heavy snow that's falling, but when she sees me she runs towards me and I catch her in my arms, burying my face in her neck.

'Are you okay?' I ask, and I feel her nod. I pull away, studying her face just to make sure, but she looks perfect as always.

Over her shoulder, I can see Eliza and Cam watching us. Eliza's holding her wrist and Cam has his arm protectively round her. *Does he really like her? Is he serious this time?* I want to believe him, but I'm not sure I'm totally convinced. Eliza has supported me through all my relationships, though. She's a ride-or-die. I know my brother inside out but maybe

I'm wrong this time. I guess all I can do is see how it plays out. I smile at Eliza, and she doesn't hide how relieved she feels. Cam nods at me, and I nod back. We know where we both stand about the relationship, but I won't get in the way.

SEVENTY-TWO

Tia

21st December

I'm sitting next to Quincy in his car with a blanket wrapped round me while we wait for Cam and Eliza to finish talking to the towing-truck guy. Her car has a huge scratch down the side and the bumper is hanging off. I offered to help pay towards fixing it with the money I got from baking the cupcakes for Seven Days, but Eliza said her insurance will cover it.

'So how did the party go?' Quincy asks.

I tell him everything that's happened with Mike, from when he started messaging me again at Seven Days up until our conversation at his party. 'Even though it was hard, I'm so glad I managed to say my piece,' I reply. 'I want more from a relationship than what Mike and I had.'

Quincy puts his arm round me. 'You deserve someone that's all in.'

Are you? I want to ask him, but the fear of hearing him saying no stops me. Mike was right about one thing – how is this going to work with Quincy when we live so far apart? Willow told me I should have a holiday fling, yet I want more than that with Quincy. What if this is just a bit of fun for him?

'Willow knows about my trip to London,' I say, deliberately changing the subject.

Quincy groans. 'I know. I'm sorry. She also knows we kissed. She announced it in front of Drew and Cam, so ...' Quincy shrugs, but he doesn't seem annoyed.

Cam and Eliza climb into the front seats, bringing with them the cold air from outside. Snowflakes cling to their hair and Cam cups his hands round his mouth and breathes into them.

'Louie will sort the car out. I told Drew we're on our way back, so I'll drop you guys home before I take Eliza to the hospital,' Cam says.

'Cam, it's a sprain. It'll be fine ...' Eliza says, but Cam gently touches her hand.

'Best to be safe, right?'

Eliza smiles. 'Sure.'

I glance at Quincy and I can see he's watching Cam's hand as it lingers on Eliza's. I can't tell if he's okay with them or seriously pissed. Cam switches on the engine and we start the journey back.

The voice of Summer Walker fills the car, and nobody

speaks. It's like everyone is caught up in their own world. I turn to Quincy who has his eyes closed, but he's tapping his fingers on his lap to the beat. The closer we get to Saiyan Hedge Farm, the more anxious I feel.

'Shit,' Cam says under his breath as the car slows down.

Ahead, I see our families standing in the lit-up reception area. I can't make out Mum's face from here, but I already know she's livid. A soft hand wraps itself round mine and I glance at Quincy.

'I've got you,' he says.

I squeeze his hand back, silently thanking him, and feel a little braver knowing he's with me.

Cam parks the car and we all get out. I wrap the blanket tightly round me, hoping it will protect me from Mum's wrath. Quincy walks beside me in silence, his hands in his pockets. I want the walk across the gravel to take for ever. I'm expecting Mum to be furious, but as we get to the door I can see she has her hand on her chest and is wiping her eyes with a tissue. *Is she crying?* Maybe she doesn't know I went to London and thought the accident happened on the way back from the fair.

'Tia!' Mum and Willow run up to me and envelop me in a hug. Mum's rubbing my back and chanting, 'Thank you, thank you!'

'Yes, thank God,' echoes Mrs Parker as she hugs Eliza, who winces.

'Careful, Mum. Eliza's hurt her wrist,' Cam explains.

'Let's get you some painkillers,' Mr Parker says, and Eliza

turns and gives me an encouraging smile as she follows him to the kitchen.

'Are you sure you're not hurt?' Willow asks me, and I nod my head.

Over her shoulder, I can see Quincy watching me. His mum is saying something to him and clicks her fingers in his face to regain his attention. Quincy's head jerks and he turns back to her.

'Why did it take you so long to get back from the fair?' Mum asks, holding me at arm's length.

I glance at Willow. She clearly didn't snitch on me, but I feel too guilty to keep up the lie.

'We didn't go to the fair,' I say quietly.

Mum frowns. 'What did you say?'

I take a deep breath. 'Eliza drove me to London so I could ... go to Mike's party.'

Mum's hands fall away from me, and she takes a step back.

'I'm really sorry, Mum. The only reason I went was to end things with him.'

'You ended it?' Willow asks surprised.

But Mum holds up her hand to silence us. 'I said you couldn't go, so can you tell me why you chose to disobey me and drag other people into your mess too?'

I flinch at her harsh tone.

'That's not what happened,' Quincy says, and everyone turns to look at him.

I shake my head, wanting him to shut up, because there's no point both of us going down with this ship.

'It's my fault,' he continues. 'I asked Tia for a favour, and in return she asked me to help get her to London.'

'Quincy, I know you're trying to help,' Mum says before anyone else can speak, 'but Tia has messed up big time.' Mum glares at me. 'What the hell is wrong with you? We're here in this beautiful home on a family holiday, and now it turns out you've been scheming behind my back this whole time. That accident could have been a lot worse, and all because . . . because you couldn't wait until we were back in London to see that little boy?'

Now Mum's fully shouting, and each word strikes my skin like a slap.

'Was it worth it, Tia, putting yourself and Eliza in danger? For Mike?'

Everyone is uncomfortable and avoids looking at me, apart from Quincy. We lock eyes and it's enough to push Mum over the edge. She points at the stairs. 'Go!'

'But, Mum!' I protest.

'Move,' she says through gritted teeth. 'And give me your phone.'

'My phone?' I repeat weakly, taking it out of my bag and handing it to her.

'You're grounded. No phone, no internet and no Winter Ball!'

'Mum!' I protest, but I'm looking at Quincy, whose mouth has dropped open.

'One more word, Tia, and I swear . . .' Mum hisses.

My whole face is burning. I've never felt so embarrassed.

I walk quickly, keeping my head down, not daring to look at Quincy again. He kept up his end of the bargain and now I can't do the same.

SEVENTY-THREE

Quincy

21st December

'You have some explaining to do, Quincy,' Mum says, her hands on her hips. She may not be yelling like Tope, but Mum's calm voice is even worse. It's hard to tell how pissed she really is. 'Go to the living room and wait for me there.' Drew gives me a sad smile as I turn to go.

After all that, Tia can't even go to the ball! Now I'm back to square one without a date. I wish I could go upstairs and check on her, but I don't dare do anything else, so I sit on the sofa and wait for the inevitable. I hear Tope apologizing to Mum for all the hassle and Mum cutting her off, telling her not to be silly.

A few minutes later, Mum comes in kneading her forehead. A car engine revs outside.

'Your dad and Cam are taking Eliza to the hospital. Her

mum is going to meet them there.' Mum sits beside me. 'What happened, Quincy? What's this about asking Tia for a favour?'

I sigh. 'I'm really sorry, Mum. I asked Tia to be my date for the ball to make Kali jealous.'

Mum frowns. 'Jealous? I thought it was a joint decision to end that relationship.'

I take a deep breath, preparing myself to finally tell her the truth. 'You remember you recently asked why Simon hasn't been around?' Mum nods, and I explain everything – the situation between Simon and Kali, the pressure I felt to have a date, the worry I'd be letting my family and myself down if I didn't. 'So I asked Tia to be my date, not just because I needed one, but because I know it would make Kali mad if she thought I was with someone new. In return, Tia asked me to help her get to London.'

Mum shakes her head. 'Quincy, this is ... Simon and Kali – *really*?'

It's weird, now that I've said it aloud to her, I don't feel as angry and hurt as before. 'I spoke to both of them at Seven Days, actually. Simon and I have managed to clear the air.'

'And you're fine with them coming to the ball?' Mum asks.

'I wasn't before, but now I don't care. Since Tia and I have been pretending to be a couple, I've found myself starting to really like her.'

'As in more than a friend?' Mum questions.

'Yeah ... The only reason she went to London was so she could officially end things with her boyfriend.'

Mum's quiet for a moment and then she puts her arm

round me. 'It makes me sad that you felt you had to lie about everything that's been going on in your life, especially agreeing to sneak Tia to London. Tope was so worried about her.'

I feel so stupid. I should have just been honest about Kali and Simon in the first place and never made up a fake girl. Though a part of me wonders whether Tia and I would have ended up spending so much time together if we'd never pretended to date.

Mum pulls away from me. 'What I'm more angry about is that you weren't going to tell me or Dad about the accident. Why would you keep quiet about that?'

'I dunno. I panicked, and I didn't want Tia to get in trouble with her mum.' I look down at the carpet.

'That's not on you, Quincy,' Mum says. 'Things have a funny way of going wrong when you're not honest. Now look where we are – Tia's grounded, Tope's holiday is ruined, Eliza's injured and you don't have a date for the ball. All of this would have been avoided if everyone had just told the truth.'

I'm hot with shame and feel guilty that Tia is getting so much shit from her mum when I'm just as big a part of this. 'Do you really think Tope won't let Tia come to the ball?'

Mum eyeballs me. 'You saw her face, right? I'll ask around about another date for you. But with the way this weather's going, there might not be a ball to go to.'

SEVENTY-FOUR

Tia

21st December

I'm lying on my bed when Mum barges in. I jump up, catching a glimpse of Willow in the corridor as Mum slams the door behind her.

'You've got five minutes to explain what the hell you were thinking,' Mum yells. 'I couldn't have been clearer when I said you couldn't go to Mike's, and you completely disregarded that. I thought you were enjoying yourself here. I'm so disappointed in you, Tia.'

My eyes start to burn and I know I'm a second away from crying. I can take Mum shouting at me, but her saying she's disappointed makes me feel like the worst daughter in the world.

'Then to top it all off, you pull Eliza into your mess and

get into an accident, because anyone can see the roads aren't safe to drive in this weather. Did it not occur to you, even for a second, that what you were planning was stupid and dangerous?' Mum raises an eyebrow at me, which is her way of saying *speak up*.

'At first I was trying to fix me and Mike's relationship, and I thought if I could get back for his party, we'd be able to work things out,' I say, keeping my eyes cast down. 'So when Quincy asked me to be his date for the ball, to make his ex jealous, I said yes as long as he could get me to London and back without anyone knowing.'

I hear Mum's sharp intake of breath, so I look up at her. Her jaw is tight, and her arms are crossed over her chest.

'But the space away from Mike made me realize our relationship wasn't working. So I went to his party to break up with him.'

Mum sits next to me on the bed. 'How did he take it?' she asks, more gently now.

'Terribly. But Quincy—'

'Quincy? What's he got to do with it?'

I have no idea how she's going to react to this next part of the story, so I say it all in one breath. 'We've hung out a lot and started to like each other for real.' I bite my bottom lip, waiting for her to respond, but she's staring into space, her forehead creased.

'I see,' she says slowly. 'Well, breaking up with Mike was definitely the right move. I always knew you could do better than him, even though you couldn't see that yourself.'

I look at her, grateful for her insight. 'Yeah. I wish I could have realized that sooner. I invested so much into the relationship and it was all for nothing.'

'Tia, you're young. There'll be plenty of other boys,' Mum continues.

'That's easy for you to say.' I squeeze my eyes shut, because I was meant to think that, not say it out loud.

'What does that mean?' Mum asks stiffly.

I sigh and look at her. 'You have guys falling at your feet almost every day. Boys don't like me like that. It took ages for Mike to even notice me, so when he finally asked me out, I couldn't believe my luck. And after everything that happened with your job and the move, I was desperate for something good to happen in my life.'

Mum looks away, but I grab her hand.

'I'm not blaming you, Mum. It was rough for everyone. But I think that's why, when Mike started showing me attention, I was all in. Except I think I leaned on him more than I should have, and that's one of the reasons we started to fall apart.'

'You should have leaned on me, Tia,' Mum says softly, squeezing my hand back. 'I was so focused on getting us through that tough time I didn't notice how challenging you were finding it. Willow and I thought we were protecting you and Banks. You were always out with Mike, and maybe I should have questioned why that was, but I thought you were happy. I'm sorry I didn't realize you needed more support. Mike's lost out big time, because you're an amazing and beautiful girl, Tia. You have to believe that in there –' she points at my heart – 'not because some boy tells you, but because you know it to be true. You can't rely on boys to bring you happiness, Tia. I've done too much of that myself and look where it's got me.' Mum sighs heavily. 'Me and your dad got together when we were teenagers. We had Willow and you when we were so young, but I didn't mind because I thought we'd be together for ever. Even when my parents told me it wasn't working, even when it was clear we were growing apart, I still didn't leave. Then we moved to San Diego and I was so unhappy. I'd relied so much on your dad for love and money and security that I felt I'd never be able to stand on my own two feet.'

Mum doesn't talk much about her and Dad so I've never fully understood why they broke up when they still get along so well.

'Your dad was my best friend, but as we grew up we wanted different things in life. After him, I dated other men, but I was still relying on them to look after us, and that's not a healthy relationship. I didn't even know who I was as a person. It took me years to realize cooking is my passion and I could go it alone. Tia, I don't want you to make the mistakes I did.'

'But what about you and Paul? You were great together,' I say. 'Can't you be your own person with him?'

Mum shakes her head sadly. 'When I met Paul, I still hadn't found myself. I was working in retail with two teenagers and he was this successful guy who wanted to look after us all. Once I had Banks, I realized I was falling down the same hole again. I loved Paul, I still love him, but I knew I had to break the cycle. I was almost tempted to invite him to spend Christmas with us, especially now he can't get up to Edinburgh because of the snow, but ... I don't know.'

'You should call him,' I say.

'No, but maybe next year we can spend Christmas all together. Who knew once I broke up with Paul I'd lose my job and then the house!' Mum smiles. 'But we've survived it, and I'm finally happy being by myself and knowing I can provide for my family on my own. This trip was a celebration of how far we've come. Now can you see why I was so excited about it?'

I rest my head on her shoulder. 'For what it's worth, I've had a good time here.'

'I'm glad.' Mum pats my shoulder. 'Because you're going to be spending more time here, in your bedroom.'

'What?' I sit up and stare at her.

Mum looks at me steadily. 'Did you really think everything was going to be forgotten? You ran away to London, Tia! You'll stay in your room with no phone, no internet – and definitely no Quincy – so you can really think about your behaviour.'

My mouth drops open. I thought we were having a heart-to-heart, but I'm still being punished.

'And as for the ball –' Mum gets to her feet and my heart leaps ... *Maybe she's changed her mind and will let me go. A day in solitary is enough to drive me crazy. Surely she won't expect any more than that?* – 'Quincy will have to find another date because I meant it when I said you're not going.'

My stomach drops. 'Mum, please! Anything but that!'

'You think you can act the way you did and be rewarded for it?' Mum snaps, her anger bubbling back to the surface, and I fall quiet. 'No way. Grab your pyjamas. We're trading rooms. You'll sleep with Banks, and I'll stay here.'

'Why?' I huff.

'Oh, you think I wasn't a teenager? I know whose bedroom is next door.' Mum claps her hands. 'Let's go.'

I groan and reluctantly climb off the bed. My holiday is officially over.

SEVENTY-FIVE

Quincy

22nd December

I tossed and turned all night and slept badly. The snow was still coming down thick and fast when I got into bed, and even though I was wrapped up in my duvet with a hot water bottle, I was still cold. My sleep was full of dreams of Eliza's car flipping over and over, and of me at the ball in my underwear while Kali and Simon laugh at me, hand in hand . . .

I wake up with a pounding headache and the winter sun streaming through the curtains. Rubbing my eyes, I reach groggily for my phone, but I sit bolt upright when I see a message from Eliza.

> Phew! Only a sprain. Mum's pissed about the car but happy I'm alive. Did you guys get in trouble? x

I'm relieved Eliza's okay, but thinking back to last night makes my head hurt even more. I look at the wall that separates me from Tia. I want to knock on her door and see if she's okay, but Mum thinks it's best to keep my distance until things cool down. But how am I meant to do that when we're in the same house? I text Eliza back.

> So glad you're okay. You missed A LOT.
> Will fill you in later x

I pull a hoodie and joggers on and head downstairs, hoping to catch Tia at breakfast, but the first people I spot are Mum, Dad and Drew in front of the TV watching the news.

'Morning. What's going on?' I ask.

'The weather forecast is predicting the snow will stop soon,' Mum says, her eyes glued to the screen.

'But have you seen the roads?' Drew says, taking a sip from her steaming cup. 'They're a mess.'

'All that money we've spent ...' Dad says, and Mum squeezes his arm.

It *never* snows around Christmas, but the one year we're hosting the ball it ruins everything. Even if the snow does stop today, the roads still aren't safe to drive on.

'I'm making a drink,' I say. 'Anyone want one?'

'Another coffee, please,' Drew calls.

I head to the kitchen and bump into Evan, the waiter, who tells me that the guests are asking about the ball.

'Just reassure them it's all in hand,' I say. 'Mum will

confirm later.' Evan gives me a thumbs up. The last thing Mum needs is complaining guests.

Cam and Willow are leaning on the kitchen counter as I walk in. A wave of guilt washes over me when I look at my brother. I was out of line in the way I spoke to him yesterday. When I found out about Kali and Simon, Cam was there for me, even willing to fight Simon on my behalf. If he's truly serious about Eliza, I want to support him.

'Hey,' I say, switching on the kettle.

'How are you feeling?' Willow asks.

'I had a crazy dream about what happened last night. Did you hear from Eliza, Cam?' I ask.

'Yeah,' he grunts, not looking at me.

'How's Tia?' I ask Willow.

'Banished to her room – well, Mum's room – and still very much banned from the ball.'

'For real?' *Damn.* I'd hoped Tope had only said that in the heat of the moment. I wonder why Tia's had to move rooms, though. Is it because of me? 'Does your mum know everything?'

Willow nods.

Great.

Cam hasn't said another word, angling his body away from me towards the window. The tension is unbearable.

Willow glances between the two of us. 'I'm going to check on something,' she says, and I know she's only leaving to give us a chance to speak.

'Cam?' I say gently, and he doesn't move. 'I'm really sorry about what I said yesterday.'

Cam shrugs. 'What do I care what you think?' he says gruffly.

I walk over and lean beside him. He doesn't move away, which is a good start. 'I was surprised, that's all. I've been so wrapped up with my own shit that I didn't notice you and Eliza had grown close. But if you say you really like her, I believe you and I'm here for it.'

Cam looks at me sceptically. 'Swear?'

'Swear.' I hold out my fist and he bumps it with his own. 'She could do worse, I guess.' I nudge him and he laughs. Even though Cam and I bicker, I hate when we fall out.

'You good?' he asks.

I shake my head. 'I want to know if Tia's okay, but her mum's got her under lock and key. I wish I could talk to her.'

Cam drums his fingers on the counter and slowly smiles. 'I think I know a way.'

SEVENTY-SIX

Tia

22nd December

Banks is on Mum's bed with the doll from the Nativity, pretending to give it a cup of tea. I'm holding a little plastic cup too, and when she looks at me I have to pretend to drink it until she's satisfied. This is torture. I can hear Quincy talking downstairs and I wish I could go to him.

'Oh no!' Banks says as the teacup she's holding slips from her grasp and falls to the floor.

'I'll get it.' I roll to the side, off the bed and land on my feet. As I do, I see a folded sheet of paper and a pen slide under the door. 'Hello?' I call out.

Nobody answers. I pick up the paper and open it.

Dear Tia,

I'm taking it old school by writing you a letter, but hopefully you think it's romantic. Are you doing okay? It's weird not seeing you or talking to you. Willow told me you're definitely banned from the ball. I'm gutted.

We don't know if the ball will even happen. The snow hasn't stopped so it might be cancelled, which will suck. If it goes ahead, I wish there was a way you could still come.

It's funny, because at first all I cared about was not turning up alone and making Kali jealous, but now I just want to dance with you – and see you in that red dress again! Getting to know you the last two weeks has been the best. I wasn't expecting to connect with another girl any time soon, but you really are special, Tia.

Q x

I re-read Quincy's words again and again. No one has ever written me a love letter. I trace his words with my finger. *Special.* That's what he thinks of me.

'No snow,' Banks says, and I pull my attention away from the letter.

She's looking out of the window, and – I can't believe it – the snow has finally stopped. So, the ball can go ahead now? I hope so, for the Parkers' sake. They must have noticed, but I can't hear any cheers of celebrations, and it's not like I can text anyone.

Banks has grabbed my teacup and is now setting it down

beside her on the bed before she scolds the doll, saying, 'No! This tea is for Daddy.'

And suddenly I have an idea that might be completely terrible, but I know I need to try it anyway. I turn the letter over, quickly write back to Quincy, then fold it up. Just then, the bedroom door opens, so I hide the letter behind my back, but it's not Mum. It's Willow.

'How you holding up?' she asks. She's dressed in jeans and an ugly jumper with reindeer on it, and when she sees my face she says, 'What? I'm running out of jumpers.'

'Can you give this to Quincy?' I hand her the folded note and Willow stares at it. 'Please? He was just checking if I was okay.'

'I can *tell* him you're okay,' she says, but she puts the letter in her pocket anyway.

'I also need your phone ... Trust me,' I add as she goes to protest. 'If this works, everyone will be happy.'

'"If" doesn't fill me with a lot of confidence,' Willow says. Reluctantly she takes her phone out of her pocket. 'Tell me what you have in mind.'

I take a deep breath and explain my idea.

SEVENTY-SEVEN

Quincy

22nd December

The snow has finally stopped, and I really hope it's for good and it isn't just taking a break. Tope insists on finishing the dessert prep for the ball and says if worst comes to worst we can eat it for Christmas dinner. Mum keeps switching between carrying on as normal and making alternative arrangements, until Drew puts a firm hand on her shoulder.

'You've worked hard on this, Mum,' Drew says. 'Right now, the weather is on our side, so let's throw the best Winter Ball this town has ever seen.'

I watch Mum's face, waiting to see what she says. She grips Drew's hand tightly. 'You're right. Let me find out when the roads will be cleared.'

There's a buzz in the air now that we're moving forward

with the ball, but even though that makes me happy, what I truly want is confined in a bedroom upstairs. I haven't heard back from Tia despite Cam walking past her room multiple times. I sigh heavily. It seems like everyone wins but me and Tia.

SEVENTY-EIGHT

Tia

23rd December

I've taken Banks' clothes for the Winter Ball out of the wardrobe and laid them neatly on the bed. She's going to be wearing a pink sparkly princess dress with matching shoes, and I can only imagine how cute she'll look. Willow's raiding Mum's wardrobe for some heels. She's going with a guy she met at Seven Days, Akil. I thought if I stopped complaining, babysat Banks and basically acted like the perfect daughter, Mum might change her mind – but no, she's not budging. I feel kind of guilty about what I'm planning to do, but as Quincy held up his end of our deal, I'm sure as hell not letting him down.

SEVENTY-NINE

Quincy

23rd December

It's five p.m. and I collapse on my bed exhausted even though I know I need to be getting ready for the ball. Drew has had me out all day, encouraging our neighbours to clear their driveways and help dig out the lanes. The snow ploughs have been out too, so no one has an excuse not to come tonight.

There's a knock on my door and Cam walks in looking sharp in his tailored black suit. His long hair is tied back and he's holding a black bow tie in his hand.

'You're not dressed yet?' He looks at me lying there in my hoodie and jeans.

I sit up. I didn't even get two minutes. 'I'm about to change, man.'

'Can you help with this?' He holds out his bow tie. 'I should have bought a clip-on.'

As I'm tying it for him, I realize how nervous he seems.

'You and Eliza are gonna look great together,' I say.

Cam slowly smiles. 'You think?'

'No doubt. Is Daniel here yet?' I ask.

'He's meeting Drew at the ball. Apparently he's got some model friend for Regal.'

I laugh. Only Regal could stress about not having a date and still find a model to accompany her. I'll be going with Bunny. She called Drew last night in a panic because her boyfriend had to pull out.

'How are you feeling?' Cam asks seriously.

I shrug. 'Tia didn't even respond to my letter.' I stand back to check both sides of the bow tie are even. 'Perfect.'

'Thanks, Q. Now get dressed!'

Once Cam's gone, I pull my suit out of the wardrobe, feeling deflated that I won't have Tia on my arm this evening. I get dressed and am just putting my phone in the inside pocket of my jacket when my fingers brush against a tightly folded piece of paper. *Has she replied?* I unfold it quickly, see my love letter staring back at me and turn it over eagerly:

Meet me under the stars.
T x

My heartbeat quickens and I smile. She replied! But what does she mean by 'under the stars'? I have no idea what time she left me this note, so perhaps I've missed her. Quickly, I put on my black shoes and hurry down the stairs.

Willow is standing in the reception. She looks stunning in a forest green one-shoulder dress. Her hair is long and black and snakes down her back.

'Well, don't you look handsome,' she says, looking me over.

'Thank you. You scrub up great yourself.' I show her the note. 'It was in my suit pocket. What does it mean?'

Willow smiles. 'Trust her.'

I nod, because I do trust Tia, but I can't help wondering what the hell she's up to.

EIGHTY

Tia

23rd December

'I think I'm ready.' Mum checks her bag for the hundredth time.

'Mum, go!' I say. For once Banks is sitting calmly in her sparkly dress, her light brown curls tied up in a ballerina bun.

'Sure I look okay?' Mum asks. She looks beautiful in a long, slinky dark blue evening gown, silver high heels and her hair in loose waves.

'Gorgeous. You never told me who your date is.'

'I'm going with Ethan,' she says.

'Ethan? The horse guy? When did that happen?'

'He asked me last week. Here.' She hands me my phone from her bag, and I take it eagerly. 'It's for emergencies only, Tia, not so you can text Quincy all night ... although I do like Quincy.'

'You do?' I ask, surprised.

'He's a lovely boy, from a good family, and you seem like yourself around him. It's Christmas Eve tomorrow so count this as your last night grounded in your room.'

'Wait, you still want me to stay up here this evening, even though the whole house is going to be empty? I was planning on watching Netflix.'

Mum rolls her eyes. 'It's not like I can stop you.' She leans over and kisses my cheek. 'Be good. Banksy, come and kiss your sister goodbye.'

Banks runs up to me and I smother her face in kisses, making her laugh uncontrollably.

'Have fun,' I say. 'And take lots of pictures.'

They head out of the room, and I hear their footsteps descending the stairs. I don't move until everything's silent and all the cars have left the farm. I know I shouldn't be disobeying Mum again when she's trusting me to stay in, but I take out my make-up bag anyway, with only Quincy on my mind. I've got about an hour until it's time.

The text comes through just as I've put on my faux fur coat. The side's still different lengths, but it's guaranteed to make Quincy laugh. I grab my bag and make my way down the stairs, holding the front of my red dress so I don't trip.

Paul waves at me from out front and I let him into the reception, greeting him with a big hug.

'Tia, you look lovely,' he says.

'Thank you – so do you.' He's wearing a black suit under a

377

smart grey jacket and is clean-shaven, but there's an anxious energy about him. 'Willow wasn't clear on the phone. Why didn't you leave with everyone else?'

'Oh ... erm ... Mum was worried you wouldn't find the venue, so I offered to stay behind.' Paul nods, believing my lie. 'Sorry the snow stopped you from going to Edinburgh.'

'It's okay. I'm here with my favourite girls, aren't I?' He gives me a one-armed hug. 'Shall we go?'

I link arms with Paul as we walk to his car. The roads are clear, almost as if the snow had never been. We start to drive and my heart thuds thinking about Mum freaking out when she finds out what I've done.

'I was so happy to get that call from Willow.' Paul grins. 'It's made my Christmas that your mum wanted me to come and be her date for the ball.'

'Mmm,' I say. I just hope Ethan won't mind if Mum and Paul have one dance together.

'It's a bit strange she didn't call me herself, though,' Paul continues.

'She's been busy cooking.' Not a lie. 'She's going to be so happy to see you.' I really don't know whether that part's true, but Paul's smile is so big it could light up the sky. And Mum did say she still loves him, so she will be happy ... right?

EIGHTY-ONE

Quincy

23rd December

I'm walking around with a smile plastered on my face, but my heart's not in it. There's no denying that the Winter Ball is a huge success. Centrepieces of red roses, pinecones and greenery adorn the tables set out round the edge of the dance floor, and gold crackers tied with black ribbon have been placed above each plate. The Christmas trees at either end of the ballroom, with candles twinkling in their branches, look magical. We've installed a fibre optic lighting kit up in the gilded ceiling, and now it looks like everyone is standing under the starry night sky.

Pretty much the whole town is here, as well as guests from further afield, and the local press. The sit-down dinner was perfect, and everyone's been raving about the food. Tope did such an amazing job, and Mum's been showing her off every chance she gets. After dinner the tables were pushed back to create space for the dance floor and the DJ has been so good. She's a friend of Cam's and has been playing a nice mix of music to appeal to all the different age groups. I've actually had a good time with Bunny, and she looks stunning in a deep purple off-the-shoulder dress. I've only seen Kali once, and she was arm-in-arm with a guy I don't know. It's weird seeing her with someone else, but it doesn't bother me the way I thought it would.

'I'll be back,' Bunny says, hurrying off to say hi to someone she knows.

'Quincy!'

I turn to see Mr Huntington in a three-piece suit, his cane by his side. Mrs Huntington is hovering next to him and is sparkling from her giant earrings all the way down to her shoes.

'Mr Huntington! It's good to see you!' I give him a hug and breathe in the smell of mint and tobacco. 'How have you been?'

'This damn leg.' He tuts. 'Mind you, nothing was going to stop us from being here tonight. You've done a magnificent job.'

'Thank you, sir,' I say.

'Now, where's Kali? I haven't seen her,' Mr Huntington says, looking around.

'Remember what I told you, dear.' Mrs Huntington smiles apologetically at me. 'Which lovely lady did you bring tonight, Quincy?'

'Bunny Vaux,' I say.

Mr Huntington pats my arm. 'Oh, to be young and single! Good times.'

'Jim!' Mrs Huntington snaps, and I have to press my lips together to hold in my laughter.

'I'm joking, Anne,' he says, but when she turns away in a huff, he winks at me.

I'm still chuckling to myself when I turn from the Huntingtons and see Simon talking to a guy in a dark blue tuxedo. *Is that . . . ?*

'Sean!' I walk over to him. I haven't seen him in weeks, since his grandma fell ill.

'Quincy, my man!' Sean slaps my hand with his own. He's shorter than me with jet black hair and light brown eyes.

'How's your grandma?' I ask.

'She's made a full recovery! . . . Yo, I had no idea Cam and Eliza were a thing.' Sean's eyes bulge. 'When did that happen?'

'Been going on for a while,' I say. 'I'm cool with it.'

'Sorry to hear about Tia,' Simon says. 'Eliza's filled us in.'

I shrug like it's not a big deal.

'Ah! There you are.' Mum walks over to me. In a gold dress with her hair styled in an elaborate up-do, she looks like a whole queen. 'And it's so good to see *you*, Sean. How's everyone?'

'Good, thanks, Mrs Parker,' Sean replies.

Mum fixes a cold stare on Simon who pales under her gaze.

'Hey, Aunty Mel,' Simon says weakly.

'We're due a chat, I think, Simon,' Mum says sharply,

and Simon nods. 'Quincy, the local paper wants to take a family picture.'

As we walk away from my friends, I turn to her and say, 'You know, me and Simon have sorted things now?'

'Yes, but I'm still not okay about it,' Mum says. 'Once I've told him exactly how I feel about his stupid behaviour, then we can move forward. Sophie's going to rip into him when she finds out.'

I link arms with her and smile. Mum really is something.

EIGHTY-TWO

Tia

23rd December

Paul parks in the overflow carpark and checks his bow tie in the pull-down mirror. He looks as nervous as I feel. I'll probably be grounded for life once Mum sees me, but there's no going back now. I quickly text Willow that we're here before I turn to Paul and smile.

'Ready?'

He takes a deep breath. 'Yep, let's go.'

We get out of the car and the music is loud enough out here that I can already feel the bass. We walk into the manor house and I can hear kids laughing and squealing to the right of me. I assume that's the kids' party that Banks is at. If she sees her dad, she'll cling to him, and he won't be able to spend any time alone with Mum. I steer us away towards the ballroom.

My phone buzzes:

Mum's on the dance floor

EIGHTY-THREE

Quincy

23rd December

The press pictures seem to take for ever. We're grouped together with our partners and, even though Bunny is a great date, I wish Tia was the one standing beside me.

'My feet are killing me,' Bunny says once the photographer is done, and I glance down at her six-inch heels. 'You mind if I take a seat?'

'Nah, go for it. I'll catch up with you in a bit,' I reply. I spot Tope in the crowd talking to some of the other guests. She catches my eye and I give her a tentative wave, so she walks over.

'Having fun?' she asks.

'Yeah. The food was amazing, by the way,' I say.

'Thank you, it was my pleasure to cook. I've made lots

of great contacts tonight.' Tope waits a beat. 'Tia has her phone now.'

'Really? I can call her?'

She smiles. 'Yes, you can.'

I smile so wide that my cheeks hurt. 'Thanks, Tope.'

Sean hurries over and watches Tope walk away. '*Who* is *that*?'

'That's Tope, Tia's mum,' I say, and Sean's jaw drops.

'Tia's mum? Damn! She single?'

I laugh. 'Dickhead.'

I take out my phone and squeeze through the throng, making my way to the door. I'm already scrolling through my contacts to find Tia's number when I look up and spot a white guy scanning the room. He looks familiar ... and then I remember it's the guy who arrived with the Solankés on their first day. Isn't he Banks' dad?

I'm about to approach him when he sets off determinedly across the room. When he reaches Tope, he taps her on the shoulder. She spins round and her eyes widen. It's obvious she had no idea he was coming. The last time he was here, she was acting like she didn't want him around, but whatever he's saying now seems to be working, because she's smiling. And when he reaches for her hand, she doesn't pull away. Instead, she leads him to the middle of the dance floor.

I have to tell Tia about this. I continue towards the door, raising my phone to my ear, and suddenly it's like everything around me happens in slow motion. The crowd parts and there she is, standing in the doorway in her beautiful red dress. I catch my breath. This must be a dream. How is she here? Tia turns, and when she sees me my heart beats in double time. She walks towards me, I walk towards her, and we meet halfway.

'Hey,' she says, a small smile on her face.

'Hi,' I respond. 'How?'

She gives me a mischievous look. 'We had a deal, remember?' She points up at the ceiling. 'And I told you I'd meet you under the stars.'

I look up, and the stars twinkle back at me. I send up a silent thank-you prayer that she's here with me.

'Even though Mum's definitely going to kill me later, so this might be the last time you see me for a while,' she adds. 'I snuck out and got Paul to come along.'

'Are you joking?' She shakes her head, and I burst out laughing. 'Your life is one hundred per cent done.'

Tia groans and leans into my chest. Her perfume surrounds me, and for a second I feel like I'm drowning in her. 'I didn't know what else to do.' She looks up at me. Her large brown eyes are outlined in black and gold specks glisten on her eyelids. 'I'll always show up for you, Quincy.' Her eyes dart round the room and she chuckles. 'People are staring at us.'

'You're drawing their attention looking like that, and they also know I came here with Bunny.'

Tia holds out her hand. 'Well, I hope she doesn't mind if I steal you for a dance ... far away from Mum and Paul.'

I laugh and take her hand, feeling complete. 'Come on, trouble.'

EIGHTY-FOUR

Tia

23rd December

Quincy leads me onto the dance floor. He puts one hand on the bottom of my back, and the familiar jolt that always happens when he touches me travels through my entire body. His other hand is warm and a perfect fit in mine.

The ballroom is breathtaking, and everyone is dressed to the nines. I spot Eliza and Cam swaying to the beat, Willow dancing with Akil, Regal hand in hand with an equally gorgeous guy, and Drew being spun by a handsome dark-skinned man. Mum and Paul are here too, looking like they're in their own world. She seems so happy. Maybe this wasn't such a crazy idea after all . . .

An Asian guy standing on the sidelines is waving at me enthusiastically. He gives me two thumbs up when he sees I've spotted him.

'Who's that?' I ask Quincy, who rolls his eyes.

'My friend Sean. Ignore him!'

I laugh. 'I love how happy he is that we're together. This ball really is something.'

'It's been a big hit, but this right now is the best part,' Quincy says, looking at me. His locs are hanging to his shoulders, his lips are plump and inviting, and those eyes seem to look deep inside me. He's so beautiful.

A white guy with a camera in his hand walks over to us.

'Quincy?' he asks. 'Can I get a picture of you both for the local paper?'

'Oh, sure.' Quincy pulls me close to him and we pose and smile. My life is definitely over when Mum sees this in the newspaper, but right now I don't care.

The guy snaps away, and I realize how much I want to capture this perfect moment too.

'Can we get one?' I ask, handing the man my phone. I look at Quincy and my eyes travel down from his eyes to his lips. He raises his eyebrows as if challenging me. I may not know where this is going with Quincy, and my mum might ban me from talking to him for a while after this, but there's only one thing on my mind right now.

I pull gently on the lapels of his jacket, and as if in slow motion Quincy bends down until our lips meet . . . Fireworks explode in my head. It's lightning and magic and bliss all rolled into one. My head is spinning and I'm dizzy on him. Quincy Parker is all mine and he's most definitely worth the risk.

ACKNOWLEDGEMENTS

I absolutely loved writing *Only for the Holidays*. At first, I wasn't sure I'd be able to fall in love with a couple as much as I had with Trey and Ariel in *Love in Winter Wonderland*, but Quincy and Tia came to me one day and I couldn't shake them.

Quincy is essentially the nice guy, and even though his story starts off with heartbreak, I wanted to prove that nice guys, in my eyes, definitely don't finish last. Tia reminds me of my younger self and of so many girls I know that need a good shaking because they can do better than the boy they're with, but luckily Tia goes on a journey of self-discovery and eventually realizes this for herself. Setting the majority of the story in the countryside is hilarious to me because, like Tia, I'm a city girl; I don't like the countryside much myself and I'm scared of horses. It was a really fun experience writing from these two perspectives, and it's such a privilege bringing another Black love story set at Christmas to life.

Thank you to God as always for helping me to write this book. Whenever I first start writing a new story, I forget that I'm more than capable of doing this and doubts creep in. But somehow I manage to get to the end every time. Thank you for answering me whenever I pray to you.

To the dream team – my agent, Gemma, the OG farm girl who I absolutely adore! I love our agent–author relationship and thank you for always encouraging me and bouncing ideas around with me, even my hungover ones. My editor, Amina – we clearly need to make a playlist together! Thank you once again for rooting for my lovebirds Quincy and Tia and spreading your magic to elevate my book. You just get me, girl. I'm so excited for all the future books that I get to work on with you.

Massive love to my publicist Ellen, my marketer Olivia, Rachel and the whole S&S team for all your support, love and belief. Sometimes I pinch myself that I'm an S&S author! Thank you for my beautiful cover that I'm obsessed with – and the pink party for *Love in Winter Wonderland* was epic. Colour-themed parties are the way forward!

Dad, Mum, Gboli and Lola – as always, you're at the forefront of what I do, and I strive to make you guys proud.

Thank you to my friends. Anneliese, for always finding the time to read my first raw drafts and somehow seeing the beauty of the book before I can. Helen, for taking me on a road trip around the countryside for inspiration and standing close to the horses so I wouldn't have to; I'll try to spend more time in the countryside with you ... maybe. Zarah, for all the baking tips; Tia may share a lot of my dislikes, but her love and talent for baking is all you, girl.

Lastly, thank you to all the booksellers, librarians, teachers, bloggers and readers for your support for my books. You guys are the backbone of this industry, and I appreciate you so much.

ABIOLA BELLO

is a Nigerian-British, prize-winning, bestselling children's and YA author who was born and raised in London. She is an advocate for diversity in books for young people. She's the author of the award-winning fantasy series Emily Knight and was nominated for the CILIP's Carnegie Award, won London's BIG Read 2019, and was a finalist for the People's Book Prize Best Children's Book. Abiola contributed to *The Very Merry Murder Club*, a collection of mysteries from thirteen exciting and diverse children's writers which published in October 2021 and was selected as Waterstones Children's Book of the Month. Her debut YA, *Love in Winter Wonderland*, published in November 2022 and was an Amazon's Editor's Choice and was featured in The Guardian's Children's and Teens Best New Novels. *Only For The Holidays* is her second YA book. Abiola is a finalist for The Black British Business Awards 2023 for Arts and Media, she won The London Book Fair Trailblazer Awards 2018 and is the co-founder of Hashtag Press, Hashtag BLAK, The Diverse Book Awards and ink!

@ABelloWrites

HAVE YOU READ?

WILL TREY AND ARIEL FIND THEIR HAPPILY EVER AFTER?

LOVE in Winter WONDERLAND

ABIOLA BELLO